Cross My Heart

CARMEN REID

CORGI BOOKS

CROSS MY HEART
A CORGI BOOK 978 0 552 56701 5

First published in Great Britain by Corgi Books,
an imprint of Random House Children's Publishers UK,
A Random House Group Company

This edition published 2013

1 3 5 7 9 10 8 6 4 2

The Random House Group Limited supports the Forest Stewardship Council®
(FSC®), the leading international forest-certification organisation. Our books carrying
the FSC label are printed on FSC®-certified paper. FSC is the only forest-certification
scheme supported by the leading environmental organisations, including
Greenpeace. Our paper procurement policy can be found at
www.randomhouse.co.uk/environment.

Corgi Books are published by Random House Children's Publishers UK,
61–63 Uxbridge Road, London W5 5SA

www.**randomhouse**.co.uk
www.**randomhousechildrens**.co.uk
www.**totallyrandombooks**.co.uk

Addresses for companies within The Random House Group Limited can be found
at: www.randomhouse.co.uk/offices.htm

THE RANDOM HOUSE GROUP Limited Reg. No. 954009

A CIP catalogue record for this book is available from the British Library.

Printed and bound in Great Britain by CPI Group (UK) Ltd, Croydon, CR0 4YY

In loving memory of my grandparents,
who served on both sides in World War Two

Herman Rittmeier (German soldier)
Maria Heinrich (wine grower)
Eleanor McIntyre (ambulance driver)
William Reid (farmer and British Home Guard)

10th May 1940

Everyone remembers where they were when they heard the terrible news.

I was in class. My teacher, Monsieur Durance, was trying to tell us about William Shakespeare but no one could concentrate. We were all straining to see out of the high windows because people were running into the schoolyard, shouting, even crying.

'Let the children out! We want our children!'

'The Nazis are coming!'

A ripple of panic spread through the classroom. We knew that Denmark, then Norway, had been invaded by the Germans; we were all wondering if Belgium would be next. My friend Lottie Rosen burst into tears and I jumped to my feet with a mixture of nerves, excitement and sheer curiosity.

'Sit down, Nicole,' Monsieur Durance ordered. 'This

is just panic and noise. We must remain calm until we know the facts.'

But then came rapid tapping on the classroom door and Sister Agnes, the lean and usually unflappable headmistress of St Teresa's, burst into the room.

'Monsieur Durance!' she cried, her voice shrill. 'Have you heard? Our army has been overpowered! The Germans are coming . . . tanks are on the way to Brussels! We are being invaded. We have to let the children go home. Everyone must leave!'

The chalk fell from Monsieur Durance's hand and then the lights went out. We all stared at Sister Agnes in shock.

'The Nazis have cut the power supply, perhaps,' Monsieur Durance said gently. 'Very clever.'

With his stick and his war-injured leg, he limped calmly to his desk. He's a tall man, round-shouldered, with a head of unruly grey hair, usually dressed in shaggy cardigans. His kind face looked very serious. He pulled open one of his desk drawers and I thought he was going to bring out a gun and prepare to fight the Germans again, like he had done in the Great War.

Instead, he brought out a large foil-covered box of chocolates and told us all to have one, because: 'The last time the Germans were in charge of Belgium, it was almost impossible to buy chocolate.'

'Class dismissed,' Sister Agnes said weakly. 'Who knows what will become of us.'

I grabbed my satchel and two chocolates and rushed out into the yard, where the infants were streaming from the other building as tearful mothers searched the crowds for their children.

'Didi!'

'Avril!'

'Esther!'

Lottie was scanning the faces for her little sister, so I helped her to look, but we couldn't find Esther.

'She's probably gone home.' I tried to calm Lottie.

'No, I need to find her. Maybe she's still inside. You don't understand, Nicole—' She gripped my arm and I could see the panic in her face. 'My family moved here from Berlin. We are German Jews and the Nazis will hunt us down. We have to leave, now! We have to join the other refugees and flee.'

'You have to become a refugee?' I asked my friend, feeling horrified.

Cars with mattresses strapped to the roof, packed with people, suitcases, pots and pans, even dogs and cats, had been travelling through Brussels for months. Foreigners from countries I'd never even heard of fleeing the Germans. They didn't have Belgian money, so they would bargain for food and medicine with silver candlesticks, gold coins, even jewellery.

Then Aurelie Van Roy ran up to us: 'I just saw your mother, Lottie. She has Esther and you're to go home.'

Lottie darted away before I could offer her a word of comfort or say goodbye.

Aurelie's pretty face, pale, with freckles and flashing hazel eyes, was smiling and excited. 'Come on, Nicole, let's go to the Avenue to watch the Germans come in. Everyone's heading there. Come on,' she insisted. 'This is a big day. Huge!'

The German army marching into our country . . . I couldn't take it in.

Then a terrible, eerie, wailing noise filled the air.

'What's that?' Aurelie shouted.

'I don't know. An air-raid siren?' I'd never heard one before.

'An air raid? Bombs?! What are we supposed to do?'

I had no idea.

We looked up and saw the plane. When dark shapes began to drop from it, Aurelie screamed. But the shapes weren't bombs; they were soldiers, hurtling towards the ground until their parachutes burst open behind them.

With my own eyes I could see what I had not wanted to believe: *the Nazis were coming.* As I hurried towards the Avenue with Aurelie, we became part of a vast crowd. The shops and offices were closed, no trams were running, and there was still no power, but at least the wail of the sirens had stopped. In the distance was the terrible rumble of gunfire and shelling on the out-skirts of the city.

I kept looking for my papa, knowing he would want to see this with his own eyes: the Germans marching back into Belgium. He fought for two years in the filthy trenches of the Great War until he was wounded and sent home to live under German occupation.

He hated the Nazis with every bone in his body and had worried about this day for the past six years, ever since Adolf Hitler became the German leader.

The news passing through the crowd was that our army had been overwhelmed.

'Are we really going to be occupied?' Aurelie asked, grinning like an idiot at every good-looking boy we passed. 'What's it going to be like?'

A tall boy rushed out of a side street to join the crowd, bumping into Aurelie. As he apologized, he stared at her, then began to stare at me too. He looked older than us; sixteen or so, with a tanned, square face, black-brown hair and dark, serious eyes.

'Do we know you?' Aurelie asked haughtily.

'Yes! You're Aurelie and Nico,' he replied. Then he grinned and I had a flash of recognition – plus there was only one person in the world who'd ever called me Nico.

'Anton?!' I blurted out, because even though Belgium was being invaded and this was surely the worst day of my life, I couldn't help grinning too, because it really was Anton and he'd come back.

Anton Morel used to live round the corner. We grew up together, playing football, hide-and-seek, all kinds of games; we climbed trees, shared books – Anton loved books – shared secrets; and four years ago when his family had moved to France I had been inconsolable.

'Hello, I'm back in Belgium . . .' he said. 'Unfortunately, so are the Germans.'

I couldn't stop staring at him. The Anton I knew was the best kind of boy: honest, open – the kind of boy who treats a girl like an equal. Through those brown eyes I often felt as if I could read his thoughts. It was almost unbelievable to see him again. He looked so different but I could still see traces of the boy I knew so well. I had about one hundred questions for him.

'When did you get back?' I began.

'Three days ago. My father's still in Paris.'

'Have you moved back? Are you staying?'

'Yes.'

'Is that really you?' Aurelie purred. 'But you look so grown-up and so handsome.' She is the biggest flirt I have ever known.

He laughed, then looked at me again. Four whole years had passed since I'd last seen him and suddenly I felt awkward. He was older, taller, definitely more handsome; more man now than boy, with a deep voice and broad shoulders. Although he still wore long shorts, not trousers, and a knitted jumper, not a jacket, he had grown up into someone new and it was unsettling.

But this wasn't the time for catching up; we were in the Avenue, waiting for the Nazis to arrive. Nothing was more important than this. We found a space on the pavement and realized that everyone was here – except the men fit to fight.

'The Germans have completely crushed us. They've invaded Holland and Luxembourg too, and they're heading for France,' Anton told us.

We waited for a long time. Shouts went up with the latest rumours.

'King Leopold is to surrender us!'

'Hitler is coming to Belgium!'

Finally, from much further down, urgent cries alerted us to a change. Everyone surged forward. Suddenly the pavement was impossibly packed with people. I was crushed against Aurelie, Anton and the people around me, everyone straining to look, desperate to know what would happen next.

There came the throaty roar of engines and a voice shouting through a loud-hailer: '*You are under German command. Put down your weapons and surrender. You are under German command.*'

I'm not tall, only one metre fifty-five on my tiptoes, so I pushed my way to the front because I had to see them. The rumble grew louder; everyone was jostling to see.

A huge formation of countless motorbikes filled the entire street. The riders' heads were held high, their goggles blanking out their eyes. The men without helmets had shining blond hair, and sunlight flashed from the metal breastplates on their chests. They looked impossibly tall and strong. Like storybook soldiers, but much more frightening – like soldiers from your worst dreams.

The crowd fell back in silence, shaken and horrified. These men were our new owners, powerful and victorious, driving in to take charge.

Aurelie put her face next to mine. 'They look rich and wonderful,' she breathed into my ear. 'Look at their shiny boots and their leather jackets . . . and so handsome. They're all gorgeous,' she gushed. 'I want a tall, blond, rich boyfriend with a motorbike.'

It made me feel sick.

Then, on the other side of the road, I caught sight of my papa and wished I hadn't. He was being forced at gunpoint to make the 'Heil Hitler' salute, and his face was streaming with tears.

Chapter One

'The Nazis are devils. The stories I've heard would make your hair curl!'

Grand-Mamie, my father's mother, is ferociously chopping cabbages at the kitchen table.

'In Germany, if you are an eighth Jewish, if even your big toe is Jewish, you can't have a job or a house – you can't even go to the swimming pool . . . and they look for any excuse to put you in prison. It will happen here too. They're already throwing Jewish people out of their jobs.'

I think of Lottie and Esther Rosen. Nothing has been heard of their family in the five months since the Nazis invaded Belgium. I hope they escaped with the flood of families heading to Spain, Britain, Switzerland or America, any country without invaders.

Yes, it's five months now since the Nazis arrived, and

in that time life has settled into a terrible new normality. The whole of Europe is ferociously at war and there is never any good news. Germany is winning.

I go to school, Papa goes to work, Mama and Grand-Mamie keep house, but we are living under military rule. Nazi soldiers and Nazi police run the country. The Belgian government has fled to London; our soldiers are all in prisoner-of-war camps. Nazis are on every street corner, demanding to see our identity papers and watching our every move.

We have ration books, which severely limit the food and clothes we can buy, and like everyone else we've become poor. Prices have trebled, even quadrupled. Food is scarce as the Nazis seize almost everything grown here and send it to Germany. We are scrabbling about for bread, growing vegetables in the garden and patching our clothes and shoes just like poor people.

I'm wearing the same jumper, blouse, skirt and coat I wore last winter; luckily I've not grown much. We've had to sell things from the house – the mantel clock, paintings, some of Mama's jewellery – just to buy food.

There's hardly any coal for heating or cooking, and even if we could find everything listed in our ration books it still wouldn't feed us. Everyone is hungry all the time. Children look grey and small, with legs so skinny their knees bulge out.

Tiny Grand-Mamie, with her shrivelled face, her black dress, rosary beads and snow-white bun, goes to St Peter's Church every day, where the old ladies must whisper all the way through mass with the amount of gossip she brings home.

'The Nazi police, those Gestapo demons, have a new *Kriminaldirektor*,' she goes on. 'He's called Johann Richter and he fought here during the Great War, lost his leg, lost his brother and hates us Belgians with a passion. Marianne's son at the Post Office, he hears these things. Richter's orders are to root out all resistance to the Nazis. Anyone who defies them will be killed. Even children. Three children who threw stones at a police car have been shot in Schaerbeek, Violetta told me.'

'Not children,' my mother protests. 'No one shoots children.'

'The Nazis shoot children,' Grand-Mamie insists. 'In Germany, the children are soldiers. They all wear brown shirts like their lunatic Führer and spy on their parents.'

I love how ferociously anti-Nazi Grand-Mamie is, because I feel just like her. Since the invasion, it has been terrible to see how most of the adults have just bowed down and accepted the new rulers. No one is fighting the Nazis. I would love to fight them, but I have no idea what to do or where to begin, so I just boil away with internal rage at the injustice of it all.

'What is the matter with Belgium?' Grand-Mamie

demands. 'We need to stand up to these devils and fight!' She brandishes a chunk of cabbage.

'Well, well . . .' Mama murmurs from the cooker, where she is bringing vats of vinegary water to the boil. As Gaspar, our big black tomcat, squeezes between my ankles I look at the vegetables spread across the counter. I'm going to have to get used to eating pickled leeks, pickled cabbage, pickled carrots, pickled everything.

'We're just trying to survive, so how are we supposed to fight the Nazis?' Mama asks gently, wiping her hands on her apron. Mama has soft skin, caramel-coloured hair she sweeps up in a bun and the most understanding copper-brown eyes. She is the kindest, most loving person I know. It's hard to imagine her fighting a bee, let alone a Nazi.

'What about Sir Winston Churchill and the British?' Grand-Mamie asks. She worships the British Prime Minister, and she has her good ear tuned to the radio at all times to make sure she does not miss a word of his broadcasts. Although listening to the BBC radio is, of course, banned.

'*We shall fight on the beaches, in the fields and in the streets, we shall never surrender!* This is the spirit,' she declares. 'This is standing up to those devils. This is why Britain hasn't been invaded yet, even though the Nazis are bombing London to pieces every night. I will fight them too. I'm eighty-three years old but I will do whatever I can. What about you, George?' Grand–Mamie demands. 'What are you doing about the Nazis?'

My father is sitting opposite me at the kitchen table, where we are making a radio out of fine wire, a razor blade, a safety pin, a chopping board and a cardboard tube, for a neighbour who can't afford a proper set.

'Wrap the wire carefully around the tube in tight coils,' he tells me, ignoring Grand–Mamie. He's wonderfully patient, Papa, a railway engineer interested in all kinds of new technology. He likes to teach me useful, practical things. He's a lean man, grown even leaner recently, with sharp blue eyes that miss nothing. But he never says much; he hides his thoughts behind his bushy black and grey moustache.

'You're lily–livered like King Leopold!' Grand–Mamie exclaims. 'What about your three brothers, my three beautiful boys, all murdered by the Germans? They would fight the Nazis if they were here now. What are we going to do, George?' Grand–Mamie persists. 'We can't do nothing.'

My father keeps his eyes trained on the radio set.

'I agree with Grand–Mamie,' I tell him. 'There must be so many people who feel like this. There must be something we can do, Papa.'

'And get shot?' he snaps. 'Like the children in Schaerbeek?'

He doesn't get a chance to say more, because now we

13

hear vehicles arriving in the street. Shouts sound out . . . then loud knocking on a door close to our own. Gaspar scoots from under the table to his basket in the laundry room.

'What's happening?' Mama asks.

Papa hurries to the front room and I follow. We see policemen swarming over the street. 'Quickly!' Papa whispers. He hurries to the old cabinet which has books on top, behind glass doors; underneath, there are many projects we have worked on together: simple circuit boards, abandoned radio sets and home-made gadgets.

I realize with a lurch of fear how incriminating these innocent projects could look if our house is searched. I crouch beside him and we quickly scoop up as much as we can.

'Where do we hide them?' I ask, panicky now.

'Follow me,' he says. Papa rushes upstairs to the attic room and opens a small door to the eaves. There's an old trunk in here, so we tumble the items inside as we hear the loud rapping on our front door.

'George!' Mama calls out. 'Shall I answer?'

Papa pushes a chest of drawers in front of the door to the eaves, then to my surprise he pulls me into a tight hug. 'Whatever happens, Nicole, don't try to fight back,' he tells me. 'The Nazis are deadly. If you try to fight, no one in this family will be safe.'

'What do you mean?' I ask, frightened by his words.

But there's no time to explain as we hurry down the stairs.

I'm in the hall with Mama, Papa and Grand-Mamie when Mama opens the door and three uniformed thugs stand there, imposingly tall and aggressive.

'George de Wilde?' one of them demands.

'Yes,' Papa replies.

'You are required for interview at Gestapo head-quarters.'

'I'll get my jacket,' Papa says calmly, turning to the row of coat hooks on the wall.

'Why are you taking him? What has he done?' Grand-Mamie demands.

No reply.

'What's this about?' she insists. Mama clutches at me. My heart is pounding in my chest.

'George de Wilde is of interest to Kriminaldirektor Richter and the new authorities,' the thug at the door spits out.

Papa walks towards them, but they grab hold of him and drag him out of his own home.

'There's no need for that,' he protests, but they drag him even harder.

I'm too shocked to cry out, but I follow them into the street, where Papa is pushed into the back of the car. Through the window, he smiles, trying to reassure me.

Of interest to Kriminaldirektor Richter . . . The words are ringing in my head. Why? Why is my papa of interest? What has he done? There must be some mistake.

The three policemen climb into the car, the doors slam shut and they drive off with my beloved papa. I'm too stunned to even know how to react.

I turn to see Mama's face, crumpled and distraught, and Grand-Mamie's defiant look.

'Time to be brave, Nicole,' Grand-Mamie says, taking hold of my arm. 'The trials of life only serve to make the strong stronger.'

Chapter Two

I glance left and right. There's no sign of a uniform or of those men in matching long overcoats and trilby hats who laughably think they are 'secret' police.

Then I bend down and slip the piece of wood I've made jagged with nails against the tyre of the Gestapo car. My heart is racing so fast I can't breathe. Maybe it gets easier; maybe sabotaging Nazi cars will feel like nothing once I've been doing it for a few weeks.

I get up and walk on quickly. My papa is still in jail and I'm determined to take revenge.

Three weeks after taking him, the Gestapo are still holding my father without charge. Mama and I have been to the prison several times. We've not been allowed even to see Papa, and all we can find out is that they believe he was a Resistance member during the last war, so he's under suspicion.

'A Resistance member? How can you say that?' Mama protested. 'He didn't do anything; he was an injured soldier. He might have delivered some leaflets, but that was over twenty years ago.'

But they sent us away.

I turn the corner now and almost walk straight into the skinny, scruffy soldier who guards our streets all day long.

'Oh, good afternoon, sir,' I gush, making an attempt at a flirty smile. I've decided to be over-friendly and charming to him so that he won't suspect me of tyre-wrecking.

'Good afternoon, mademoiselle. You don't have to call me sir, you know. I'm Private Stapenhorst, but you can call me Stapie.'

'Hello, Stapie, I'm Nicole.'

He smiles back and asks, 'So where are you off to, Nicole?'

'To meet some friends.'

'Where do you go?'

I wonder why he has this boring job, guarding quiet streets. Maybe he's injured in some way or not a very good soldier.

'To the library,' I lie, because the thought of him suggesting he might come and meet me after his shift is too horrible for words. Lots of girls have German boyfriends now, but I'd rather be single for the rest of my life.

'Have a good time,' he says. 'Maybe I'll be allowed off duty one day and I'll be able to join you.'

I almost shudder.

I make the twenty-minute walk through our dismal, drab Brussels. Even in the daylight windows are blacked out with felt or newspaper; everything and everyone looks dirty and neglected. The only cars with fuel to drive through the streets are police or army ones. Everyone else is walking, and we are a depressed and ragged lot in our patched and worn clothes, our shoes held together with cardboard and glue. Every so often, we have to pass through checkpoints, show our papers and empty our bags – further proof that we are under military rule and no longer free.

'Hey, Nico!' I turn to see Anton running the last few paces to catch up with me. 'You're early,' he says.

'Or maybe you're late,' I suggest.

When he smiles straight at me, my chest tightens with happiness. We've spent a lot of time together lately: talking, walking, getting to know each other again, visiting cafés with friends. But no matter how much time I spend with him, I still want more.

I feel as if I can talk to him about everything; even my little revenge plots against the Nazis. I trust him completely, and when he talks I just want to listen.

He's standing in front of me smiling and I realize with

a rush of excitement and confusion that I don't want to be Anton's friend. For the first time, I want much more. I want to be his girl. And more than anything, I want to know if he feels the same longing to be together that I do.

I want to hold his hand, touch his cheek. I want Anton to be all mine. Does he feel the same? I don't know, and suddenly this feels impossible to bear.

'So . . . are we going in?' he asks, breaking eye contact and gesturing to the café.

It's cheerful inside, packed with teenagers and students smoking, laughing, trying briefly to forget about the Occupation and the war. There's music playing. We see our friend Padrice at a table close to the door, along with Anton's older brother Henri and Henri's girlfriend Madeleine.

I notice Henri's arm draped casually over Madeleine's shoulder as I take the seat next to Anton's.

'What is there to drink?' I ask, and suddenly I dare to place my hand lightly on the back of Anton's neck; my fingertips tingle at the touch of his skin.

'Probably coffee made from acorns . . .' Anton replies, glancing at me but not moving away from my touch.

'Yeah, rotten acorns and mud,' Padrice jokes; he sees what I am doing and his eyebrows jiggle with amusement. Padrice is a total joker and I hope he's not going to tease me.

'Or you can have tap water, but at a price,' Madeleine adds. 'I have to go.' She kisses handsome Henri full on the mouth while Padrice whistles and I try not to stare, then she heads out of the café.

'So, how's your knitting?' Anton asks me. My hand slips down into his and he clasps hold of it. This is new and thrilling, quite electrifying, but we both pretend it's normal.

'Good. I made another sock today,' I reply. 'And you?'

We are talking about how many tyre-ripping devices we have placed. But like everyone, everywhere in Belgium, we have to talk in code.

'Four.'

'How are you, Nicole?' Henri asks. 'Have you heard when your father's going to be released?'

I shake my head.

'All the missing fathers,' Henri says, and I know he's thinking about Monsieur Morel, stuck in Paris without a travel permit. 'They'll be home soon, hopefully.' He pats my arm and looks at me so kindly that a lump begins to form in my throat.

'Oh my good God! Is that Aurelie?' Padrice asks, jerking his head towards the window. 'She's not coming in here with him, surely?'

Walking through the café door is my friend Aurelie; her hair is curled under her jaunty beret, her face is rouged, her lips bright red and she is arm in arm, laughing, with a Nazi policeman. He is young, blond and undoubtedly handsome, but I would like to poke her eyes out for this. There are all sorts of rumours about Aurelie's father: he's a collaborator – a 'collabo' – who works for the Nazis and even helped in the invasion. Clearly, Aurelie has turned into a Nazi sympathizer herself.

As she sweeps the room, she sees us and waves. I shake my head in warning, but still she comes over, the German oaf in tow.

'Nicole, this is Franz!'

There is so much fun and excitement in her face. I'm embarrassed, but I will not shake her Nazi by the hand and invite him to sit down with us. I cannot.

'I'm sorry, but this table is full,' I say.

'Full? Don't be silly,' Aurelie trills. 'Move up. Franz will bring two chairs.' She still doesn't get it. She still doesn't seem to understand that most of us are horrified at the thought of socializing with our invaders.

I don't move; neither do Anton, Padrice or Henri. We sit still and sullen, and now the German has noticed.

'Move,' he commands, 'or I will ask you all to leave this table.'

'We were just leaving,' Henri replies, pushing back his chair and preparing to stand up.

'Sit down! Now!' the German orders.

'So charming, your new boyfriend,' I say to Aurelie, although I know it's foolish and dangerous.

The German glares furiously, and I do not know what might happen, but then there are frantic shouts outside. They grow louder and people are running past the café windows with uniformed men chasing behind.

'*Eine Razzia*,' Franz declares, looking delighted. We all know this means a raid. I've heard of them, but I've never been in one: the Nazis block both ends of a street and search all the properties, stoking up terror and looking for anything hidden or forbidden, anyone not carrying identity papers.

The music stops and a sense of fear grows in the café; voices have lowered and some of the girls have begun to cry. I wonder if there is anything in my bag . . . any wood or nails which could land me in fatal trouble. I touch my jacket pocket and feel the reassuring smoothness of my identity card.

The door bursts open and two uniformed officers enter, guns drawn; behind them is a third man in a long overcoat and brimmed hat. As he walks stiffly forward, it is clear this man has a cumbersome wooden leg, but he is wearing polished black riding boots with simple metal spurs at the heel. Maybe he was a cavalry officer before he became Gestapo.

I can't take my eyes from him. He has small round

gold-rimmed glasses, small mean eyes, and there is a menacing sneer across his face.

'Sixteen or younger, line up at the door,' he barks in French with a harsh German accent. 'We will inspect your papers and your bags. If you are in order, go home, study or do something useful. No more sitting about in cafés like degenerates. Line up!'

I take hold of my bag, grab Aurelie's hand and head for the door. Padrice follows, but Anton does not move. He and Henri are staring at the Nazis, their faces strained.

'Seventeen or older, good news,' the Gestapo devil announces. 'We have work for you. There are factories all over Germany needing good, strong workers right now. Today! So form a second line: papers out! If you're fit to work, we will send you.'

Gasps and cries of shock greet this announcement.

'Line up!' one of the officers barks.

Still Anton is glued to his chair. For a few more months, he's sixteen, so he needs to line up with us. But of course, his brother Henri is eighteen. Surely that can't mean Henri's about to be taken away? Without any warning? He's a medical student, a future doctor . . . is he going to be rounded up like a criminal?

'Come over here,' I urge Anton.

'Silence!' one of the officers barks.

Beyond the café window, more soldiers are massing,

guns hanging from their shoulders and those terrible Alsatian dogs howling, straining at their leads, trained to outrun you and drag you to the ground. Two lorries are rolling up and I understand immediately: they're here to take the older teenagers away.

Helpless rage bubbles up inside me again. Bursting a few tyres is hopeless; it means nothing. There is nothing we can do to really fight back against our invaders.

'And what about you?' The Gestapo devil limps with his wooden leg towards Anton. This must be Kriminaldirektor Richter, the one who lost his leg to the Belgians and hates us with such a passion. 'Young enough to run home to Mama or are you coming to Germany to work like a man? If you're nearly seventeen, we can make an exception for a big strong boy.'

'No!' Henri protests, a desperate edge to his voice. 'My brother is sixteen and he stays at home.'

With the back of his hand, the devil strikes Henri hard in the face. Something on his hand, a ring perhaps, slices Henri's cheekbone and draws blood.

'Silence, you impudent brat!' Richter commands. 'I'm Kriminaldirektor Richter. I decide — and you, brat, are the first into the van.'

Chapter Three

I stamp my feet and slap my hands against my arms but I'm still freezing cold. I've been standing in this queue for coal along with hundreds of other people for almost three hours. The only good thing is that Anton is queuing beside me and we try to keep our spirits up with jokes and stories.

We don't talk about the people painfully missing from our lives: our fathers, and now Henri, marched at gunpoint into the back of Richter's lorry while we could only stand by desperately and watch. It will be our turn to be taken to the work camps soon enough.

This is the coldest November I've ever experienced. There's already ice inside the windows in the mornings. If winter carries on like this, we risk not just starving, but also freezing to death.

Craving a little warmth, I slip my hand into Anton's

pocket and curl it around his. We are both wearing woollen gloves, but still I'm sure I can feel a tingle at his touch.

We often hold hands now and sometimes Anton's arm slips round my waist or shoulder, but we've still come no closer than this. We remain on the verge of getting close and I'm desperate to know when it will happen. What can I do to make it happen?

A call goes up from the front of the long queue: 'No coal left. Come back next week.' The doors of the store are quickly shut and bolted against the shouts and distressed cries of the waiting crowd.

'This is criminal! How are we supposed to survive?' a woman demands.

'My children will freeze to death in their beds,' another cries.

'Let's go to the square. Come on, people are there celebrating the King's Feast Day. Let's go and demand some coal,' a man urges.

This captures the imagination of the crowd. Cries of support rise up.

'Yes!'

'Let's go.'

'Let's tell them.'

'What have we got to lose?'

The square is not far from here, so the crowd turns as one and begins to march down the street.

'Are we going too?' Anton asks, although we are already following.

'Yes!'

I'm marching forward. I know how dangerous this is, but there are hundreds of us and there really is courage in numbers.

'Something's changing,' I tell Anton. 'Maybe it will be like Remembrance Day. People are standing up to them. We want to be part of that, don't we?'

He smiles.

Four days ago, on the 11th of November, we were all warned not to mark the end of the Great War. Mama and Grand-Mamie wouldn't let me out of the house, but thousands of people went to memorial sites all over the city to lay flowers in defiance of our Nazi rulers. There were protests, scuffles with soldiers and many arrests.

Today is the King's Feast Day – a ceremony in honour of our King who is under house arrest – and the service being held for him in the cathedral could be the focus for another protest.

The closer we get to the square, the angrier the crowd becomes.

'We want coal! We need coal! We demand coal!' The chanting becomes louder and more powerful, and more people join us as we make our way towards the square. Soon we are a river of people filling the narrow streets; chanting and shouting furiously. Even if Anton and I didn't want to go, it would now be difficult to fight our way against the flow.

As we round the corner towards the square we can hear chaotic noise ahead of us. There is shouting, screaming, the noise of sirens and vehicles, ominous cracks which I suspect are gunfire, and above it all the booming of the cathedral organ.

We are still being marched forward, still trying to be brave as we approach this upheaval.

'It sounds like a riot,' Anton says grimly, but his jaw is set. He has a tight hold of my hand. I don't want him to let go, so I link my fingers with his. 'Are you ready?' he asks.

'Yes.'

We begin to jog forward as the speed of the marchers increases.

'Give us coal!' we are all chanting together. 'We demand coal!'

Propelled by the crowd in front and the crowd behind, we rush into the square, where a riot is in full swing. Furious men, women, teenagers, even children are hurling anything they can find at the line of Nazi uniforms which has ringed the cathedral grounds. People are shouting about everything: soldiers kept in prisoner-of-war camps, the lack of food, the lack of coal, teenagers being rounded up and taken away.

I find I'm furious too, and in the crowd I have the courage to say it.

'You've got my papa!' I scream. 'Where is my papa?!'

'And Henri!' Anton shouts. 'And my dad!'

'You evil scum!' I shout.

Someone has collected stones, bottles and chunks of metal into a pile, and buoyed by the courage of everyone around, we join in, scrambling for items and throwing them as hard as we can at the soldiers.

When I manage to hit a Nazi on the knee and he drops to the ground, I feel a rush of achievement and throw my next stone even harder.

'Always a great aim,' Anton says as he pitches a stone too. 'Remember the apple cores?'

I do. The two of us perched in an apple tree firing cores at passers-by and trying to knock off their hats.

Vehicles roar into the square, scattering protesters. Reinforcements are on their way. There are so many more of us than them, but they are armed. Loud-hailers urge us to disperse and go home. Then the soldiers around the cathedral, on command, all fire their guns together into the air.

After the shocking, explosive sound, there is smoke and a bitter burning smell. For a minute or two the crowd quietens down, and maybe we are quailing, maybe we are thinking of leaving before it gets too ugly and dangerous.

But then something extraordinary happens. We can hear the cathedral organ and it's playing the British national anthem. This is wonderful, outrageous defiance. The Belgian national anthem would make us sad, would make us think of our defeat, of our imprisoned loved ones, of everything we have lost. But the British national anthem – at once we are inspired by the nation that has not been invaded, that fights on.

The shouting, screaming and throwing begins afresh, with renewed determination. I watch a big glass bottle soar into the air and burst into flames at the feet of the guards, finally scattering them from their line.

But then the guns begin to crack rapidly. Screams follow: terrified, wounded screams. The soldiers are not firing into the air any more; they are firing *at* us.

'Nico!' Anton shouts; he grabs for my hand and pulls me along. Two jeeps loaded with soldiers, machine guns at the ready, are charging towards us. 'This way!'

We run, swerve and dive into a little side street. We run because people are running behind us. Panic has broken out. If we fall, we will be trampled.

'They're firing at the crowd,' I gasp. 'Unarmed civilians, women, children . . . they're *firing*!'

'We need to get away!'

But as we run down this street, a handful of others are running past us, towards the square: young men with grins on their faces, some carrying old-fashioned handguns.

'Be brave! You've rattled them!' one calls out

31

cheerfully as he passes. 'Now we'll go and pick a few off.'

'Join up!' another urges. 'Join the Resistance and we'll get rid of them for good!'

A girl not much older than me is handing out flimsy newspapers from a bag slung over her shoulder. '*Le Libre*: read the real news,' she says as she thrusts copies into our hands.

We keep on running and only when we are in a quieter street, sure we are not being chased any more, do we pull into a doorway and collapse against the walls, eyes locked on each other, grins wide.

'That was intense!' I say, almost dizzy with relief.

'Yeah!'

I look at the paper in my hands. It is not like anything I've seen before. It has photographs not of Nazis marching triumphantly from yet another victory, but of anti-Nazi ambushes and recent sabotage explosions. The headlines are anti-Nazi too: BRITAIN WINS AIR BATTLE TO KEEP OUT NAZI INVADERS.

'Who publishes this?' Anton asks, searching through the pages. He starts to laugh. 'Look at this!' He points to a paragraph, where the publication address given is: *Gestapo Headquarters on Avenue Louise*, the editor's name: *Peter Pan*.

'That's just brilliant.' I read out the message below: '*Join us, find a Resistance friend, start a cell, never, ever give up on this fight!*'

I take hold of Anton's hand. I see a little scar on the back of it and suddenly remember dropping his penknife when I was ten or eleven and impaling him right there. It makes me feel more closely connected to him than ever.

'We have to join,' I tell him, squeezing his hand. 'No matter what my papa says, some things are more important than staying safe.'

'I know, Nico. We'll join together.' Anton turns to me.

We search each other's faces for the endless courage and determination we will have to find to do this. I am burning to kiss him, blazing with the need. But we can hear the rumble of army trucks on the move. We have to get out of here.

Chapter Four

When I step through my front door I can tell at once that something is different. Mama and Grand-Mamie are not in the kitchen; there is the smell of a wood fire in the sitting room.

'There you are!' I hear Mama call. 'We've been so worried.'

'What's happened?' I ask, hurrying into the sitting room.

Both Mama and Grand-Mamie are huddled together on the sofa in front of the fire; Mama looks as if she has been crying.

'What's the matter?'

'We've been back to the Gestapo to ask about your papa . . .' Mama begins, but she can't continue.

'What?!' I ask, rushing over to them.

Mama begins to sob, her face in her hands.

'They don't have him,' Grand-Mamie says.

'They don't have him? What do they mean?' I exclaim.

'He was moved to another prison yesterday, outside Brussels, but he went missing on the journey. They can't tell us anything more,' Grand-Mamie adds.

'He went missing? Do they mean he's escaped?' I'm filled with a burst of hope.

Mama shakes her head. 'Surely he would contact us; somehow he would let us know. He must be dead . . .' she sobs. 'They've killed him. They've murdered him and they don't want us to know.'

At the thought of this, I crumple into a heap at their feet, feeling punched, winded, utterly defeated. But Grand-Mamie immediately puts a soothing hand on my back.

'Please, Nicole, Elisabeth, I don't think we should assume the worst.'

When I can find my voice again, I ask lots of questions: which prison was Papa moved to? When did this happen? Have they spoken to his friends? Nothing brings me any answers.

'Where have you been, Nicole?' Mama asks eventually, lifting her head and looking at me with swollen eyes. 'Do you have any coal? We've had to burn a post from the garden fence.'

And then I make my mistake. I launch into the story

of the coal queue and the march on the square and the soldiers firing at us. Brimful of bravado, I tell them about *Le Libre* and how the will to fight back is growing and how we must all be a part of it.

'So Anton and I—'

'Enough!' Mama interrupts me. 'I have heard enough.' She sounds distraught. 'What did your papa tell you?' she demands. 'What was the last thing he asked you to do before he was taken away? I know, because I heard him.' Her eyes are fixed on my face and I have never seen her look so wildly upset. I've never heard her voice raised like this.

'Not to fight back,' I mumble.

'You have no idea what you are meddling with here. These men have no mercy. They are attack dogs trained to follow orders, trained to break us.'

'So what are we supposed to do?' I can still feel the hot flame of defiance burning in my heart.

'You are to stay safe, to keep your family safe and to do as you are told,' she orders.

'Then we are going to either starve or freeze to death!' I protest. 'There's no food, there's no coal. I'll sneak out to the railway depot tonight, shall I? Apparently that's where people go when they are desperate. They climb over the fence in the dark, they fill their pockets with lumps of coal from the mountain the Nazis keep for the trains, and they don't mind being fired at by guards with machine guns because if they don't get the coal home they'll all freeze anyway!'

'Don't be so dramatic!'

I've never heard my mama talk like this. Furious now, I blurt out: 'Papa was in the Resistance the last time. I know it! We have to be like him. We have to join up and fight the beasts! We're doing nothing and I'm ashamed—'

Smack!

My cheek is suddenly on fire, my ears ringing; all my words have fled from my mind. My mama, my beloved, gentle mama has slapped me. Hard.

'Don't you dare,' she says, pale with anger. 'Your papa delivered leaflets and nothing else. Everyone was doing it. And girls don't fight. Girls can't make a difference. No good comes of resistance. It just makes the Nazis worse. Every time a Nazi is killed by the Resisters, innocent people pay the price. Is that what you want? The death of an innocent person on your conscience? One day the war will end and it is my duty to keep us safe until then.'

Tears of rage are burning in my eyes. There are a hundred arguments I could make against hers, but instead I get up and run to my room.

'Elisabeth, that was too harsh, the girl has spirit,' I hear Grand-Mamie defending me. 'We cannot crush the spirit of the young, or what hope is there?'

★ ★ ★

Later my mother calls me down to dinner. She hugs me, she apologizes and she kisses my bright red cheek, but otherwise says nothing.

I still feel furious with her. *Girls can't make a difference.* I still can't believe she said that.

There is a linen cloth on the table, as well as napkins, soup bowls, side plates and the butter knives with the ivory handles, although there has been no butter for months now. And I miss butter, almost more than anything else.

Mama brings in the soup tureen but smiles apologetically as she sets it down. 'I'm afraid it's a poor meal tonight.'

'It will be delicious,' Grand-Mamie declares, and it's true: Mama has a talent for making even the most meagre ingredients tasty. But no one complains about food any more. No one even speaks when they eat any more. We are all too ravenously hungry.

Mama takes the lid from the tureen and heaps my bowl. I say thank you, but yet again I'm faced with a watery plateful of boiled barley, thin strips of cabbage and what looks like wild dandelion leaves and nettle tops.

'Very nice,' Grand-Mamie says unconvincingly.

Then we hear the rumbling. At first, I think it's Gaspar, our cat, purring. But as the sound grows louder, I realize a vehicle is approaching.

Through the lace curtain, we see a car pulling to a

halt outside our house. Two men in the grey and black uniforms of the dreaded Gestapo get out.

We hardly dare to breathe.

The two policemen knock so violently at our front door I expect it to fall off its hinges. Mama jumps up, a terrified expression on her face. Grand-Mamie and I follow her into the hall, where the policemen have already barged in.

'Can I help you?' Mama asks, her voice trembling.

'Where is your husband, George de Wilde?' one of them barks.

'I don't know . . . we went to the headquarters today and they couldn't—'

Before she's finished her reply, the man barks: 'Stay here.'

Then the pair begin to search the house. Despite our protests that Papa is not here, they overturn chairs and the sofa, search behind curtains and out in the back garden. Then they head upstairs, emptying the wardrobes and searching under the beds. I listen closely when they are in the attic room, but I can't hear the door to the eaves being opened.

When they come downstairs again, they look furious.

'Where is he?' one of them shouts. 'Tell us now or you will be in terrible trouble.'

'We don't know. Maybe if you'd listened the first time . . .' Grand-Mamie dares.

One of the policemen steps towards me. With his gloved hand, he takes hold of my neck, underneath my chin, and squeezes tightly.

'What are you doing?' Mama gasps. 'She doesn't know anything. Please, what are you doing?'

'*Ruhe hier!*' the man shouts. Silence.

Mama claps her hand over her mouth.

'Tell me right now where your husband is or she is coming to prison too.' He squeezes harder to make his point.

Mama's eyes are wild with fright. I can't breathe. I can't bear to look at her and I can't bear to look away. I am bursting to do something . . . so I reach over, grab the handle and throw the front door open as my mother gasps with horror. Now that the door is open and others can see in, the policeman lets go of my neck.

'We don't know,' my mother whispers. 'We honestly know nothing.'

'If he returns, you have a duty to inform the authorities immediately,' the policeman insists. Then, with a heel click and a salute, they leave the house, get into their car and drive away.

As soon as they're gone, Mama bursts into tears. We all look at one another, then fall into a hug of relief.

'I have to go out,' I announce, because there's a plan I have to set in motion this minute.

'No!' Mama howls. 'Haven't you been through

enough? You will stay at home, safe. It's nearly the curfew.'

'Just to Anton's,' I insist.

'No!' Mama pleads.

I feel terribly sorry for her, and I never, ever want to hurt her, but if I don't break free from her anxious care, I'll never be able to do anything.

'Just ten minutes, I promise. Please, Mama . . .'

Before she can stop me, I grab my coat, far too small now, shoot out of the front door and begin to run. I'm soon at Anton's house, where he opens the door.

'Nico?' His eyebrows arch up in surprise.

'Hello.' I step inside, and for a moment we stand in the hallway just looking at one another. He pushes the dark hair from his forehead. His serious eyes meet mine and for the first time since we were children, I have the sense that we are reading one another's thoughts once again.

'You're ready?' he asks.

'I am.'

'Nicole? Is everything all right?' Anton's mother calls from the sitting room, where I know she is in her arm-chair, darning clothes or maybe writing a letter to Henri or her husband.

'I need some help with my maths homework,' I fib.

Anton turns towards the wooden staircase and I follow him up to his bedroom. When I was younger,

I was often in this small room, decorated with a shelf of books, posters and a collection of painstakingly built model aeroplanes. But now it feels intimate to be standing right beside his narrow bed.

'The Gestapo have just been at my house,' I whisper.

'Why?' Anton asks.

'They're looking for Papa. He escaped on the way to another prison.'

'Really? He *escaped*?'

'Yes. We thought he might be dead . . . but if they're looking for him, then he must have got away from them.' Some small sense of relief returns to me with these words.

'Are you OK?' Anton puts his hands on my shoulders and I feel steadied.

I nod, then tell him: 'Come on, we need to do this. Did you get the information? We need to join up and get these monsters out of Belgium.'

'Yes, we need to do this,' he agrees. 'I found the boy whose sister I saw handing out *Le Libre*. He's told me what to do.' Anton opens an atlas and pulls two forms from between its pages. His hands are shaking slightly. 'We fill these in – using codenames – and put them into a postbox I've been told about.'

The paper in front of me is an innocent-looking library application. I hover with Anton's fountain pen over the form.

'*It is not in the stars to hold our destiny, but in ourselves,*' Anton quotes.

'I like that. Is it Schiller?' I ask.

'Shakespeare.'

'Ah, Shakespeare – you should meet Monsieur Durance.' With the pen, I write 'Coco' in my best hand in the space marked 'name'.

'Why "Coco"?' Anton asks.

I shrug. 'I think it's glamorous – you know, like Coco Chanel.'

His mouth is twitching as if he's trying not to smile. Yes, I am a girl in an outgrown coat and an outgrown skirt and scruffy shoes, so it's ridiculous to pick the code-name Coco. But joining the Resistance is glamorous. It's bold and big and . . . quite terrifying.

As the wet ink shines before it dries into the paper, I have the feeling that I have just done something very serious, very grown-up and irreversible. I'm going to join the Resistance. I'm going to be part of a growing movement fighting the Nazis. I'm doing this for my papa, for Henri, for Madame Morel sitting downstairs, and all the other mothers all over Europe writing love letters to their exiled husbands and children.

I'm doing this because it's the right thing to do.

I watch as Anton begins to fill out his form.

'What's my codename?' he asks, his grave eyes looking up at me.

I glance around the room and fix on the shelf of books. I've never known a boy to read so much, and proper literature too. There's Schiller here, Shakespeare, Victor Hugo and Goethe. Behind those books, I know he hides a stack of the books we're no longer allowed: poetry by Heine, Jack London's *White Fang*, even *Emil and the Detectives*, a children's story banned because the author is Jewish.

'You're the "Poet",' I tell him.

As he laughs and begins to write out his codename, I'm incredibly glad that we're joining up together. With all the games and dares we did together as children, we were building up the friendship and the courage for this.

I smile, hand him my form and say, 'Coco and the Poet are going to war.'

Chapter Five

I study my face in the mirror: grey eyes, thin lips, high cheekbones and a small nose. I think I am quite pretty but not startlingly so, like Aurelie.

I'm proudest of my hair, which is light brown with touches of gold and falls below my shoulders with a slight curl. I often wear it in a ponytail or plait, but today I need to do something different. Today I'm going with Anton to meet our first Resistance contact, and I need to look not like a schoolgirl but like an adult who can be trusted to carry out dangerous work.

I pull my hair back and twist it up into a bun, pushing hairpins into my head to keep it in place. I take a stub of red lipstick I've found in Mama's chest of drawers and drag it carefully over my lips. Then I clip pearl earrings onto my lobes. Two drops of Mama's precious perfume go behind each ear.

Finally, I choose a dark jacket to go over my jumper and skirt in the hope that it looks a little more grown-up.

When the doorbell rings, I shout down, 'It's Anton, we're going to the library!' and scoot out of the front door before Mama or Grand-Mamie catch sight of me and wonder what I've done to myself.

'You look different,' Anton says as he links arms with me. I feel the excitement of not just being with him but also of our shared secret. No one else knows about this.

'I'm trying to look older,' I say, and pout at him with my red lips.

'I see . . .'

'Do you like it?'

'I'm not sure. You don't look like yourself . . . you don't look so fierce any more.'

'What do you mean, fierce?' I want to snatch my arm back. Is this how he thinks of me?

His mouth makes that twitchy trying-not-to-laugh movement. 'I just mean . . . fierce as in determined, strong, willing to charge into things. It's a good thing.'

I still feel annoyed. He's obviously trying to look older too, in a white shirt, tie and woollen coat. Anton has more clothes than anyone, but no one can feel jealous because these are all the clothes his brother left behind when he was bundled into a lorry that day and sent to work.

'Don't be sulky, I brought you something,' he says. He reaches into his pocket, and there in the palm of his hand is a glossy Belgian chocolate. I haven't seen one for months; just as Monsieur Durance warned, chocolate has become almost impossible to find.

'For me?' It's a small gift, but I'm very touched.

'All yours.'

I bite off half and hold out the remains to him. 'It's totally delicious. You have this bit.'

'No, it's for you.'

'Have it!' There's a pause. Although it's mad, I'm telling myself if he eats the chocolate, he'll kiss me one day. If he doesn't, he won't.

He eats it and a jolt of happiness rushes through me.

'Are you nervous?' I ask him.

'Not too bad. Are you?'

'No.'

This is true. I'm excited. I'm fizzing with curiosity, and I can't wait to join up and get started . . . so I don't feel nervous at all.

'Codenames at all times,' Anton reminds me.

'Of course, Poet.' Although I chose it, his codename still makes me giggle.

'Mademoiselle Nicole, are you off to the library again?' Stapie, the soldier from the corner of the road, peels himself from the wall he's been leaning against and throws the butt of his cigarette into the street.

47

'Hello, Stapie, yes, we're a very studious bunch.'

'Have a good time.'

He looks so bored and fed up that I feel I have to stop and talk to him for a moment.

'Where are you from, Stapie?'

'A dairy farm . . . in the countryside near Ludwigsburg.'

'Oh . . .'

This is unexpected. I've not thought before of what the German soldiers might have done before the war. Stapie looks as if he'd be more at home in the fields than standing guard over a quiet street in Brussels.

'I don't know how my father and mother are managing without me. But there was no choice. I had to join the army.'

Anton nudges me in the ribs; it's time to go.

'Well, here's hoping you'll get home soon,' I say.

'Yes . . .' He looks as if he can't decide whether I'm being friendly or cheeky.

I give him a little wave and walk on, smiling cheerfully. I don't introduce Anton, who just glares at him.

'What's that about?' he hisses once we are out of earshot.

'If Stapie thinks I'm his friend, he's not going to suspect me of being a Resister, is he?'

'Suppose . . . but you don't have to pretend you're in love with him.'

I can't help smiling. Is this proof that Anton is jealous? 'What do you think Stapie did to land the most boring job in the army?' I wonder.

'Probably failed to whittle the Führer out of an acorn at Hitler Youth camp.'

Maybe because I'm so tense and hyped up, I find this hysterically funny.

'Please stop laughing,' Anton hisses. 'Your German boyfriend is staring at us.'

'Oh, ha ha . . . my German boyfriend.' I smack Anton on the arm.

It is ten to four when we find the café on Rue du Choeur. We have been told to sit at an indoor table and wait for someone to do something very precise. A man with a blue scarf is going to come in at 4 p.m. He will ask the barman the time and for a glass of tap water. He will sit down, drink his water, blow his nose with a red handkerchief, drop his paper on the floor, pick it up again and walk out of the café.

We are to wait several moments before following him to a park where we can talk.

Anton and I order ersatz coffees and take a seat. We sip and try to keep up an ordinary conversation, but now I'm beginning to feel nervous.

'I'm glad you're here,' I tell him. 'When I'm with you' – I slip my hand over his – 'well . . . I'm just glad we're doing this together. It makes me feel braver.'

His eyes meet mine and he breaks a small smile: 'Me too, fierce girl.'

At one minute past four, a man with a walking stick and a blue scarf walks in: he approaches the bar, he asks the time, he asks for a glass of water. He sits down and opens up the detested *Le Soir* newspaper which is run by Nazis and collabos. He blows his nose with a big red hanky then makes a slightly ham-fisted job of dropping the paper on the floor and picking it up again. Finally, he drinks his water and gets up to leave.

I flash an urgent glance at Anton. I can't say anything obvious. But somehow I need to let him know that this man is not the mysterious stranger I was expecting. This man is Monsieur Durance! My teacher from school.

Anton is already on his feet, although it seems too soon. 'I'll pay for the coffees,' he says.

I stand up, put my satchel over my shoulder and head for the door, trying to look relaxed. Monsieur Durance has turned right.

I don't know what to say to my teacher . . . I don't know what he will say to me. He knows me; despite my lipstick and my bun, he knows I'm fifteen and probably too young to join up.

'That's my teacher from school,' I whisper to Anton, as we begin to walk along the pavement.

'What?! Are you sure?'

'Of course I'm sure – it's Monsieur Durance.'

'We're to call him the Owl.'

We're only a few metres behind Monsieur Durance now; although he limps, he walks at a brisk pace. He looks left and right and I'm sure he's checking to see who's following, but he makes it look graceful and casual. No one would suspect him of anything.

It takes us just a few more moments to reach a small park, abandoned because of the intense cold and because metal feet are all that is left of the benches. The seats have all been stolen and chopped up for firewood.

Then he turns to face us.

'Good afternoon,' Anton says.

Monsieur Durance smiles. 'Good afternoon.'

'Coco and the Poet,' Anton whispers, sounding a little embarrassed.

'So nice to meet you,' Monsieur begins, but then he looks at me properly and sees past the lipstick and hairdo.

'Coco, I know you.'

'But Monsieur . . . Owl – I can help,' I whisper. 'We want to do everything we can to get the Nazis out.'

'Coco and the Poet,' Monsieur Durance repeats, 'you are brave to look for us and to want to join. But you both look too young for the work we do.'

'No,' I protest. 'We already burst car tyres and we're not too young to help. You know the Gestapo have taken my papa away. I have to fight back.'

Monsieur Durance nods.

'The Poet is sixteen,' I add, 'plus we're brave and willing to do everything you ask. Soon there will be no one older left – the Germans are sending them all to work camps.'

'I do know you, Coco,' Monsieur Durance says gently. 'You are full of spirit but you still have to learn patience. We do very dangerous work. Can I trust you to follow orders to the letter, Coco? Can I put the lives of my friends in your hands?'

I look at him pleadingly and somehow try to convey my desperation to be part of this without words.

'Please make use of us in any way you can, sir,' Anton says finally. His voice is deep and serious and I can feel myself, like a climber losing a foothold, falling just a little further in love with him.

I hear a tiny rustle and look round. There is nothing to see, just shrubbery, but it reminds me how dangerous this meeting is.

Monsieur Durance looks as if he's trying to decide. I realize there is nothing I want more than to be allowed to join. I can't fight the Nazis on my own; he has to let me in. He has to agree – we have to be allowed to help him. I press my hands together and beg without words.

'Are you really ready?' he asks.

We nod.

'Do you really understand that *when* you are caught –

we never say *if* – you will be cruelly tortured for the names of everyone involved, then killed?'

I swallow and nod again.

'No deals can ever be made with the Nazis. As soon as they learn you are involved with us, it will always be worse for you. You can admit nothing. Your only hope of release is to deny everything. Play innocent to the last.'

Anton and I cannot take our eyes from Monsieur Durance's face. He is smiling gently while he talks about torture.

'You can still walk away from us. No harm is done. I'll trust you to keep my secret.'

'No,' I say immediately.

'Never,' Anton adds.

After a long pause, Monsieur Durance begins: 'My friends, there are two important things you need to learn first of all. Please memorize this address: sixteen Rue du Clair. It is in your part of town.'

'I know it,' I say eagerly.

'Beside number sixteen is the entrance to a little alley. One third of the way up, on the left-hand side, low down, you will find a loose brick in the wall. This is your dead drop. Check under the brick at least once a day, maybe twice. You will find instructions and necessary information from Group K, which is our cell.'

I can't resist grinning . . . he means we're in, doesn't he? Coco and the Poet are being invited to join Group K.

'The instructions are always in code. Do you have a copy of *The Complete Works of William Shakespeare*? In English? If not, you can find one in the library . . .'

We both nod.

'The play is always *Henry V*. The first word of the message you will find in the opening twenty lines. Lots of nonsense words will follow. To translate them, use an alphabet which begins with the first letter of the word in the play which follows the codeword. So, if your alphabet begins with g, then "a" is "g", "b" is "h", "c" is "i" and so on.'

I don't really get this, but Anton is nodding, so I hope he can explain later.

'What do we do first?' I ask Monsieur Durance. 'How can we help?'

He smiles. 'Patience,' he says. 'You must do the little things well. You must build your nerves and your courage . . . *All things are ready if our minds be so.*'

Little things? I feel disappointed and I think he's quoting Shakespeare at me, just like he does in class.

'But Coco, even the little jobs are vitally important: surveillance, simple sabotage. Two tips . . .' he says and does his graceful, casual look around once again. 'Always be smiling, cheerful, whistling, never act suspiciously . . .'

'Easy,' I say.

Suddenly the Owl breaks into a belly laugh and throws his arms around me. 'My dear, happy news!' he cries. As his head moves forward and I wonder if he greets all his new recruits like this, he whispers urgently into my ear, 'Someone's watching, time to leave.'

'Lovely to see you, Uncle!' I trill, and grabbing hold of Anton's arm I fairly skip out of the park and onto the pavement.

'What's going on?' Anton hisses.

'Time to lose a follower,' I whisper, and we duck quickly into a side street. I hear footsteps behind us and alongside my fear there is a burst of thrill. We are being chased. We are properly in the game. 'Speed up,' I urge Anton.

The footsteps behind us speed up too.

'We'll have to run,' I say, my heart pumping wildly.

Anton looks down the road. A tram has stopped not twenty feet in front of us. 'We'll jump on at the last minute,' he whispers.

We walk briskly towards the tram. The conductor is already ringing the bell; it's about to pull off. I keep walking, for as long as I can bear; then, just as the tram starts to move, I leap for the door, Anton right behind me.

As we look out of the window, we see a man in a long grey overcoat running to catch up. But he's too late.

I squeeze Anton's hand and joke, 'Coco and the Poet, one; secret policeman, nil.'

Chapter Six

I crouch beside the wall in the alley, searching for a brick that seems loose. I touch many bricks in turn until at last, one wobbles.

I wish Anton was here, but after our encounter with the secret policeman we've decided to stay apart for several days. Looking left and right, trying to be as graceful as Monsieur Durance, I check I'm alone, then quickly pull the brick out, snatch the scrap of paper from underneath then push the brick back in place.

The scrap goes into my shoe, then I race home, where I can look at it in private. I sit on my bed with a copy of *The Complete Works of William Shakespeare* beside me and unfurl the scrap.

Brightest. Ybl kl uljr zpe-lpnoa avupnoa. Pm luitf: zovba 'klupzl'. Zahuk ha 15-21, dhajo zpeallu. Jvumpyt.

I stare at the letters in horror. I'm never going to make sense of this. This is impossible. Brightest? What does it mean? I try to remember what Monsieur Durance said.

I open the book at *Henry V* – that much I can remember – and scan the opening lines. 'Brightest', yes: there it is, not far from the top. The next word begins with 'h'. So I'm to write out the alphabet, then write a code alphabet that begins with 'h'. So 'a' is 'h', 'b' is 'i', 'c' is 'j' and so on.

I write the two alphabets out. So now I tackle the first word: Ybl. When I rewrite it in the decoded alphabet, it magically turns into 'Rue'. I've got it! I can do this.

It doesn't take long to uncover the other words: 'Rue de Neck six–eight tonight. If enemy: shout "Denise". Stand at 15–21. Watch sixteen. Confirm.'

Here it is: my first assignment. I'm to stand lookout outside a house numbered sixteen from six o'clock till eight. I scribble my coded 'Confirm. Coco' ready to take back to the loose brick in the lane. Already I'm wondering how I can be inconspicuous. How I can stay alert? How I can stay warm? Will I manage? I'm sure I will. I can. I will. I'm a little disappointed to have just a look-out job, but didn't Monsieur Durance say I had to learn to be patient?

★　★　★

The Rue de Neck is quiet when I get there well before 6 p.m. I find the house I'm supposed to be watching, cross the road and stand opposite. This might not be an exciting job, but I'm going to do it well. Whatever's going on in that house, people are depending on me.

Some children are huddled in a doorway further along, chatting, but almost everyone else has gone in because it's cold and dark. I'm wrapped up in all the clothes I can find. I'm going to walk up and down the street and sit in a doorway from time to time. I will constantly be watching for Nazis. In the house I'm guarding they could be making bombs, or a secret radio broadcast. Their lives could be at risk and I can't lose focus for a moment.

'Who are you? Who are you looking for?'

Within fifteen minutes of walking up and down this part of the street, two little boys have attached themselves to me and are asking tireless questions.

'I'm just waiting for someone to come home.'

'Who?'

'It doesn't matter. What's your name?' I'm hoping to distract them and make them go away.

They are skinny little boys in ragged clothes with filthy hands, knees and faces. One has an unruly blond mop; the other has hair cut almost to his scalp, probably to keep head lice at bay.

'I'm Alfonse,' the blond one says.

'I'm Pierre.'

'Alfonse, I know your mother,' I fib. 'She would want you home by now.'

'My mother's dead.'

'Oh . . . sorry, I've made a mistake.' I feel terrible.

'Why are you here?' Pierre asks. 'Why are you standing outside my building?'

'I'm just waiting . . . really, it's boring.' I keep my glances at the boys as brief as possible. Almost all of my attention is on number sixteen.

A figure is approaching the house, in a thick coat and scarf, hat pulled low over the ears, but I would recognize that figure no matter where. It's Anton. He hasn't seen me and I'm sure I shouldn't let him know I'm here.

I sink back into a passageway as he knocks on the door. After a brief wait, he's let in. Now my heart begins to jump in my chest. I'm not just guarding the lives of Resistance workers I've never met before; I'm now guarding Anton's life.

'Do you know someone who lives over there?' Pierre persists.

'I'm just waiting, honestly. It might take a while. You shouldn't—'

And then it happens: two cars, from both ends of the street, speed in and screech to a halt in front of me. For a moment I'm paralysed with shock, but then as soldiers jump from one car and police from the other, I know I have to act.

'Denise! Denise! Hello! Over here!' I begin to shout, jumping and waving like a mad thing. 'Denise! Denise!'

All I can think about is Anton. He can't be caught. He has to get out of there.

The uniforms ignore me and begin to head straight for number sixteen. I have to do something, anything, to hold them off a little longer. I rush across the road and beat them to the door.

'Denise!' I shout wildly, then again, even when a soldier shouts at me to be quiet and get out of the way. 'Denise! Denise!'

'Silence!' a policeman orders. He grabs me by the hair and pulls me from the doorstep.

I manage one final 'Denise!' before he claps his hand over my mouth. I am alone in the street with the Nazis. The little boys must have run away as soon as the cars appeared.

While I'm held with my heart pounding with fright, my hands behind my back and a gloved hand over my mouth, the door is broken open with a smash. As soldiers and policemen storm into the house, a third car pulls up – low, black and expensive-looking. Even before the back door opens, I have a horrible feeling I know who is going to step out.

I see the slicked-back hair and gold-rimmed glasses

first; then comes the trailing stiff leg and the polished cavalry boots with glinting metal spurs. Sneer in place on his face, it's Richter. Now I'm properly terrified. Anton and I could be in the Gestapo's prison tonight. I think of Monsieur Durance's warning of torture and feel like I might be sick.

'Who's the girl?' Richter shouts.

'Must be their lookout,' the soldier holding me replies.

Somehow I must think calmly and make up a story.

The uniforms come out of the house now with an old man in their grip. 'Where is your son?' Richter shouts at him.

The man shrugs and is smashed in the face with a rifle butt. I want to look away but I can't. I hear the crunching impact and see the spurt of blood. The old man buckles in pain. But he's thrown without ceremony into the back of a jeep.

'Who else is in there?' Richter demands.

'No one.'

'Have you searched? Get in there. Tear it apart. Others must be hiding.'

The men rush back inside as Richter walks towards me. He comes right up close. One of the uniforms flashes a torch beam at us, revealing his white, shiny skin and eyes the palest shade of blue. I look straight into his face.

'What is your name?' he asks.

My knees are trembling and the only idea I can think of is to copy the sing-song voice of a girl who lives on our street and is said to be 'simple'.

'I am Nico,' I say with a smile. 'I wave at Denise. Hello, Denise . . .' I wave with my hand. 'Hello, Denise. She is my friend.'

'Have you checked her papers?' Richter asks the man holding me.

'Papers!' the policeman orders.

'I am Nico,' I repeat.

The policeman opens my coat roughly and grabs the identity card from my pocket. 'Nicole de Wilde,' he reads out. 'Rue Houblon.'

'Hello, Denise,' I say, waving my hand again. I try very hard to show no fear, but under my five layers of clothing I am running with sweat.

'You're wasting your time with an idiot,' Richter spits out and turns away. 'Let's get into the house and flush out the vermin.'

As soon as the policeman releases me, I'm torn between the desire to run home as fast as I can or to wait here to see if they bring Anton out. I know I need to keep up my act so I begin to walk slowly down the road saying, 'Hello, I am Nico . . .' and 'Hello, Denise,' every now and then.

I duck into a doorway and look back, my mind full of panic. Could I have raised the alarm more quickly? Should I do something else? More soldiers run into the house with guns at the ready . . . they're going to find Anton!

Chapter Seven

I wait and wait and wait.

I can't feel my feet; I can't feel my fingers. The curfew began over an hour ago and now I'm breaking the law by being out. But I keep waiting, my eyes trained on the house.

The soldiers come and go. They shout at one another. They bring in guns and axes. I hear the tearing and chopping of wood, then short bursts of gunfire.

I cringe, tears squeezing from my eyes. Have they found more Resisters? Have they shot them?

Finally I'm so cold I can barely stand and I know I have to go home. I sneak along as quietly as I can, hugging walls and buildings, peering round corners to make sure I don't run into a soldier on patrol. When I get to my street, I'm nearly at my front door when I see Stapenhorst. He's at the end of the street, talking to another soldier. I keep my eyes fixed on them as

I slink as close to the walls as I can towards my house.

I'm two doors away when Stapenhorst turns. I push myself up against the wall. I need a hedge to hide behind, but none of the houses in our street has a front garden. I hold my breath, panicked about what I'm going to say when he catches me. Then his colleague calls him back and I don't waste a moment. I race across the road and into the little alleyway there.

I think I'm safe, but a dark figure peels from the wall and grabs hold of me. The scream is almost out of my throat when I realize it's Anton.

'You! It's you!' I gasp, astonished, delighted, slightly delirious. 'Is it really you?'

'Yes. I've been waiting for you,' he whispers. 'Hoping you got away. Going mad at the thought of you not getting away.'

'I've been waiting for *you*. How did you escape?'

'Over the rooftops with two others. I was so worried about you, Nico. I heard you down in the street. You were so brave.'

We're holding onto each other's arms, pulling close. I'm so happy, so relieved to see him, that we hug tightly, my face pressed against his chest. Then I look up. The burning need to kiss him is welling up in me, and this time I reach upwards and search for his lips with mine.

I feel the touch of his mouth and it is like nothing else. Here I am opening myself to him, offering this tender part of me for the very first time, revealing my heart, my longing for him.

And he kisses me back.

It's magical. The touch of his lips is caring, curious, questioning. I kiss back, feeling electrified with happiness, every nerve ending tingling.

He likes me. He wants *me*. I'm his girl.

Nicole and Anton.

Coco and the Poet.

I've never felt so happy. I never, ever want this to end.

The message under the brick the next morning instructs us both to come to St Agnes's Church on Rue de Jean to help with Red Cross work from 6 p.m.

Red Cross work is an excellent excuse to give my mama and grand-mamie, who are still upset that I came home after the curfew last night. I told them I'd been studying with Anton and lost track of time, but I was only just believed.

As I reach the corner of my street now at 5.45 p.m., I can't help smiling to see Anton already waiting for me ahead. I say a brief hello to Stapenhorst and walk on. When I reach Anton, he squeezes my hand and brushes my cheek with a kiss. We can't help laughing at each other. This is still so new and thrilling.

'I've brought you flowers,' he says with a hint of a blush.

'Flowers? In Brussels? In November? When we can't buy anything?!'

From behind his back he brings out a tiny posy of holly leaves and hawthorn berries clinging to bare branches. It's unbearably sweet and I wish I'd thought to bring something for him.

'Thank you . . .' I say, taking the posy; then I have to blurt out the huge worry on my mind: 'What if we're being called to this meeting so they can tell me off? They might not want me to work for them any more. I should have given the warning earlier . . . that poor old man.'

'You did everything you could – no one could have done more,' he reassures me. 'I'll tell them that.'

Picking our way carefully through the pitch-dark streets, we soon arrive at the church. Because of the blackout, it's hard to know if anyone is inside or not, but we go to the back door and knock. After some time the door opens.

'Mr Owl,' I whisper at the sight of Monsieur Durance.

'My friends, here for the Red Cross meeting?' he asks with a cheery smile.

'Yes.'

He lets us in, closes the door behind us and leads us down steps to another solid wooden door. He gives ten taps against the door, but in a rhythmic la-*la*, la-*la*, la-*la* sort of way.

'Iambic pentameter.' He turns and winks.

'The heartbeat of the poets,' Anton says.

'Ah, a fellow admirer of a well-turned verse.'

I can hear bolts being drawn on the other side, then the door is opened on a spacious underground crypt, lit with paraffin lamps; it is all set out with boxes, tins of food, bottles of medicine and bandages, piles of paper, lists pinned to the walls. It looks exactly like a Red Cross meeting, but it is also a Group K meeting. I'm so proud to be here and immediately desperate to know what the other members are going to be like.

'Hello, new people, good to meet you, I'm La Belle.' A dazzling girl maybe a few years older than me gets up from a collapsed leather armchair and shakes my hand.

'Hello, I'm . . .' Just as I'm about to say my real name, I remember: 'Coco.'

La Belle – *the beautiful one* – has the perfect code-name. She is the most gorgeous and glamorous girl I've ever met. On her head is a tiny, eye-catching hat trimmed with a pink, fully blown rose. Her hair is bright blonde and falls below her shoulders in perfect waves like a film star's. Her lovely fine-boned face is luminous with pale make-up and a slash of red lipstick. She wears a chic black dress, cut to show off her figure, and a gold necklace glitters at her throat. Where on earth have all these luxury items come from?

'Hello, I'm Hope.' A young woman steps forward.

She has a kind smile, shorter, dark hair, and the sort of capable handshake that makes me think she is a practical person. I'm certain she has children, because her hand is dry with short nails, her flowery dress and cardie are a little mumsy and she looks like she could balance babies on her hip while making dinner. 'And this is . . . Raven,' she adds with a slight giggle.

My hand gets a vigorous shake from a handsome, dark-haired man who grins enthusiastically. He's scruffily dressed in a shrunken mustard sweater and very faded cords. He shakes Anton's hand too and claps him on the back.

'You both did very well last night,' he says. 'We didn't expect a raid – it was a baptism of fire and you both passed the test.'

I can't help smiling with relief.

'Nearly everyone was very lucky,' Raven adds.

'How is the old man?' I ask.

'We don't know yet,' Monsieur Durance replies, 'but let's hope for the best.'

Raven moves to Hope's side and slips his arm round her waist, proving they are a couple. I see Hope's ring and wonder if he is her husband.

'These two are very young,' Hope says, directing her comment at Monsieur Durance. 'Maybe too young. We're really a sabotage group, so maybe we should point them towards a surveillance group.'

'No, no,' La Belle protests. 'I'll get Coco a nice dress, do her hair and make-up, and she could have a very informative, generous Nazi boyfriend just like mine. Think how much we'll find out. So many extra new places to bomb.'

Anton and I exchange glances. He won't like a Nazi boyfriend . . . I will hate a Nazi boyfriend. Although it perhaps explains where La Belle's make-up and jewellery comes from.

Monsieur Durance shakes his head. 'They are young, but they're brave, clever and determined to help. Coco doesn't need a Nazi boyfriend – she needs to keep wearing plaits, carrying her satchel and whistling, then no one will suspect her of a thing. Think what a powerful weapon that makes her.'

This is a relief.

'Are you in the army?' Anton asks Raven. You hardly see any twenty-something men around because they are all soldiers, airmen or sailors, either trapped in France or in prisoner-of-war camps.

Raven shakes his head. 'I'm a children's doctor at the Infirmary. At the moment they still need us, but when they've starved all the children to death, we might be surplus to requirements,' he adds grimly.

'I'm so sorry about last night . . .' I say. 'I gave as much warning as I could but I wish I'd done more. I'm sorry. I hope you don't think I can't—'

Monsieur Durance holds up his hand to make me stop, just like he does in class. 'You did the best you could, Coco,' he says. 'Our enemy is clever and dangerous, and for the moment we are outnumbered. We must always be careful, cunning, and strike hard whenever we get the smallest opportunity.'

Mr Durance and Raven look at one another.

'My dear Poet, we'd like you to come with us tonight,' Monsieur Durance says. 'I hope you have a steady hand and a head for heights. Coco, talk to La Belle who will explain your first courier mission.'

As the door closes on Anton and the men, I wonder what they've gone off to do. If it's something dangerous, something risky . . . I'm hit by the crushing realization that now we are Resisters, every time Anton and I part, we may never see each other again. And I didn't even say goodbye.

I turn to my two new colleagues. They begin parcelling up food and medicine into boxes while they talk, so Group K must actually do Red Cross work too. I marvel at how cheerful and gossipy they are as they pack cans and medicines. But as I join in with the chat I realize that down here in the crypt we are free. We can talk without worrying if a Nazi or collabo is listening and about to report us. Plus, we are all on the same side, united by our hatred of the invaders.

This is a place of hope. Everyone here thinks they can make a difference.

'Do you think they will release the Clog?' La Belle asks, and I wonder if they mean the old man.

Hope says, 'Only if he keeps telling them he is totally innocent. There's no other way.' Her eyes meet mine with deadly seriousness. 'As soon as the Gestapo discover that you know something, they will never let you go. They come for your friends, your family, for everyone you know. Then they kill you. This is the most important thing you must learn.'

I wonder what she may have gone through to learn this lesson.

La Belle ties a parcel tightly with string and adds, 'We don't want to frighten you. I know the Owl must have warned you and you've decided to join us anyway, but everyone involved in this mission has to prepare for pain and death.'

'If you believe the pain will end, you can stand it. Just tell yourself over and over that it will end and you will find a way to bear it,' Hope says.

I nod. I've thought about it, of course. We are beginning to hear about the terrible punishments being inflicted on Resisters. But what's the alternative? Sitting at home doing nothing? Waiting to starve or be sent to a work camp? At least fighting back, there is hope.

I suddenly think of Papa holding me tight, telling me not to fight back, and I hope that when we're reunited, one day, he'll forgive me.

'So you're a sabotage group . . .' I begin. 'How many missions have you—'

Hope is shaking her head and putting her finger up to her lips. They're not allowed to say, of course.

'Where do you send the parcels?' I ask next, hoping this is a safer question.

'Prisoner-of-war camps and those terrible work camps where they use our teenagers as slave labour,' Hope replies.

Now I think of Henri and I know that being here is the right thing.

Hope turns to La Belle and asks, 'So what information do you have for us from Gestapo HQ?'

La Belle leans close to whisper answers as Hope writes them down in a number code.

A boyfriend at Gestapo HQ? I'm beginning to understand how brave these people are. La Belle is in a terrible position. The Nazis would kill her in a moment if they knew about her work here, and yet certain Belgians would kill her too; anyone thought to be collaborating with Nazis is a target.

'Have you heard anything about Johann Richter?' La Belle asks when she has finished whispering to Hope.

My eyebrows shoot up my forehead.

'Do you know something?' La Belle looks at me quizzically.

'He led the raid last night when the old man was

caught. I've also seen him round up teenagers to send to camps. He took the Poet's brother. Apparently he hates Belgians with a passion.'

'Excellent!' She smiles. 'I have a job interview with him tomorrow. Apparently he's looking for a secretary.'

As I gasp, Hope grins. 'You'd be the best-placed spy in the whole of the Resistance!' she exclaims.

'It's perfect.' La Belle adds, 'It might get very hot though. I mean, if I work there, at Gestapo HQ, well, then I really am entering the lion's den.'

'Did your boyfriend put you up for this?'

La Belle nods.

'So . . . what is my first courier mission going to be?' I ask.

'It's simple,' La Belle replies. 'The Owl is going to give you some ingredients tomorrow. Then you and I are going to deliver them to the Hawk.'

'Who's the Hawk?'

'Most groups have one carefully protected member, the radio operator. Unfortunately the Clog has been caught. But because we do sabotage, we have another member we keep deeply protected. Even the Owl doesn't meet the Hawk face to face.'

'So what does the Hawk do?'

'Well, he's a very clever man. He can take ordinary, everyday ingredients and turn them into bombs.'

Chapter Eight

Monsieur Durance wipes the blackboard clean as everyone packs up their satchels for the day.

'And Nicole, if you could stay behind for five minutes, I must give you some exercises for your truly indecipherable handwriting,' he says so convincingly that even I'm expecting a lecture about my scribbles as the other girls file out of the classroom.

'I'll see you outside,' Aurelie calls over her shoulder.

'Will that be a problem?' Monsieur Durance asks me as the door closes on the last girl.

'What?' I ask, because I am a numbskull.

'Well, my dear Coco, the Owl is about to give you a special package to deliver to a special person. Will it be a problem if Aurelie is waiting for you in the playground? She is not exactly secret about where her sympathies lie. I believe her father is actually working for the Gestapo now.'

Finally, I catch up. 'No, Aurelie won't be a problem. She keeps trying to be my friend, but I've practically ignored her ever since she started . . . "fraternizing". Will I fit everything into my school bag?'

'I don't think so.' He opens the cupboard beside the blackboard, moves a stack of books to the side and I see packets and packets of . . .

'*Sugar?*'

Monsieur Durance nods. 'I have a holdall. Could you use that?'

'Yes . . . if anyone stops me, I'll say I'm making jam.'

'Be careful, Coco,' he warns. 'No one could have this amount of sugar without the help of the black market. You only have to get to the Rue des Ateliers without being stopped. There you will meet La Belle, who has a wonderful hiding place for the rest of the journey. Are your papers all in order? You may have to pass through a checkpoint.'

I nod. My palms feel sweaty. 'Let's load up the bag . . . I'll get rid of Aurelie,' I say.

And I do, surprisingly easily.

She's waiting in the playground and as soon as she sees me, she asks, 'What's in that bag? Are you running an errand for Durance?'

I just shrug and tell her, 'Taking some of his old books to the Red Cross. Shouldn't you be off meeting hunky Franz and learning how to do a Heil Hitler salute?'

'Are you jealous?'

'As if . . .'

'You better watch yourself, Nicole – we all know your father's in prison because of his suspected Resistance sympathies.'

'Shut up!' I say, suddenly furious with her. How dare she even mention my poor papa. Isn't he suffering enough? Whenever I think of him, I'm stabbed with the pain of loss. 'Just go off and enjoy some Nazi time,' I blurt out. 'Go get your brainwashed boyfriend to teach you some songs of praise to that Führer nincompoop!'

I could be in trouble now . . . I glance around to see who else might have heard this. And with precious sugar for the Hawk in my hand! But Aurelie storms off without another word.

With my satchel over one shoulder and the bag packed with sugar over the other, I walk out of the playground into the street and suddenly feel completely conspicuous. As if I'm carrying a sign saying: 'Bomb-making material in here. Look now!'

I try my hardest to be casual. I start to whistle . . . then quickly whistle something else when I realize I've picked the national anthem. When I pass a street guard, I can feel sweat breaking out. But still I force a whistle through my dry lips and even give him a half-smile. I almost walk straight past La Belle at the corner of the Rue des Ateliers because she is pushing a pram.

'Hello! How are you?' she gushes and treats me to one of her radiant, lipstick smiles, even kissing me on the cheek as if we are old friends. I take in her fitted tweed coat, high heels and perfectly dressed hair with more than a little envy. She is so gloriously lovely. But I'm excited to be working with her, desperate to get to know more about her. We begin to walk along the road together. There's a big, smiley baby boy in the pram, maybe nine or ten months old. He's called Max, La Belle tells me.

'Hello, you! Are you coming for a walk? Are you?' I ask him with a big grin. I love babies.

'We'll just stop in this doorway here,' La Belle says after we've walked a little. 'I know it's a quiet one.'

We pull into the apartment doorway where she asks me to put down my bag and hold the baby. 'Hello, sweetheart, hello, Max!' I coo as the heavy bundle is placed into my arms.

Then with several deft moves, La Belle has stripped out the mattress and sheets of the pram, stuffed in all the sugar bags, then set up the baby's sheets and blankets on top.

When I settle him back in, he is higher than before and the pram seems awkward to push, but baby Max doesn't mind. He babbles and points as we walk along.

'Is he your baby?' I ask.

La Belle laughs and shakes her head. 'No, he's my

friend's. She doesn't know anything about this or she would *kill* me. He's lovely. I wish he was my baby.'

'Me too. He's gorgeous,' I agree.

'But I won't have children,' she says, still smiling at Max. 'I won't live that long. I'll be lucky if I'm alive in six months' time.'

She says this so simply, so matter of factly that I find it hard to hear. 'No,' I protest. 'Surely if you're careful . . . ?'

She turns to me. 'I thought that too when I joined. Everyone thinks it won't be them. But when you see even the very clever ones, the very skilled, being caught, then you realize it won't be long. I'm lying to my Gestapo boyfriend every day. They'll find out sooner or later.'

We walk on for a little while, then I ask, 'How long have you been with the group?'

'Three months. My brother was a member, and I joined when he was killed by the beasts.' Her white face seems to turn even paler with these words.

'I'm very sorry.'

'Me too. But every time one of us dies, many more flock to the cause. That's what gives us courage,' she adds. 'Our work is vital, Coco: we give Nazis doubts and Belgians hope, but we're flies in the web and soon enough the spider comes to find us. And here they are . . . the spiders.'

At the end of this road there is a checkpoint: wooden

barriers and sand bags block the way and two soldiers stand guard with guns. It's too late to turn away; they would find that suspicious and come after us anyway.

'They'll want to know why your bag is empty . . .' La Belle whispers, although there is a smile set across her face.

'I dropped some old books off at the Red Cross,' I say.

'Good . . . all right, just relax, let me take the lead.'

As she is smiling at the soldiers, I do too, but my heart begins to race.

'Good afternoon, officers,' La Belle says flirtatiously, charming, giving them an instant promotion.

They straighten up at the sight of her. This must be what it's like to be beautiful; people pay you a great deal of attention.

'Your papers, *mesdemoiselles* . . . and if we could look inside your bags. Please tell us where you are going?' As one soldier searches my satchel and the empty holdall, the second looks in La Belle's handbag. Then he tells her, 'I hope you won't object to a quick frisk.'

With a sigh she puts up her hands and lets the soldier feel all around her body. I notice he slowly runs his hands over her chest and her buttocks several times.

'We're just making a quick visit to my grandmother – maybe we'll see you again on the way back,' she says, still charming despite the groping.

It has the right effect. The soldier stops feeling her up

and smiles, delighted at the thought of doing it all again on the return journey.

I push the pram through the checkpoint.

'Should we look under the baby?' the other soldier asks.

'Only if you want a wet hand,' I joke, wondering how I can sound so cheerful when I'm tense enough to be sick.

La Belle laughs. 'Or worse,' she adds and we are waved through.

Not until we are down the street and round the next corner do we dare to even let out our breaths with relief.

'Would they really have arrested us for sugar?' I ask.

'It's a lot of sugar and we're hiding it. They would have been far too interested.'

We are in a quieter part of town now. The houses are lower with generous front gardens; some have signs on the pavement offering vegetables for sale. It's so quiet here that it's a shock when a sleek black police car suddenly appears. It speeds down the road and passes us. But then stops and reverses.

La Belle speeds up, so I do likewise. But the car is level with us now. I glance inside and see four Gestapo officers, all with the same look of arrogant superiority on their faces.

'It *is* you. I knew it was you . . .' one of the officers says, leaning over to look out of the driver's window.

'What are you doing here?' The question is for La Belle.

'Oh, Yann, what a surprise!' La Belle gushes with a delighted smile. From this, I guess that Yann must be her boyfriend.

'Are you visiting someone?' he asks.

'No . . . I . . . I really shouldn't . . .' She gives a silly giggle. 'We thought we might buy some vegetables. I'm sorry – that's very bad, isn't it?' She gives a sweet smile.

'Tut tut. If you want to waste twenty francs on some worm-eaten bit of turnip, go ahead. But a good Belgian, a Gestapo officer's girlfriend, should not be doing such things.' He looks a little stiff and formal as he says this.

'No. I'm sorry.'

'There's some trouble with your application. I'm just waiting to hear about it.'

'Really?'

Baby Max is squirming and restless. I'm only too aware that he is sitting on a sugar mountain and we are now far too close to the Gestapo. The sooner we can get out of here the better.

'Apparently you have another surname. I know you foreigners like all sorts of combinations. In Germany we prefer one surname per person. Much simpler for the paperwork.'

'Oh . . . I use my mother's name usually . . .'

'But we don't like that. We're looking you up under

your other name too . . . I put you forward for this job. I hope I can trust you.'

'What are you talking about? Of course you can trust me . . . don't be silly,' La Belle trills.

'Hmmm . . . we'll see. *Fahren Sie weiter*,' he adds curtly. Drive on. Yann gives La Belle a final nod, then the window is rolled up and the car glides off.

'That's not good. That's not good at all,' La Belle hisses. She begins to walk again, much more quickly, pushing the pram ahead.

'What's wrong?' I ask.

'Since my brother was killed . . . ever since I joined up, I've used my mother's name. Changed my papers. I never wanted them to find out about my family connection to the Resistance. Now maybe they have . . . it's not good.' She looks tense and troubled. 'C'mon, we need to deliver the sugar and get out of here.'

I walk beside her at a brisk pace. We turn right into a road – the Rue du Moulin. It has a patch of land divided into allotments beside it. A few old men are about, digging in the frozen soil, maybe unearthing a potato or two. One glances at us, but goes back to his digging. We pass several ramshackle huts. The last hut in the row is off the path a little. No one is in sight.

La Belle approaches this hut and looks around. The old men are not paying any attention and there is no one else about. Max, maybe sensing our nervousness, is quiet too. La Belle lifts the hook holding the door shut and pushes it open with a creak.

I realize I'm nervous all of a sudden. The car full of Gestapo officers and La Belle's anxiety about her name has rattled me. As we go forward into the dark, musty space, Max begins to cry.

'Shhhhh, it's OK, we're going back to Mama. Yes we are,' I soothe him.

My eyes adjust to the light and I see a perfectly ordinary shed. Pots stacked neatly, rolls of string, trowels and a spade. A pair of battered gloves lies on a worn wooden counter. It smells of earth.

'Here,' La Belle says, and points to a scrap of paper pinned to a wooden door beneath the counter which reads: *Jam supplies*. She opens the door to reveal dusty jam jars. I lift Max from the pram and sit him down on the earth floor. Then I begin to unpack the sugar bags and help her stack them in the cupboard.

Poor Max is still crying. 'Just a minute, just a little minute, my darling,' I tell him.

As soon as the cupboard is packed, we settle the crying baby back in the pram and head out of the shed, then up the lane.

We start on the long walk back. I push the pram now, thinking about the sugar and wondering what the Hawk is going to bomb. I just hope I can play a part. My hatred of the Nazis grows by the day and

I want to inflict damage on them. Serious damage.

'Don't worry, we're going home to Mama,' I tell Max. At least he has stopped crying now.

As we round a corner and approach the houses offering vegetables for sale, I'm startled to see the black car with the Gestapo officers again; it's driving slowly, deliberately towards us.

'Let's turn round and get out of here,' I hiss.

'Too late, they'll chase us . . . we'll have to talk our way out of it,' La Belle says. She's already putting a smile on her face, but it doesn't reach her eyes. 'If anything happens, Max's address is tucked into his nappy,' she whispers.

'Nothing's going to happen . . . what could happen?' I whisper back, but I realize I'm saying this to try and calm myself.

Yann and another officer step out of the car and begin to walk towards us.

'How nice to see you again,' La Belle chirps. 'We're just going home now. Baby Max needs his supper.'

Yann doesn't smile. He marches up to La Belle and grabs her, pulling her arms behind her back.

'What are you doing?' she cries. My stomach clenches with fear.

'You're coming with us,' Yann says.

'What? Why? What on earth's the matter?'

'You're Vivienne Fontaine. Your brother was a traitor

hanged for his treachery. You're coming with us!'

'No. No . . . you're wrong!' La Belle protests, but she is dragged to the car by the officers.

'Wait! Wait − there must be some mistake,' I say, hurrying after them with the pram.

La Belle is shaking her head; she turns and glares at me. I take this as a warning to shut up. As they push her into the car, she shouts, 'I hardly know this girl − she's nothing to me. Let her take the baby home.' The doors slam shut and just before the car drives off my eyes meet La Belle's. She looks fragile and very scared.

The Gestapo have her and I don't know what to do.

Chapter Nine

The next morning, I get dressed under the covers because it is so cold. I'm worrying about La Belle, wondering if anyone got my coded message about her, which I left under the brick as soon as I could yesterday. I went back to the school to try and find Monsieur Durance and I also knocked on St Agnes's Church door. But there was no reply. Then I had to run home because it was curfew.

'Nicole! Breakfast!' my mother calls.

On my plate there is a slice of the dreadful grey, sticky mess that passes for bread nowadays. Chestnut flour, bark and who knows what else goes into it. Our poor baker is embarrassed to hand it over and take his outrageous fifteen francs.

But beside my slice of terrible bread I'm astonished to see . . . a boiled egg in a blue egg cup. 'Mama! An egg!'

I exclaim. 'Where did you get it? I can't eat this. You should have it. You and Grand-Mamie are looking much skinnier than me.'

'Eat the egg,' Mama says, sitting down opposite me, a smile breaking over her face. 'Nothing will make me happier than watching you eat a delicious egg.'

'You'll have half,' I tell her.

'I won't have one mouthful,' she insists. 'The Foulards have two hens in their garden now and they gave me this egg for you.'

Grand-Mamie comes in from mass and we make a big fuss of her, tucking her into her chair, pouring out her ersatz coffee.

'Ugh!' she says after her first mouthful. 'This is the daily cruelty they inflict on us. Every time we put a mouthful of this horror to our lips we know we are under their heel. Have I told you that my friend Violetta is a cleaner at the Gestapo HQ now?'

'No!' I'm horrified. 'How can she clean for them?'

Grand-Mamie gives a crafty laugh. 'Ah ha. It's not like that. At mass, I give Violetta the latest copy of *Le Libre*, and when she's finished swabbing the floor, dusting the lights and cleaning the blinds, she hides it in amongst the papers on Kriminaldirektor Richter's desk. Apparently he screams with fury every time he finds it.'

'No, this is too dangerous!' Mama protests.

'One must do what one can,' Grand-Mamie says,

taking another sip and screwing up her face. 'They need to know that they have not broken our spirit because that is the only thing that truly frightens them.'

'Would you like some egg?' I ask her. 'Please, it's delicious.'

'No. Eggs are for spring chickens, not withered old birds like me.'

There's a knock at the front door. We all startle; now that the Gestapo can barge in whenever they like, we no longer feel as secure as we once did at home.

'Maybe the post,' Mama says, wiping her hands on her apron. Within moments she's back in the kitchen with a letter in her hand.

Grand-Mamie looks at her with concern. 'Oh, Elisabeth, this reminds me of those dreadful telegrams,' she says quietly, 'about my dear boys. The postboy looked so sorry to hand them over to me: two in the same week.'

I pat Grand-Mamie's hand gently as Mama rips open the envelope, unfolds the paper and begins to read. To our horror, she lets out a howl of distress and collapses into the nearest chair.

'Mama! What's the matter? Is it news about Papa?' I ask, rushing to her side. I would do anything for any news of him: good or bad – anything to end the dull agony of not knowing what's happened to him.

'Oh . . . oh . . .' But Mama can't go on because she begins to sob.

I take the letter from her hand and I'm shocked to see my name at the top.

'*Nicole de Wilde, 11 Rue Houblon, Brussels,*' I read out. '*Mademoiselle de Wilde is to report to the district HQ today, 26th November, 1940, at 09:30 hours. She will bring a rucksack with suitable spare clothes and toiletries. She will be assessed for fitness to work in Germany.*'

Mama is sobbing into her apron. 'Oh no,' she says. 'Oh no, oh no. I can't bear it. No one comes back from Germany. No one's children have returned.'

I put my arms around her and press my face against her shoulder. 'It's OK,' I try to soothe her. 'I won't let them take me. I know you need me.'

'Oh no, oh no,' she sobs, gripping me tightly by the arms. 'I won't let you go. You won't go to their head-quarters, Nicole; I won't let you. No! Nothing is going to happen to you, George promised me. George . . . where is he? When is he coming back?'

Grand-Mamie gets up and puts her arm round Mama's shoulders. 'Take her to the school first and see if that fine Monsieur Durance has any good advice,' she says. 'We'll plead that she's a schoolgirl. Please, Elisabeth, she won't go to Germany. We will keep her safe.'

Mama nods and puts her face into her apron, trying desperately to stop crying.

'Come on, Mama, we'll be OK, I promise.'

I hurry upstairs and try to put a bag together. My

hands are shaking and I can't seem to find anything I need. When I'm finally ready to leave the house, it's hard to say goodbye to my grand-mamie. I try to be brave and smile and reassure her that I will be coming home later. But what if . . . ?

'Be brave, my lovely grandchild, my precious girl. Find your courage,' Grand-Mamie says as her skinny arms hold me tight and I kiss her withered cheeks.

We are outside the Gestapo HQ.

Mama turns to me, holds my face in her hands and looks deep, deep into my eyes. 'You're my only child,' she says. 'I tried to give you brothers and sisters, but the pregnancies didn't last.'

'I know,' I whisper back. 'It's all right. It's going to be all right.'

'You must come back to me,' she insists. 'Life without you and without George is not worth living.' Her face is pale with shock and fright and I want to say the right thing to comfort her.

'I'll come back. I won't let them keep me, I promise.' I put my hands over hers. Despite all the cooking, the carrying, the laundry and the cheap soap, there is still warmth and softness to her hands. My lovely mama.

Then, full of uncertainty, it's time for me to leave her amongst the crowd of weeping parents outside the building. As I step into the lobby, I see many, many other teenagers are here, clutching papers, bags and rucksacks and looking sick with worry. I scan the faces, hoping to see no one familiar. I've had no time to find out if Anton or any other friends have been summoned.

I'm wearing my hair in two girlish plaits, because Monsieur Durance's first piece of advice when we met him this morning was to look as young as possible. This isn't hard for me because I'm small and I'm wearing my school clothes. Then he gave me a phrase in German: '*Ich bin ein Einzelkind, ich muss nach Hause.*' I am an only child; I need to go home.

I managed to slip a piece of paper into Monsieur Durance's hand, asking if he'd heard anything about La Belle; in reply, he shook his head.

I repeat my German phrase over and over in my head to memorize it. Then I hear my name being barked out over the crowd and I come forward to the desk.

The guard looks at my papers and writes down some details. I try out my German phrase on him: '*Ich bin ein Einzelkind, ich muss nach Hause.*'

He just points to a long corridor and orders me to go down it. I take my bag and trudge along. Maybe I will be sent to one of their filthy work camps. All I know about them is from the postcards Anton receives from his brother. There is little food, no medicines, no pay. Everyone has to work twelve hours a day and people regularly become so ill that they die. Once in a camp, there doesn't seem to be any hope of returning home until the day we all pray for: when the war is over.

When. I can't bear to think of 'if' . . . of the war lasting for the rest of my life. Or even worse, of the war ending because the devils have won.

A guard uses his machine gun to direct me into a big room filled with teenagers in various states of undress. Two men in white coats are carrying out physical examinations. One boy has his mouth open while a dentist looks inside. The room smells of disinfectant and sweat and there is the hush of real fear.

I hand my papers over to the clerk and try out my phrase on him. '*Ich bin ein Einzelkind, ich muss nach Hause.*'

He just points at a bench, where I sit, rucksack in my lap, feeling small and entirely insignificant; just another name, date of birth and address, to be filed, stamped and catalogued. It must make them feel so terribly important, ruling us, running our lives with their countless rules, regulations and orders from on high.

Suddenly, the door bursts open and a cluster of Gestapo men in long raincoats swoop in. I'm horrified to see Richter at the back of the group and I shrink down behind my bag. It's not long since he caught me in the street and held me right up to his face. There is every chance he will still remember me . . . and I will have to play simple again. It could be a very dangerous game to play here.

One of the Gestapo men has a list in his hands and he shouts out several names, ordering the kids to stand up. Two boys and a girl get to their feet in different parts of the room. They are immediately grabbed and dragged out. It is vicious and violent to watch. I have no idea what these kids have done. Maybe nothing; maybe this is to make the rest of us docile and afraid.

'You! Come over here!'

I realize with a shudder that Richter is pointing to me. I approach him timidly.

'Do I know you?' he demands.

I shake my head, saying nothing.

'Yes, I know you,' he insists. 'I never forget a face.'

I take a breath and begin my line, my one hope, my only chance of getting out: *'Ich bin ein Einzelkind, ich muss nach Hause.'*

School finished several hours ago, but I tap on my classroom door, hoping that I will still find my teacher here.

'Come in,' he replies.

I open up, and although Monsieur Durance smiles he can only manage a weak: 'Hello . . . thank goodness you're back.'

'I had to wait for hours, but when they realized I was still only fifteen, they let me go,' I tell him, stepping in and closing the door behind me. I don't want to think any more about all the teenagers who weren't let go, who were marched past me, clutching their rucksacks, desperation on their faces.

'So the great Third Reich still makes the occasional paperwork error,' Monsieur Durance says, his voice husky.

'What's the matter?' I ask.

He puts his face into his hands and groans gently. 'I'm very glad you're back,' he says. 'I didn't want to lose another. I couldn't bear to lose another.' His shoulders heave and he makes an odd coughing, gasping noise which I realize is a burst of tears.

'Monsieur Durance, what's the matter?' I come up close, put my hand on his back, on his matted old cardie and rub gently. 'What's happened?'

'It's La Belle . . .' His voice sounds choked and I feel myself go cold.

'Is she OK?'

He shakes his head. 'They've already killed her.'

I struggle to take this in. But his head stays in his hands and his shoulders heave again as he cries.

'They've killed her,' he repeats. 'They didn't mean to. They would have liked to keep her alive longer and try to get information out of her . . . but she . . . she bled to death in her cell.'

Beautiful La Belle . . . it can't be true. I was with her less than twenty-four hours ago.

Monsieur Durance looks up at me. His eyes are wet

and his nose is running and he fumbles in his pocket for a handkerchief. 'Do you know what they did to her face? No . . . I shouldn't tell you.'

I'm stunned. I don't know what to say or do, or even what to feel. But I know that I need to know this detail. Whatever the Nazis did to La Belle's face, I need to know so that I can use it to drown out my fear and my horror and feed my fury against them.

'Of course you should tell me,' I say. 'I need to know what I'm dealing with here.'

'They carved the word "traitor" onto it,' he whispers.

'Onto her beautiful face?'

He nods.

I can't help it; hot tears leap up into my eyes and I begin to cry too. 'Oh no . . . oh no . . .' I gasp and I'm crying, even though I can't really believe she's dead.

'We'll have to wind the group up,' Monsieur Durance says, trying to calm his sobs. 'I can't do this. I can't send young people to their deaths any longer. You're my pupil . . . I have a duty of care.' He wipes at his tears with a big white hankie but more keep coming. 'This "New Order", these vicious, robotic thugs . . . they are trampling down everything civilization has ever built. They are vandals, wreckers . . . I barely knew what I was fighting for in the last war, but now it's as if we are fighting for humanity itself.'

'They're not going to win,' I say quietly.

'I think they are . . .' Monsieur Durance replies.

'Every time someone dies for the cause, more people come. That's what La Belle told me. If you close Group K now, she'll have died in vain. We can't close, monsieur, we have to find others,' I urge him. 'We have to grow every single day.'

He shakes his head. 'We are fighting men without mercy, men without any human feeling,' he protests. 'To fight them, you'll have to become like them. I can't train you to do that.'

I grip his arm and make my point even more fiercely than before. 'They *can't* win. They *won't* win. Look how much force they have to use to keep us in place. They're trying to starve us into submission. No one believes in their silly ideals. Their idiotic leader. They've been brainwashed. They will not win. More and more people will join us. I promise.'

I think of La Belle's beautiful face, carved with the hideous word. I think of my papa, taken away. I look up at Monsieur Durance and know I have to inspire him. He needs to know that I'm not a hopeless schoolgirl. I'm ready to fight for freedom.

'Many, many more will join us,' I insist. 'This is war.'

Chapter Ten

Wednesday, one week later, is freezing cold and wet as I trudge with Anton to the Church of St Bartholomew. As we walk up the church path, I see other mourners dressed in dark clothes and hear the organ playing. I've only been to the funerals of old people before and I keep thinking of La Belle pushing baby Max in his pram and telling me that she knows she won't have children. I think of her bright lipstick smile and I ache with pain for her, even though I still can't believe I won't see her again.

As we approach the wooden door, Anton takes hold of my hand and squeezes hard, but there is nothing comforting to say. We step inside the church and join a queue waiting to shake hands with a small man all in black who is unmistakably La Belle's father.

Monsieur Fontaine has the same elegant nose and

high cheekbones. Beside him is a pale boy of about four-teen or fifteen with a head of blond hair not quite as vivid as hers was, then there is a blonde-haired sister, younger than her brother.

When I see their faces, pained and white, straining not to cry, I suddenly have a rush of understanding. La Belle is dead. She has really gone and she's not going to return. Her father will grow old, her brother and sister will grow up; life will carry on mercilessly without her. I'm so overwhelmed that I begin to sob. I try to stop my tears, but they keep on falling. As we approach the family, I wipe my hand over my face and try to hold myself together, but tears still stream down my face and I clutch at Anton's hand.

'I'm sorry . . .' I begin as I shake Monsieur Fontaine's hand, but then I am choked with sorrow and unable to speak.

He leans forward and puts his arm around my shoulder. 'She was the spirit of Belgium,' he says, looking right into my eyes. 'I am bursting with pride for her.'

In a blur of tears, I shake her brother's hand, then hug her little sister. 'She was wonderful,' I say into the girl's hair.

And she was. She gave up her chance at life to wage her own little war against the Nazis.

I see baby Max in the arms of his mother, whose eyes are swollen with crying. Despite their simple disguises,

I recognize Monsieur Durance, his face half hidden in a scarf, Hope in clumsy glasses and a bearded Raven sitting together in a pew. Anton guides me into the row behind them, as they do not make any greeting or acknowledgement; neither do we. Sometimes I forget how careful we have to be and I turn up my coat collar to shield my face.

I cry as quietly as I can through the brief funeral service. The priest is deeply sad and solemn. He tells us he baptized Vivienne and took her first communion, and he talks about her lively happiness. For a moment, I try to imagine what Father Bruno, our parish priest who has known me since I was three, would say at my funeral.

Vivienne's priest tells us she had a fierce spirit and unswerving determination to serve her country, and I realize he must know something about her work. When applause follows his words, I feel a fresh surge of hope. There is a growing will to fight back.

When the service has finished, Vivienne's father and brother, pale and serious, are the front coffin-bearers, carrying the simple wooden box with rope handles out of the church. I see Monsieur Durance turn and pass a hymn book to Anton, who slips something from it and into his pocket. New instructions for a new mission? I wonder. Then we file out and follow the coffin and the small crowd of mourners to the church graveyard.

Vivienne's grave is the next one in a row of graves so

recent they are still unmarked with headstones. War must keep the gravediggers busy, I think grimly. As the priest leads the prayers and her coffin is lowered into the ground, I think of her words: '*I'll be lucky if I'm still alive in six months' time.*'

I wish I'd had the chance to know her better. I wish I'd joined Group K months ago. She could have taught me all sorts of helpful things. I start to weep again and shake with the cold; Anton's arm is the only thing holding me upright. Now all this knowledge is being buried with the bravest of girls, left to bleed to death in a prison cell, her face destroyed so that her family could not even have the comfort of one last look at her. Everything feels bleak and dreadful.

Then a car pulls up at the entrance to the church. We turn our heads and see two Gestapo officers get out and begin marching towards us. Anton's grip around my waist tightens.

'Is this the grave of Vivienne Fontaine?' one of them demands.

We all nod or answer 'Yes'.

'Fill it in,' the officer commands the two gravediggers waiting nearby with their shovels.

We all stand back as the earth is piled with awful thuds onto the coffin. The priest approaches the officers to ask, 'Please, is it possible to leave this grieving family in peace?'

'This is the grave of a traitor,' the officer barks. 'Where is Monsieur Fontaine?'

Vivienne's father steps forward. 'Can I ask you to leave us in peace?' he says, calm and unbowed.

'Certainly not,' the second officer replies. 'You are to stamp on this grave. You will spit on this grave and denounce your daughter as a coward and a traitor.'

There is some courage in numbers, so as a crowd we protest: 'No!' 'Please, no!' 'Not possible.'

But the officers take their machine guns from their shoulders and point them at us. 'Fontaine, stamp on the grave or we will arrest your other children,' the senior officer demands.

Monsieur Fontaine walks slowly to the mound of earth. He looks down at the ground, puts his foot on the earth and taps without any conviction.

'Tell us what she was?!' the officer demands.

'She was my beautiful child,' Monsieur Fontaine replies.

'What was she? We will take your other children!' the officer shouts; he's losing his temper.

'She was . . . she was . . .' His voice is cracking with pain. 'A coward . . .' He makes a terrible sob.

'And what else?!'

'A traitor . . .'

'Stamp!' the other beast demands. 'And spit.'

As one, we turn away. It's the least we can do to show

our solidarity. But as we turn, the vicious beasts shout, 'Watch! Every one of you. You watch as this man denounces his filthy, cowardly, traitor daughter!'

They bring out a camera. I see Hope and Raven turn to one another and embrace so that their faces are hidden. I understand that Anton and I need to do the same. I put my head against his chest and hide his face with my arms. We are mourners at a Resistance funeral. The Gestapo are here to take notes, photographs and write down names. They will ask questions. How do we know Vivienne? How long have we known Vivienne? I do not have answers. We have to get out of here.

I think of the slip of paper Anton pocketed. If he's caught with a coded message, it will be his funeral next. But his arms squeeze tightly around me, willing me to be brave, not to lose hope. He leans his face down against my ear and whispers lines from a poem I've heard many times before: '*Sing, Belgians, sing. Although our wounds may bleed, although our voices break . . .*'

He holds me tight, tight, whispering reassurance, and I find my courage. Together we can get through this.

Monsieur Durance, standing not far from me, turns and removes a vast red handkerchief from his pocket. As he blows his nose and coughs loudly, I'm sure I see a movement in the thick hedge bordering the graveyard. Just moments later there is an ear-splitting bang from the other side of the hedge.

'Wait here!' the officers command before leaving the graveyard at a run.

Monsieur Durance places his hands on Anton and my shoulders. 'I'm afraid a few of us will have to slip away,' he says, 'before our charming friends can return.'

Chapter Eleven

Raven's eyes move from Anton's face to mine.

'This is a drawing of the railway track. On one side is a wide field, then a road. On the other side is the embankment and a smaller road. You're going to be here, at the bottom of the embankment,' he explains, wanting to make sure we're following. 'The railway passes over the road on a little bridge there. See?' Just the three of us are in the crypt and he's very serious, giving us careful instructions for our first sabotage mission.

'By 7.15 p.m. the Hawk will have laid the device on the track on the bridge; by 7.32 p.m. it will have exploded. He works with us on the understanding that no one knows who he is, so keep out of sight and don't look for him. Your job is to guard the bridge and the device from your side. After laying the device, the Hawk will cross the field and guard the other road. This is a quiet, unwatched section of track, nothing should happen . . . so please stop looking so worried!' He gives a little smile. 'By 7.36 p.m. you'll hear the train in the distance, so retreat. Watch what happens so you can report back to us, then run for it. After the derailment, no matter what, please leave as quickly as you can.'

'Why's this train being sabotaged?' I ask. 'Is it carrying something special?'

'The Hawk has information from railway workers. This is a new, high-speed engine made in *Deutschland*. It's going to be used to rush troops, weapons and factory equipment from Germany to France and back. It's a very, very expensive machine and we're hoping to topple it and put it totally out of service tonight. It won't hurt if it damages the bridge either.'

He grins and it's infectious; I grin back and see Anton smiling too.

'Just bags of sugar – is that all the Hawk uses?' I ask.

Raven laughs. 'I don't think so. I'm not a chemist, but I think he uses all kinds of ingredients.'

'And what sets the bomb off? I mean . . . you need a lot of power or vibrations or heat to set off a bomb.'

'I've no idea – you're very curious.'

'Just interested. My papa's an engineer and we used to talk about things like that.'

'You don't need to worry about the device,' Raven

assures me. 'You just need to keep your eyes on the road and make sure no one is about.'

'What if someone does turn up?' Anton asks.

Raven presses his lips together. 'Well, we don't have any weapons we can give you . . . so you'll have to improvise. Don't fight unless you have to. And if you have to fight . . . well, what can I teach you in a few minutes? Apply hard things to soft places.'

'Like what?' I wonder.

'Boots and fists to faces or crotches . . . or whatever you can find.'

Anton and I exchange a nervous glance. Anton's been a cadet, but that doesn't exactly fill me with confidence.

'Look, please try not to worry. According to the Hawk, no one watches this stretch. Hopefully you'll just sit back and enjoy the fireworks. Good luck, my friends. You'd better get off now – don't want to be late!'

'What are you doing tonight?' I ask.

Raven smiles and shakes his head. 'Need-to-know basis, Coco, my curious friend. Good luck,' he says again, and then in a gesture which makes me ache for my papa, he kisses us both on the forehead.

'Good luck to you too,' I tell him.

'Do you have your own copy of the map?' I ask Anton as we walk out of the church.

'Under the rubber grip of my handlebars,' he says cheerfully. 'I got the idea from a spy story.'

'I'm glad all that reading's coming in handy. You maybe should have brought a book to bash any Nazis over the head.'

'I'm sure we'll think of something. What's in your bag?' He points to my shoulder bag which I've filled with the most useful emergency supplies I could think of.

'Paper, pencils, apples, strong garden twine, scissors, a metal ruler, sandwiches and some other stuff,' I tell him.

'Garden twine?!'

'It's cover for bringing the scissors. I thought we could also use the scissors as a weapon, if we have to.'

'Yes, and rap any soldiers really hard over the knuckles with your metal ruler,' Anton teases.

I button my coat up over my three jumpers and put on my gloves, hat and scarf. It's bitterly cold but we climb onto our bikes and begin the six-kilometre journey out of the city to the place.

I hate cycling. I'm unpractised and wobbly compared with Anton, but he slows down and waits for me to catch up.

'Out of breath?' he teases.

'No, my bike's a heap of rust and I can hardly turn the pedals,' I complain.

'Let me look at it after school tomorrow; I'll oil it up.'

School? It hardly seems possible that we'll both be at our separate schools tomorrow morning, trying to learn Latin and listening to playground gossip after a night like tonight . . . after helping to bring down a railway engine. I'm longing to leave school for good and fight the Nazis full-time.

We cycle to the edge of the city, detouring via back alleys whenever we suspect a checkpoint is ahead. The roads out of town are quiet, but we listen anxiously for vehicles. If we hear a patrol car, we have to get off the road and hide. We've already decided that if we're stopped, we're going to say we're sneaking off to be together against our parents' wishes. Just thinking about this excuse gives me butterflies . . . I would like to sneak off with Anton, but tonight we have other plans.

After about forty minutes' hard pedalling, Anton slows up.

'We're here,' he says. 'We just passed the signpost and the cottage I was told to look out for.'

We're at the bottom of a steep railway embankment, ten metres or so below the railway line. At the top is a small bridge which takes the railway over the road below. I look at my wristwatch: it's 6.55 p.m.

'Do you think the Hawk's up there?' I whisper.

'We're not supposed to look for him,' Anton reminds me, 'so stop looking and let's hide the bikes.'

We find a ditch and push them in. No sooner have we done that than we hear a vehicle in the distance.

'Over here,' Anton urges, heading towards a clump of bushes.

We push our way through the branches, crouch low and peer through the tangle of leaves. A jeep pulls up and drops off two soldiers. We look at each other. Our fear and inexperience scares us both. We wait and we watch.

The soldiers are cheerful and chatty. They look casually about; then, to our horror, one of them begins to climb up the embankment.

'What do we do?' I whisper right against Anton's ear.

'I'm thinking . . .' he whispers back.

'The Hawk could still be up there . . .'

'I know!'

But before we can come up with any kind of mad plan, the soldier comes back down. He and his colleague sit on the ground, not more than twenty feet from us, and talk. One takes out a cigarette, the other offers to light it and they smoke it together.

I glance at my watch: 7.10 p.m. I wonder if the Hawk is still up there on the bridge or if he's already set the bomb, crossed the field and is now guarding the road.

The jeep is approaching again; it's obviously making an inspection round. It pulls up and one of the soldiers jumps on board.

'*Bis später,*' he shouts. I'm sure that means 'till later', so the jeep must be coming back. But I can tell from Anton's face that he is just as relieved as I am to have only one soldier to deal with now. Two teenagers against one soldier seems better odds.

Anton moves his head next to mine to breathe out the words: 'We'll have to try.'

My eyes widen. I want to ask: 'How?' 'When?' 'With what?' But he's right. We will have to try.

I can see Anton undoing his belt buckle and slowly, silently, slipping the leather strap from his waist. We sit in silence, watching our man. Watching as he gets up, paces about, then comes back towards us again.

'When he turns his back . . .' Anton breathes into my ear.

The soldier walks past, closer to the bushes than he's been before, and I know this is our chance. Anton jumps up and I rush after him. As the soldier turns in surprise, Anton leaps onto his neck and pulls the belt tight around it. I grab for the soldier's flailing hands and try to pin them to his sides.

But he's strong and putting up a terrible fight.

Anton grunts and gasps as he pulls the belt tight around this blond boy's . . . no, don't look at his face, just look at his uniform, his horrible tin helmet. Think of poor La Belle.

The soldier wheezes and gurgles as I wrestle with his gun strap until I've pulled the rifle from his shoulder. As soon as it's in my hands, I'm hit by an immense wave of relief. The power has shifted: we are in charge.

I want to laugh. In fact, I do give a laugh. But the German can't hear because he has collapsed to the ground. 'Is he dead?' I ask. His face looks white against the grass. I don't want him to be a threat, but now that I see him helpless on the grass, I don't want him to be dead either.

Anton crouches over him, taking the handgun from the soldier's holster. 'I don't know . . . I don't think so; maybe we should shoot him.' He sounds very un-certain.

'No. If he's unconscious he can't hurt us.'

'We'll tie him up; his hands and feet, then we'll put something into his mouth to gag him.'

'Good thing I brought my twine then . . .'

'Yes.'

It takes us some time to make the soldier's hands and feet secure. Anton uses his sock to make a gag, but only once we've thought to rip out the incriminating name-tape and store it carefully in a tight pocket.

When I look at my watch, I see it's 7.30 p.m.

'The bomb's about to go off,' I hiss at him.

'We should move back, just to be safe.'

We get back into our hiding place in the bushes and wait, counting down the seconds.

'And fifty-nine . . . sixty . . .' I stuff my fingers into my ears.

Nothing happens.

We watch another whole minute tick by on my watch.

'Why hasn't the bomb gone off?' I ask. 'We need to go up there and check everything's OK.'

'Nico, that's not a good idea.'

'But the train will be here in a few minutes . . . I need to see if there's anything I can . . .'

Before Anton can get a hold of me, I begin to scramble up the embankment. It doesn't take long to get up to the track where I begin to search for any signs of the Hawk's device. When I find the pile of wired packages tucked in beside the rails, I realize this is a dangerous place to be.

'Move back!' Anton's hands are on my shoulders and he is pulling me away.

'Something's wrong,' I tell him. 'It should have gone off by now . . .'

The breathy quiet of the night has changed, and in the distance now I can hear the rumble of an express train approaching at speed.

'It should have gone off,' I insist. 'It's 7.34. The train will be here in less than two minutes.'

'Will you get down?' Anton insists. 'It's about to go off and we're going to be blown to bits!'

But I break away from his grip and go back towards the packages. I know it's crazy. But I just have a feeling . . . I try not to think about the rumble, growing louder; instead, I crouch down and look carefully. The packages have been set inside the rails against the huge bolts that hold the tracks onto the wooden sleepers. Clever. The bombs will explode and push the rails outwards, so the engine will be forced to jump forward onto the wooden sleepers. The stress of the explosions and the weight of the engine should weaken the bridge enough to topple the train. It might even destroy the bridge itself.

I follow the wiring from the packages to a simple circuit board and my heart gives a little start. I know all about circuit boards from evenings with Papa. I run my fingers along the wiring. I find a battery and I understand. The batteries are supposed to send a charge through this tiny fragile wire, to overheat it; then, when it burns through, the shock wave will pass up this thicker wire, into the fuse and light the packages.

Clever . . .

Except the wire connecting the battery has come loose.

I push it back into place and realize I've started the countdown. I back away as quickly as I can. 'Down!' I tell Anton. I grab for his hand and we hurtle down the embankment.

When we are at the bottom . . . still nothing. The clickety-clack of the engine, flying along at speed, is much louder now.

'What did you do?' Anton whispers.

'The wire was loose, so I pushed it back in and started the countdown . . . I've no idea how long—'

'You're a lunatic!' he tells me. 'But in a good way.' His arm around me, he pulls me down into a squat. The train is beginning to roar.

'That's a big engine.'

'Huge,' Anton agrees.

And then it happens. A muffled boom seems to grow and reverberate, shaking the air all around us. Waves of sound pulse through my ears. I can hear nothing and yet a huge noise at the same time.

'The bomb!' I shout.

A splatter of earth and wood splinters fly over us. The roar of the huge metal engine increases with every second. The train is charging towards the bridge. I put my hands over my ears. Please let this work; please let the engine derail . . . then I look at the embankment directly above our heads. We need to be further away! I grab hold of Anton's arm and tug.

As we run, I glance back to see a vast black engine bearing down on the bridge in a cloud of smoke and steam. Then comes a terrible smashing, splintering, grinding sound as the engine ploughs off the rails, throwing up wood, grass, stones – everything in its path.

The noise is immense, dreadful; every soldier for kilometres around is going to rush over here. Then the engine tilts and begins to tip, slowly at first, but gathering momentum until the vast metal body rolls onto its side, gouging its way down the steep hill, crashing past our hiding place, toppling and rolling with violent noise until it is lying on the road gushing with steam.

An amazing wave of excitement and achievement rushes over me. I throw my arms around Anton. I kiss him frantically and he kisses back. I break off, wanting to cheer in triumph, but then over the roaring hiss of the steam and the grinding of the moving metal, we can hear cries for help, cries that aren't in German.

'The driver!' I shout to Anton.

'Our orders were to leave,' Anton insists. 'The jeep will be back – every soldier in the whole area will be here.'

But I've already turned. I'm running towards the engine. Not far away, I can see the soldier we fought struggling with muffled cries against the loops of string holding him tight, and I can hear Anton racing after me. The driver is Belgian or maybe French. He's not a German, so I'm not prepared to just leave him there.

'Nico! We have to go!'

'Help! Help me! Please help! For pity's sake, get me out of here!'

The metal beast is on its side, still bellowing boiling hot steam. Somehow we'll have to pull the driver out of the door, which is now eight feet up in the air. We scramble to the other side of the engine, away from the blasting funnel.

'Boost me up,' I ask Anton.

'No, you keep watch. You've got the rifle,' Anton replies. 'Watch the soldier.' He begins to climb up before I can argue.

I can hear him cursing and pulling, then finally comes the creaking, grating sound that suggests he's got the cab door open. Anton's voice and the groaning of the injured man follows. Then legs appear over the top of the engine.

'Grab him, Coco,' Anton urges, somehow remembering to use my codename.

The broken, bleeding man is bumped and manhandled down as best we can. As we lay him on the grass, he groans in pain. He has a gash on his head and his arm is twisted and out of place.

'We'll try and get help,' I tell him, bending low to get close to him. Although I'm not sure how we can. We'll have to rely on the soldiers who will be here any moment to help him.

The driver opens his eyes and an ugly expression comes to his face. 'Did you do this? Did you derail the engine?' he asks harshly. 'Did you break the tracks, you stupid cow? They'll shoot me when they get here, if I don't die first.'

At first I'm too stunned to react. But then I manage: 'I'm sorry you're hurt.'

'You stupid, filthy cow!' he shouts out.

I want to reason with him, make him see that we are right to do this. We have to resist, otherwise what are we? We are nobodies, just objects allowing the Nazis to rule.

But now we hear sirens rushing towards the scene.

'I'll give them your description, you silly tart!' the driver shouts after me.

I pretend to myself that I've not heard his horrible words. 'The bikes!' I turn to Anton.

'Too late,' he shouts back. He grabs my hand and we run. We run like dogs after rabbits, like horses in a race. We run as we never imagined we could run before. Through fields, over ditches, scrambling through fences, through mud, grass and clumps of trees. We run and run until we can't hear even the faintest sound of sirens any more.

We run until we find ourselves in a little wood, far away from the train crash, where we finally feel safe enough to stop. We collapse into a hollow littered with fallen beech leaves and realize how exhausted we are. My feet ache, my legs ache, my breath is rasping in and out of my chest.

But none of this matters because, lying flat on my back, leaves in my hair, a machine gun slung over my shoulders, I find I am giggling with exhilaration, with joy and a dizzying relief, difficult to describe. Anton begins to laugh too.

'That was something,' I gasp. 'That was really something.'

'I still can't believe you rewired the bomb, you lunatic! You could have blown your head off.'

'I didn't rewire it; I just pushed a loose wire back into the battery. That's all.'

'Oh, you just "pushed a loose wire back into the battery" and nearly blew your head off.'

'Were you scared?' I ask. I prop myself up on an elbow to look at him.

'Was I scared? Let me see . . . yes, yes and yes, completely, utterly terrified. For the whole thing, from the moment the soldiers arrived till . . . the moment the soldiers came back.' He's joking about it now, but it's true, we were both terrified almost all of the time.

'The engine driver . . .' I begin. 'I didn't expect that. He was Belgian and he didn't want us to do what we did.' I still feel shaken, baffled by his response.

'He was in shock . . . maybe he didn't mean . . .'

'What if he'd been killed?' I ask. 'He wasn't a soldier.' I suddenly remember my mama's warning the day she slapped me: '*Is that what you want? The death of an innocent person on your conscience?*'

'Would you do it again?' Anton asks me, and despite the driver, I already know my answer.

'Yes. One thousand times yes.'

He turns to hold me tight in his arms and kisses me hungrily on the mouth. 'Yes,' he says. 'Yes, yes, yes, but I want you to be with me, every time. You give me the courage.'

'You to me too.'

I kiss him back, again and again, over and over. I've never felt like this: desperate for his touch, crackling with happiness and life. These are the most desperate times, but we are alive and fighting back.

Chapter Twelve

We walk for several hours, avoiding patrol cars by leaping behind walls and hedges whenever we hear them. On the outskirts of Brussels we bury the machine gun and the handgun we took from the soldier under a road sign, so we'll be able to find them again.

It's after midnight when we finally get back to our part of town. Although we crouch behind a wall waiting for Stapenhorst to leave the corner of my street, he doesn't, so because I am now faint with hunger, cold and exhaustion, Anton insists I come home with him.

'But my mama,' I whisper. 'She'll be frantic, she'll be leading a search party and alerting the police. She's become even more anxious since Papa was taken.'

'We've made it all this way without being caught by anyone, we have to get off the street,' Anton whispers. 'An engine has been derailed, Nico. They'll be tearing everything apart looking for suspects.'

So I creep with him towards his house. The guard in his area watches three streets at a time, so it's easier to dodge him and slip in through the unlocked front door.

'Anton!' Madame Morel cries out. Within moments, she's at the sitting-room door in a battered old dressing gown, her hair in a wild bun. She looks totally bewildered. 'Oh, Anton' – she throws her arms around him – 'I thought they'd got you; I thought they'd taken you . . . Oh, Anton. Where have you been? And Nicole . . . what are you doing here? What's going on?'

I can see someone standing beyond her in the sitting room, and for a moment I'm terrified it's a Nazi. But I realize who it is just as Anton sees him and rushes forward.

'Henri? Is it really you? Henri!' he exclaims, his voice cracking. The brothers fall into a heartfelt hug.

Once handsome, Henri has grown grey, gaunt, thinner than anyone I've seen, even in Brussels where we're all slowly starving to death.

'Did you get out? Did they let you go? Did you run away?' Anton's questions tumble out. He hugs his brother again for much longer this time and tries very hard not to cry.

Meanwhile I have a few moments to come up with an excuse for our incredibly late arrival back. It involves a Red Cross job and a roadblock. It had better be good because I'll have to tell the same story to my mother in the morning.

When I open my eyes, I look up at a white ceiling that isn't my own. My eyes search the room and for a moment I can't remember . . .

Then I recognize the map of the world on the wall and realize I'm in Anton's room and I have to get home immediately. I swing legs that ache and burn from the longest cross-country run I've ever done out from the covers. I'm still dressed, so I just lace up my shoes, put on my coat, hat and gloves, pick up my bag and slip out of the quiet house.

'Hi, Stapie, busy night?' I march past Stapenhorst quickly, giving him a cheery wave, and keep going before his sluggish brain can think to ask why I'm up so early.

I push open the door of our home, always unlocked, and tiptoe in. The sitting-room door is open and I can see my mama asleep on the sofa. Gaspar the cat has curled up beside her. In her hand is one of those old-fashioned romance novels we tease her for reading. But I realize, full of tenderness for her, that these books with their heroines in crinoline dresses and flowery bonnets are some of the few little treats she allows herself. I crouch down and stroke her forehead. I look at the lines etched across it and hope I've not caused too many of them.

'I'm home,' I whisper. 'I'm sorry I'm so late.'

Her eyes flutter a little then finally open, but she's not fully awake yet.

'We were making a delivery and then there was a roadblock,' I fib. 'We were stuck for hours. There were all these patrols . . . I made it to the Morels' house and I had to stay there to avoid meeting that twit Stapenhorst and getting into trouble for breaking the curfew.'

'Nicole,' she whispers and puts her hand over mine. 'I was so worried, I was so afraid for you.'

'I'm sorry,' I tell her. 'I hate to worry you. Can you forgive me?'

She holds onto my hand as if I were a little girl. Maybe I'll always be a little girl to my mama. 'I couldn't bear to lose you, my darling, I couldn't bear it. We've already lost your papa . . . who knows when he'll come home? What if he never comes home?'

'It's OK,' I tell her, stroking her hair gently. 'We need to trust in Papa. Henri's home, Anton's brother, he's been allowed back. So there's hope. And you need to trust in me.'

One day I'll tell her about derailing a train and running for hours to escape the Nazis, hand in hand with the most wonderful, caring, daring boy . . . but will she ever believe me?

Chapter Thirteen

The next day, we are settling down for a maths lesson when Monsieur Durance looks up and barks: 'No newspapers in class and certainly no copies of *Le Soir*, Clementine. The definition of censorship, if you please?'

'Sir, it's when people aren't allowed to speak freely and newspapers and radios aren't allowed to report news which has not been approved by the Germans.'

'By the authorities, Clementine. I'm sure there are other regimes all over the world who would like to compare themselves with our Nazi rulers.'

'But sir, this paper is different. Everyone was reading it on the train; it's got a *Le Soir* cover, but inside it's totally different.' She brings the paper to Monsieur Durance's desk for inspection and when we see the surprise on his face as he turns the pages, we all leave our desks and crowd round to look.

'But how?' he gasps. 'It has the official front page . . . where did you buy this?'

'At the newsstand at the tram station – everyone was queuing to buy it, so I thought there must be some special announcement. But inside, it's news of . . . the *Resistance*.' Her voice drops to a whisper, as if just saying the word could get her into trouble.

'They must have organized the printing, the distribution. Oh my goodness!' Mr Durance exclaims. 'The Gestapo will have a tantrum.'

As he turns the pages, the first thing I see is a photograph of *our* engine lying on its side . . . I recognize the embankment, the bridge, and my heart leaps with pride. I come and stand beside Monsieur Durance so I can see the article, headlined: OUR BRAVE RESISTERS DESTROY NAZI SHOWPIECE ENGINE, and now I spot the sketchy drawing of a girl's face which has been partly covered with thick black lines. Underneath are the words: *Wanted: saboteur! Codename—*, but a thick black line covers the final word. *We censor the Nazis for a change* is the caption.

Could that be me? Is that supposed to be me?! I tingle with panic. The train driver must have given them my description. They've got a sketch of me! I don't dare to look at Monsieur Durance in case my face gives something away. Have I brought the group into danger?

I scan the article. The writer wishes me courage but warns that Kriminaldirecktor Richter is determined to find me. He's stamping out all signs of Resistance, particularly in idealistic teenagers.

'A girl?' Clementine asks, pointing to the drawing. 'A girl brought down a Nazi train?'

'Teenagers all over Belgium are resisting the Nazis,' Monsieur Durance says, although it is a dangerous thing to claim in a classroom.

'We should not be reading this paper. It's full of filthy lies.' All this time, Aurelie has been standing back from the crowd. Now, hand on hip, she says, 'Get rid of this paper. Or I will report you.'

'Sit down, Aurelie,' Monsieur Durance says firmly. 'In this classroom, we follow my rules, not Nazi rules.'

There is an uneasy silence. Everyone goes back to their desks and Monsieur Durance folds the paper up and puts it in his drawer while Aurelie glowers at him from under her hair.

When the bell finally rings for the end of lessons, we gather up our books and bags and head out to the schoolyard.

'Nicole, I never see you any more,' Aurelie says sweetly, coming up beside me.

'Oh, and I wonder why?' I snap. It's hard to believe she was once my best friend; ever since that day in the café, I can hardly bear to look at her.

'You need to be careful, Nicole. I hear some of your new friends are dangerous.'

I spin on my heel and glare at her. 'What are you talking about?'

'When you're in the company of important people, you hear important things.'

'And what do you think you've heard?'

'Monsieur Durance sympathizes with the Resistance and so do the Morels, that's why Papa Morel isn't allowed back into the country . . . so what about you? Do you know more about the Resistance than you're letting on?'

I go on staring at her. She's bluffing; she knows nothing that isn't common gossip. She's hoping I'll spill some information and give her a titbit to rush to her Nazi boyfriend or her Gestapo-loving dad.

'I don't believe in censorship, Aurelie; neither does Monsieur Durance. If you think that makes us Resisters, then you've been brainwashed just like the rest of them.'

She's stopped walking, and she's looking right at me with her beautiful eyes, framed with their long lashes. I suddenly feel a little sorry for her. We were once such close friends. What's happened to her?

'Why aren't we friends any more? Is it because of Franz or because of my dad?' she asks in a hurt voice.

'Maybe both,' I reply.

By now I'm at the school gate and catch sight of a cluster of girls at the corner of the street. Some have their hands over their mouths in shock, but most are weeping and several run away.

I hurry over to see what's happened, Aurelie at my heels. Over the shoulders of the other schoolgirls crowding round, I see a little newspaper stand, just a simple table with stacks of *Le Soir* and a tobacco tin for money. Behind the table the wall is splattered with thick blood, still sticky, not quite dried.

On the pavement, the newspaper seller – the elderly man who is always on this corner outside the school – is lying dead. Half of his face is missing.

I reel back. This must have something to do with the sabotaging of the newspaper. He's been killed in retaliation. He's lying in a bloody pulp on the pavement as a result of the Gestapo tantrum Monsieur Durance promised.

'Distributing filth!' Aurelie says loudly and turns away from the scene.

'I can't be your friend,' I tell her. 'And it's because of you.'

I rush home as quickly as I can to find that Mama is out and only Grand-Mamie is in the kitchen.

'Cup of the revolting muck the Nazis are trying to brainwash us to drink?' she asks me cheerfully as I drop my books on the floor and flop into a chair.

'Just hot water, please – it tastes better.'

'You look miserable.'

'I am miserable.'

'Why?' Grand-Mamie asks.

'Because our country's been invaded by the Nazis, remember?'

'Oh, that. Well, it's no worse today than it was yesterday.'

'Yes it is! The Nazis shot the newspaperman at the stall beside the school. He was selling *Le Soir* and the Resistance people had sabotaged it and—'

'Oh dear, yes, I was reading that paper in church. Poor man.'

'Did he deserve to die? Did he deserve that? The Resisters killed him!' I exclaim.

'Nicole.' Grand-Mamie looks at me fiercely. 'The *Nazis* killed him. Never forget that. And this is a war, Nicole. All kinds of innocents die in a war and there is nothing anyone can do to prevent that.'

I slump my head down onto the table. I'm exhausted. I miss Mama's baking; when I came home from school there always used to be fresh biscuits or cakes or toasted bread with home-made jam. Now there is a cup of muddy hot water and my mama is off helping in a soup kitchen. Tears of self-pity trickle out of my eyes and down my nose.

Grand-Mamie runs her knobbly fingers over my hair.

'I'm sorry,' she says. 'It must be hard to be young and to try and make sense of it. But we must stand strong and do what we can to fight them . . . I know you have thought about this.'

'I have thought about it,' I sniff. 'I do what I can . . . but it's not much. It's not enough. And I can't say anything more.'

'All the Red Cross work . . . Is something else going on?' she asks, still stroking my hair.

'Grand-Mamie, I can't say anything, you understand.' I meet her beady bird-like eyes.

'May the Lord bless and keep you,' she says with great sincerity, her hand on my cheek now.

'Thank you.'

'Please stay safe. It's very dangerous, too dangerous.' She shakes her head. 'Come on, my darling, I think we need to cheer ourselves up. Shall we go to my room and see what's playing on the radio?'

I understand immediately; we are going to tune in to the British BBC and see if there is any news.

'Our friend, Winston Churchill, is making a speech at his old school today. I'm sure it will be very interesting,' Grand-Mamie says, fairly hopping up the stairs ahead of me. The thought of Sir Winston has put a spring in her step.

We sit and fiddle with the radio dials for ages. Loud German marching music keeps blasting out at us. The

Nazis are always trying to jam the channels to prevent people from listening to the BBC. But we are patient; we move the dial millimetre by millimetre until at last we hear the unmistakable booming British voice coming over the airwaves to us. We both straighten our backs at the sound of it.

'*Never give in, never give in, never, never, never, never – in nothing, great or small, large or petty – never give in except to convictions of honour and good sense. Never yield to force; never yield to the apparently overwhelming might of the enemy.*'

Grand-Mamie and I look at each other and grin. Never, never, never, never. He repeated it four times. He repeated it for as many times as I needed to hear it.

For a few moments, the dreadful marching music interrupts again. I leap up to retune and we catch the very end of the speech and the unshakable resolve in his words: '*We can be sure that we have only to persevere to conquer.*'

'You see!' Grand-Mamie says, eyes shining. 'We must only persevere. Think of Violetta. Whenever a new Resistance paper comes out, she puts a fresh copy on the Kriminaldirektor's desk. Apparently she hides it in her underpants. No one wants to search an old woman's underpants. So we must all do what we can.'

We listen to the news and then from the radio comes the totally disembodied message: 'The pigeon prepares to fly to the owl and raven.' Then the German marching music starts up again.

'Never mind,' says Grand–Mamie, switching off. 'We have heard as much as we need: *never, never, never, never give in!*' she repeats, shaking her fist.

'*The pigeon prepares to fly to the owl and the raven . . .*' I whisper to myself. Group K has an Owl and a Raven. Could it be possible that the BBC has a message for us?

Chapter Fourteen

The next evening, as instructed by a note, I go to the crypt and find Hope, Raven, Anton and Monsieur Durance already there, drinking bad coffee and packing boxes. I glance about and realize with a jolt that I'm looking for La Belle.

She isn't here and she never will be.

'Aha, it's the famous Coco. You made the newspapers,' Raven greets me.

'It's my fault,' I admit, still worried that I've put the whole group in danger. 'I went back to help the driver, even though you and the Poet told me not to. He was a collabo and must have given them my description.'

'Unless it was the soldier . . .' Anton adds. 'We should probably have shot him, but—'

'My goodness, no! You're young, we wouldn't ask you

to shoot anyone,' Monsieur Durance protests. 'I'm sorry you were faced with a soldier – that was unexpected.'

'Luckily it's a very poor drawing of you,' Hope adds. 'It doesn't do you justice, Coco.'

Raven comes over and puts a hand on my shoulder. He's stubbly with purple smudges of exhaustion under his eyes but his expression is endlessly kind. 'You shouldn't have gone back for the driver, Coco,' he says, 'but we understand. We all have to make difficult choices every day. Sometimes innocent people die as a result of our actions, and when it happens it's devastating. But we do this because we think our cause is more important than any one life.'

There's a pause while we all let his words sink in. Then Monsieur Durance, bushy eyebrows raised, says, 'I heard from the Poet that you fixed the bomb's detonator circuit. Now, I don't think you learned *that* in school.'

We've not let anyone here know that we are teacher and pupil. 'My papa is a gadget man who loves to teach,' I say. Of course, Monsieur Durance knows my papa, knows he is missing, and when I catch the look of sympathy in his eyes, I suddenly feel such a weight on my chest that I have to change the subject. 'There was a message on the radio about the owl and the raven and a pigeon . . .' I begin.

Monsieur Durance, Hope and Raven begin to laugh.

'Aha . . . so what do you know about radios?' Raven asks.

'A little . . .' I admit. 'I can build a simple one, with help.'

'What do you think of this?' He pulls a sheet from what I thought was another stack of boxes. A beautiful wooden radio set, lovingly waxed and polished, is revealed. 'It obviously won't work down here in the basement,' he says. 'We'll need to get it up into our eyrie. But would you like to have a play with the dials?'

I go over to the machine and take a look.

'She should learn our frequencies and our codes,' Hope says, looking to Monsieur Durance.

'Yes. I think she's proved herself,' he replies. 'Coco, Group K has a special radio frequency and codewords which let us contact other Resistance groups. Only Hope and I know them, and they would obviously be very valuable to the enemy, allowing them to contact other groups pretending to be us. But we think we'd like you to be a code-keeper as well. My friend, the Poet, don't feel left out. You will know all about where the radio and the aerial are to be placed.'

Anton nods. 'Coco is a really good choice,' he agrees. 'I'd trust her with my life.'

For a moment, our eyes meet so intensely I can't look away, but then I feel aware of the others looking at us and I turn, remembering to thank Monsieur Durance and Hope for their trust.

'You can't write anything down,' Raven explains. 'You'll just have to think of ways to remember the numbers. Think of birthdays or ages or any other notable numbers.'

Monsieur Durance adds, 'We say "Any news from the henhouse?" and the proper reply is, "The chickens are laying." Silly, but everything is so serious these days, we must have a little humour.'

I smile.

'You boys pack up the boxes. I'll sit with Coco and help her memorize the frequency,' Hope says.

As we sit in front of the radio, she gives me the number and shows me how to turn the dials to the right place.

'The problem is always finding the frequency,' she says, 'like a needle in a haystack. It takes skill and a special kind of patience. We'll take you up to the eyrie soon and let you practise. Did you listen to the BBC broadcast tonight?'

'Yes, I heard that message about the pigeon: was it really . . . did they really mean us?'

She nods. She looks thinner than before and the restless tapping and fluttering of her fingers reveal her nervousness. 'We are going to be part of something much bigger,' she says. 'The British are helping groups to mobilize. They want to give us weapons, explosives and important targets.'

'That's amazing!' Help from the British. I can hardly believe it. We're going to be so much more powerful.

'And frightening . . .' Hope admits. 'Working with other groups on big missions – much more chance of being discovered.' After a pause she asks quietly: 'So your friend, the Poet . . . ?' She's watching me carefully and I can't help colouring up a little. 'You both have strong feelings for each other.' She doesn't ask; she's matter-of-fact because she knows it's true.

'Yes,' I reply.

'All the excitement and danger. It can make those feelings very intense. More than they would be in normal life. You need to be careful, guard your heart a little.'

'No.' I shake my head, knowing that my heart is already completely unguarded. 'I trust him. I've known him for most of my life and he's very special.'

I've not noticed that Monsieur Durance has moved to sit just behind us.

'Ah . . . the young romantics, the Romeo and Juliet of our group. No, no, I mustn't say that, too gloomy, and in reality I find our supposedly tender hearts are usually made of stronger stuff.'

'Really?' Hope asks.

'Oh, yes,' he replies, holding out a tin of tiny little mints. 'Please take one. When one love comes to an end, the heart flies free and often settles very happily on another.'

'I didn't know you were such a cynic,' Hope says with a smile.

'A realist,' Monsieur Durance replies. 'An optimist. By the way, Coco, if anyone asks you, "What's my favourite colour?" the correct reply is, "Romeo and Juliet". A favourite code, but not my favourite play . . . *But soft! What light through yonder window breaks?*' He pats my shoulder and goes back over to the boxes.

'You and the Poet are both very special to do what you do,' Hope says, putting her arm around my shoulder. 'You were incredibly brave on your mission.'

'Thanks.'

'Fifteen is still young, Coco. Part of me wants you to be a child for as long as you can. But what we do makes people grow up quickly.'

Just then the special iambic pentameter knock sounds out against the door to the crypt.

'A British plane packed with explosives, weapons and supplies is flying to us very soon,' Raven says, a broad grin across his handsome face. 'Hopefully these are the new recruits who are going to help us land it.'

He unlocks the door and in walks our joking, teaser friend Padrice, and then the pale, blond boy I recognize at once as La Belle's younger brother.

Chapter Fifteen

I'm as surprised to see Padrice as he is to see me. He immediately raises his arms for a hug and blurts out: 'Hello—'

'Shhhh!' I warn him. 'It's codenames only here!'

'Oh yes, of course, of course. Don't worry, I'll get the hang of it. I'm Plum . . .'

'Plum!' I repeat, trying not to laugh.

'And why not? Who are you?'

'I'm Coco.'

He comes over and I get the hug. Padrice feels big, strong and solid. It will be good to have him here, teasing us, keeping our spirits up.

'Delighted to meet you, Coco.' Then he kisses my cheek, because he is a rogue who always takes every single liberty he can. 'This is going to be fun.' He shoots me a wink.

Anton approaches him, along with the others. 'I'm the Poet,' Anton says almost too seriously, shaking his friend's hand.

'Of course, what else would they call you?' Padrice asks, giving him a wink too.

I turn to La Belle's brother. He looks young, pale, shy and he reminds me painfully of his sister. 'It's very brave of you to come,' I tell him.

'The Owl says I'm still too young to go on missions but I want to help in any way I can. I'm the Torch.'

'Honoured,' I reply, shaking his hand.

For the next hour or so, Raven and Monsieur Durance outline the preparations we need to make to help the British plane to land. We've not been given a date, time or location yet. Apparently the flight can only happen on a clear, moonlit night, 'a bomber's moon', so we'll only know at short notice. The location is a close-guarded secret, only to be revealed at the last minute.

'Check your dead drops twice a day for messages, and be ready to leave as soon as you get word,' Raven advises us.

Then I catch sight of Anton's wristwatch and see we're already half an hour past the curfew. 'I have to go home,' I say, jumping up. 'I was so late the last time my family is asking questions.'

Padrice gets up too. 'I'd be happy to walk you home, Coco.'

'No, that won't be necessary.' Now Anton stands up. 'I'll make sure Coco doesn't . . . fall into enemy hands.' He glowers at Padrice and I push down a smile.

We say goodnight and leave the church, walking hand in hand through dark streets that look deserted but are patrolled by dangerous soldiers and policemen.

'How's Henri?' I ask in a whisper.

'He's recovering . . . he's been granted a holiday, and he's even been given a ration book so we can feed him up a little. But there must be a reason for his release. Maybe the Nazis want him to go to a different factory, or do something more dangerous. I'm worried about him. He asks a lot about what I'm doing with the Red Cross. I haven't told him what it's really about, but he's guessing. When he's well enough, he'll want to join us.'

I pull on Anton's hand because I see a shadowy figure crossing the street ahead of us. We move into a doorway and huddle together.

Anton puts his arms around me and searches my face. 'Are you OK?' he asks.

I smile at him and nod. 'I am now.' I put my face against the soft skin of his neck.

'I'm a little worried about Padrice joining us,' he says.

'Don't you think he'll do a good job?'

'He'll do a great job – that's why I put the idea in his head . . . but you two, out at night on missions together . . .'

'Are you joking?' I ask with a smile.

'He's quite the ladies' man, Padrice.'

'So if I go out on missions with Padrice, you're going to be more worried about us flirting than about us getting killed?'

Anton clears his throat and looks a little embarrassed.

'I really like Padrice, as a friend,' I say. 'I'm not interested in him.'

'No? Not at all, not even a tiny bit? What if I was dead?'

This is meant to be funny, but in our situation, when someone we know has already died, it isn't funny at all. I don't smile back; I hold Anton's face in my hands and tell him, 'I'm very interested in you.' My voice sounds dark and serious. I have been longing to kiss him all evening.

'And I'm very interested in you,' he says.

'What do you like about me?' I whisper, just the smallest distance away from his lips.

'Everything,' he replies, 'but especially . . . especially the look that comes over your face when you've made up your mind to do something. A little line forms between your eyebrows' – he touches the place tenderly – 'and you're unstoppable.'

I move towards him slowly, enjoying the anticipation of this kiss. At first I just brush his lips with mine. Once we begin to kiss deeply, it's difficult to stop. We know we have to go home, but being here with him, feeling more alive than I've ever done before . . . just one more, just one last time . . . we can't let go of each other.

'I need to take you home,' Anton says finally when our lips are tingling, swollen with kissing, and we feel breathless with want, 'even though I'd rather stay here all night.'

Good old Stapie is in my street, so I decide to sneak in through the back alley. I tiptoe across our garden, push open the kitchen window and scramble through the little opening, sending several spoons on the draining board clattering.

The house is dark and quiet, so I creep into the hallway. For a moment, I'm confused. Have Mama and Grand-Mamie gone to bed? Without me? No fuss? Have they just trusted that I'll find my way home later? This doesn't seem right. My next thought is panicky. Has something happened to them? Have the Gestapo been back? But then I hear Mama calling my name from the sitting room.

I find her sitting in the armchair, waiting. 'Nicole, where have you been?' Along with her concern there is a sharpness to her voice.

'I was at my Red Cross meeting—' I begin, but she interrupts.

'Surely that would have finished well before the

curfew? Nicole, it's nearly ten o'clock. Where have you been?'

I swallow.

'Nicole?' Even in the dim light of the remains of the fire and a small paraffin lamp, I can see that Mama looks very serious. 'Please don't lie to me, my darling. Please, never lie. Nicole' – her voice drops low – 'are you working for the Resistance?'

I stand very still. I'm frightened to breathe. Has she found something? In my room? Has she found some clue?

'Nicole, no one in the world cares more about you than I do,' she says. 'I deserve an answer.'

I go and crouch at the foot of her chair. I look into her face and I can't bear to lie to my lovely mama. She can't know, she must not know, for her own safety. But I need to tell her something that has truth. She knows me so well, she would recognize a lie.

'I've wanted to tell you,' I begin, 'but I don't know how to . . . I'm frightened you're going to be angry.'

'Oh no,' she whispers, her hand going over her mouth. 'Papa warned you, he said—'

'I'm seeing a boy. It's serious. It's very serious. I can't help myself,' I reply, and I sound totally convincing, because what I'm saying is true.

For a moment Mama is silent. She just looks at me wide-eyed. 'Oh, Nicole . . . a boy? Thank goodness!'

Really? Now it's my turn to be surprised. She's glad I'm sneaking out at night for a boyfriend? 'You don't mind?' I ask.

'Of course I mind!' She sounds sharp again. 'Of course! But anything is better than imagining you've joined up and you're putting your life in danger.'

'When I'm out at night . . .' I begin, thinking ahead to the airdrop, which is surely going to be another very late mission, 'I don't want you to worry about me. I'm safe. I'm with a good person.'

'But . . . what would your papa say if he was here?'

'Please.' I take hold of her hands. 'Can you try to trust me?'

Chapter Sixteen

'Have you got everything?' Anton asks in a tense whisper. We're in his small bedroom, making our final preparations.

'Yes. Torch, some food, drink, the first-aid supplies and a roll of my magic garden twine,' I answer.

After delays, false hopes, cancelled dates, we've had word that the British plane, packed with bomb-making supplies and weapons, is due to land tonight, the 11th of December. Group K is meeting with Groups D and E at a special location well out of the city to help guide the plane down and unload it. If we are caught, we will surely all die.

'I'll keep my papers in my coat,' I tell Anton. We both have new identity cards: ingenious fakes with the addresses of safe houses, which will not connect us to our friends or families if we are caught, because everyone related to us might be imprisoned too. We are not supposed to know who made these elegant forgeries, but I'm sure I recognize Monsieur Durance's elegant copperplate handwriting.

Anton is now Charles Briand, and I am Eglantine DuPont, still fifteen, maybe because Monsieur Durance thinks the Nazis might go easier on a young girl.

Not from what I've heard. Henri has brought back terrible tales from his work camp. He doesn't talk about it much, but when he does we all wish we'd not heard the stories he tells. Whatever cruelties your mind can imagine, the Nazis can always invent something worse.

'Where does your mother think we are going tonight?' I ask Anton.

'I've told her we're on important Red Cross business and we may be late.'

'Do you think she believes you?'

'Yes, but I'm not sure if Henri does . . .'

Just then there is a knock on the bedroom door and Henri comes in. 'You two look as if you're going out,' he says, looking us over carefully.

'We've got important work to do for the Red Cross tonight,' Anton replies.

'Such as?'

Anton hesitates. He's not as good at excuses as me.

'We're taking first-aid supplies to a depot out of town. A whole group of us are going in the lorry to help unload and organize the whole delivery. If it gets too late to travel back, we might have to spend the night there and come back in the morning,' he replies, sounding a little wooden.

'Which depot?' Henri asks. 'Where is it?'

'I'm not sure we're allowed to tell you. Careless talk costs lives and all that,' I say breezily.

'At least tell me roughly where you're going . . . if anything happens, if we need to know where to look for you, at least give me the area.'

'Well . . . sort of the Drie-Egypten area,' I reply. 'Near Kwakenbeek. I'm not sure exactly.'

Anton glares at me, I'm not sure why. Yes, we are going to Drie-Egypten, but if Henri thinks we are doing Red Cross business there, then what's the harm? 'Look, we have to go,' he says, buckling up his rucksack.

'Are you sure?' Henri is looking at us very seriously. 'You're just kids – you don't want to get mixed up in anything serious.'

'We're fine. We're on Red Cross business. It's fine,' Anton says firmly, swinging his bag over his shoulder.

Henri stands in the doorway and for a moment I think he's going to block Anton's way.

'Come on, let us through,' Anton says. He looks strong and broad compared to his frail older brother.

'Are you sure?' Henri asks once again.

'Yes,' Anton insists.

★ ★ ★

Because we had to leave our bicycles behind the night we derailed the engine, Raven has managed to find us two hopeless old bikes with seats as hard as stone and tyres covered in lumpy patches. We have to pass through three checkpoints, show our new papers, remember to call each other Charles and Eglantine, and explain our fictional first-aid mission to guards too oafish to understand anything, even when we try to speak German.

We keep a mental note of where all the checkpoints are, because when we come back later we will have rucksacks no longer full of bandages, disinfectant and aspirin but packed with British sabotage equipment. I can't pretend it isn't going to be very frightening bicycling along at night with bomb-making equipment in my rucksack.

Before we get to the grass field which has been picked as a landing strip, Anton and I have another job. We have to dig up the guns we buried after the train mission. It's a detour of forty minutes, but the guns are essential. As Monsieur Durance put it: 'If the Nazis find out what we're doing, we're going to need all the help we can get.'

When we find the signpost, we start to dig with our hands. The guns are not down deep and we unearth them quickly. Anton insists on carrying them both, because if we are found with guns, we will no longer be able to claim we're on a Red Cross mission; we'll be taken straight to prison.

'Better if one of us can get away,' he says, then asks, 'By the way, Nico, do you know how to use one of these?'

I shake my head.

He looks at his wristwatch and decides we have enough time, so he gets back on his bike and I follow him to the edge of a wood. We go into the trees on foot, pushing the bikes. When we've walked in for five minutes or so, he stops, unloads his rucksack and takes out the handgun. It's so dark he needs his torch to explain how to load the gun and how to fire it. There are six bullets in place.

'How do you know about this?'

'Cadets,' he says. Obviously.

To my surprise, he adds: 'I can't just talk you through it – you'll have to have a go.'

'Here? Really? But someone might hear.' I realize I'm reluctant to actually try the thing.

'We'll use a silencer.'

'But we haven't got one.'

He unwinds his scarf.

'That's not going to work.'

'It should do something.'

Once the muzzle is wrapped up, Anton hands me the gun. It feels heavy, cold and deadly. I'm a little frightened of it.

'You'll be fine,' he says. 'Use both hands and two fingers if you like. Squeeze gently, aim low because you'll bounce up when you fire, because you're inexperienced. Not tonight, but the next time you shoot at something, fire several times because you'll probably miss the first time.'

I lift the gun and aim in a wobbly sort of way at the tree in front of us. I begin to squeeze, bracing myself, clenching my jaw and raising my shoulders towards my ears.

BLAM!

My hands shoot up into the air. The noise, the force, the ricochet – it takes me completely by surprise. I'm way off target, the whip of branches up in the trees showing that my shot has gone wildly high.

There's a thud and I'm astonished to see a pigeon land on the ground in a whirl of feathers. Anton bursts out laughing. 'Not a complete miss then. You shot one sleeping bird and my scarf.' He picks his scarf up from the ground and examines the holes in it. I go over and look at the dead bird. It has a bloody wound in the centre of its chest. I'm horrified. What on earth must it feel like to shoot a person? A real, living, breathing person?

Then we hear an engine, which stops, as if the vehicle has pulled up.

'Sounds as if someone's come to investigate,' Anton says. 'Time to get out of here.' He takes a tight hold of my hand and we run for the bikes.

Chapter Seventeen

After another hour or so of anxious cycling, we are at the rendezvous. It's already 10 p.m. and dark. The little map Anton has hidden behind the rubber grips on his handlebars has been accurate. We're on the edge of a wide, flat grassy field enclosed by a sturdy barbed-wire fence.

'Do you see the little hut over on the other side? That's where we're meeting everyone,' Anton whispers.

We hide our bicycles in a ditch, shoulder our rucksacks and scramble over the fence. Once we're on the other side, we crouch down, watch and listen. It seems deserted so, keeping low, we walk towards the hut.

'What are the codes again?' I ask Anton. I'm feeling very nervous now.

'Hello, my brother is a pilot,' he whispers back.

'Oh yes . . .' I look at him. This mission is dangerous – really, truly dangerous. 'Anton, you will be careful,' I say.

He turns and for a moment I'm gathered up tightly in his arms. 'Never mind careful, let's be brave,' he replies, and kisses me firmly on the mouth.

'You're right,' I say, feeling my courage flood back at his touch. 'Time to meet the others.'

When he pushes open the door of the hut, in the dim light inside we see a huddle of people, some standing, several sitting on the floor.

'Hello, my brother is a pilot,' Anton says.

'Hello! My brother is a captain,' one of the men replies, which I remember now is the proper response.

'And my brother is an idiot!'

A ripple of good-natured laughter greets Padrice's joke. He waves at us and as my eyes adjust to the light, I see Hope and Raven too, sitting close together, with Monsieur Durance and at least eight or nine others who must be members of the other groups. Some of them are young like us, but there are also two much older men with grey beards.

Although we must all talk in whispers, the mood is cheerful. 'A Lysander,' one of the old men is saying. 'Now that is a beautiful plane – it can take off and land on a tablecloth if it has to.'

'So long as he keeps to the middle of the field,' another says, 'he'll be fine.'

We have an hour or so to pass until the plane is due, so provisions come out of rucksacks: a few biscuits, apples and sips of wine are shared around. Some stories are told, but nothing too personal or downbeat. We are all quite nervous enough. We play a word game, then Anton points out that it is nearly 10.45 p.m. and surely time to get out onto the 'airfield' and provide landing lights.

I've already been told what to do. We're to stand twenty metres or so apart all the way down the runway and shine our torches straight up into the sky when we hear the plane. When we see the plane, we must shine our torches right at it.

When I'm in place with my torch in my hands, every nerve ending jangles. Can I hear the plane? Or is that an army jeep? Can I hear anything at all over the sound of the wind and the violent chattering of my teeth?

After an age . . . after I've lost all the feeling in my hands, my feet, my face, after I've lost all hope of the British turning up at all, there comes the distant hum of a propeller. It's far away but it's definitely coming from above. I look over at my colleagues. One of them punches the air in excitement. As the first torch is switched on and pointed to the sky, fear and excitement course through my veins like hot water, bringing me back to life again.

The drone grows louder surprisingly quickly. Maybe the plane has been circling, and now that it can see us it's dropping down to land. We point our torches and search the sky. Suddenly we are lighting up the metal belly of a small plane.

There it is! Swooping out of the sky towards us. The noise is startling; I've never been this close to an aeroplane coming in to land. It's a small plane, but it's dropping down at speed and looks as if it's going to fall onto our heads. I want to run out of the way but know I have to stand firm, point my torch and guide it in.

The crew in there have risked crossing the Channel, they have probably been shot at all over France and Belgium, they may not make it back alive. The least I can do is stand firm and shine my light for them.

With a roar and bumping skid, the plane hits the grass and jolts along for several hundred metres. It stops, engines and propeller still running, and as we race towards it, the cargo doors fly open.

Two British airmen, laughing and shouting encouragement, are in the hold already, throwing boxes at us, each one small and manageable enough for one person to handle.

Every second we are here longer than we need to be is deadly. So they are unloading at speed, grinning and wishing us luck. Within minutes, the hold is empty, the crewmen wave and salute us, the cargo doors go back up again and then the plane is speeding over rabbit holes, lurching and wobbling back up into the air.

Just for a moment, I enjoy the sight of the boxes heaped on the runway. They look professional, military-issue. They look packed with hope, defiance and proper weapons.

Then our heads turn, our voices stop. Faintly, oh so faintly, only just above the noise of the wind, we can hear trucks and the ferocious barking of patrol dogs.

Chapter Eighteen

A full-scale panic with purpose breaks out. Everyone grabs hold of as many boxes as they can carry. I see now there is a small farmer's truck parked beside the hut. A tattered, innocent-looking vehicle.

We rush towards it and throw in as many boxes under its tarpaulin-covered hoops as we can. The driver jumps in, starts the engine and races towards the fence. Just as I wonder how he's going to break through, someone runs ahead of him and opens a gap, which must have been cut into the wires earlier.

There is a momentary sense of relief as the truck gets away, but now, once the engine noise has retreated, we can hear the barking growing louder. There are vehicles heading this way too.

'Open the remaining boxes, take everything you can

and run away,' Monsieur Durance orders. 'Poet, my friend, I'm going to need that machine gun of yours. Give Raven the handgun.'

Anton rummages in his bag and brings out the weapons.

'Split up, people, go in twos or threes, get into the woods,' Monsieur Durance advises, 'and be brave. Be brave, my dear friends. "Stiffen the sinews, summon up the blood".' Then his hand is on my shoulder as I frantically cram slim metal tubes and plastic-coated packages into my bag. 'Run, Coco,' he urges. 'You can get away. I'm very proud of you and I know your father would be too.'

There isn't even time for me to reply. Anton grabs my hand and we begin to run, Padrice and Raven beside us. Through the gap in the fence, over the road, then we search the ditches for our bicycles.

Laden down with my bulging rucksack, I clamber on and pedal off on my lumpy tyres at a painfully slow pace. This is no good; surely I'd be quicker running?

'I can't get up any speed!' I protest.

Raven, just ahead of me, urges, 'C'mon, keep going! We'll pedal to the woods and get off there.'

I push and push on the pedals. Gradually I build up some momentum. Padrice is way ahead in the distance, then Anton, then Raven. I can see that Anton and Raven keep glancing round to make sure I'm keeping up.

Behind me come others. Hope must be there – I saw her get onto her bike after me. But what about Monsieur Durance? I glance behind, but can't see him.

On and on we pedal desperately, the sound of the jeeps growing louder.

'Here's the wood,' Padrice shouts, 'but some of us should bike on – we need to go in different directions!'

I can't pedal any more. As soon as I get off my bike, I see Anton does too. I'm so relieved, as I always feel safer with Anton. Raven joins us, but he waves Hope on as she flies past on her bicycle. We begin to run, trip and stumble through the woods.

I glance back. 'I've still not seen Monsieur' – somehow I remember to correct myself – 'I mean, the Owl . . . where is the Owl?' I ask Anton and Raven desperately. 'We have to go back. We have to go and look. We can't let anything happen to him! The Owl is the kindest . . . the cleverest.'

'You can't go back,' Anton says, taking hold of one of my arms. 'Please!'

As I slow down, trying to turn back, Raven takes hold of the other. 'We have to keep moving forward, Coco,' he insists. 'This is what the Owl asked us to do. We have vital equipment. Many people have risked their lives to get this equipment to us, so we have to keep running.'

'But where is he? What is he doing?'

'He's staying at the airfield to hold them back for as long as possible,' Raven replies grimly.

Strong arms are tugging me forward and my legs keep running but I start to cry. 'The Owl,' I sob. 'But he can't stay there! They'll kill him . . . they'll torture him. We need to go back for the Owl . . .'

'He wants us to go on,' Anton says. 'He ordered us to.'

I can hear them now. The dogs. They are barking, howling with excitement. They are still straining on their leashes, but once the soldiers let them go they'll be bounding through this wood after us. No one can out-run a dog. We'll be pulled down, their muzzles ripping through our clothes and tearing at our skin. I speed up along with Anton and Raven. They're holding me up, keeping me plunging forward. I do not want to be hunted down by animals. Terrible fear keeps me running, faster and faster than I've ever run before.

'We need water,' Raven says, and gestures with his head the direction we're to go in.

I wonder how he can think of a drink at a time like this, but as we race downhill towards a wide stream I realize we need water for a different reason. We plunge towards the dark stream, calm on top. Before I can protest, before I can say that it looks deep, it looks cold and how can we let ourselves get wet on a December night as cold as this when we are so far from home, the ice hits me.

First my legs, then my stomach, then my chest; it's so cold I gasp and cry in pain. It's like a freezing vice of cold.

'Upstream, upstream!' Raven says, his voice gasping and shaking too.

For much longer than I think I can bear, we wade waist-high through water colder than snow. I feel as if metal bars are hammering against my body. I don't think I can bear it. Then Hope's words about enduring pain come into my mind. 'It will end, it will be over,' I whisper.

'We will get through, we will get out,' Anton answers me.

'Just a little longer,' Raven tells us. Then: 'Over there.' He points to a stony patch of ground, like a miniature pebbled beach, and we wade towards it.

As soon as we get out of the water, I expect to feel relief, but now the wind is on my wet clothes and I'm colder than ever. The barking is wild, fierce and scattered; the dogs are on the loose. We need to keep going. Despite the terrible, teeth-chattering cold, we link arms, hoping to gain a little comfort and support from one another, and stumble on.

On and on, breaths rasping in our chests, laden rucksacks bumping against our backs. Through the woods, tree trunks flying past until we rush out onto a road.

'We'll follow it,' Raven suggests, so we carry on

running, three-abreast, soaked, exhausted, near delirious with cold, not sure if we are running towards the enemy or running away, when suddenly from round a corner we are confronted with huge car lights.

'*Dive!*' Raven shouts.

All at once, the comforting arms that have held me up all this time disappear. For a moment I stand like an idiot in the light. Then I hear that voice with its unmistakable delight at being in control:

'There! There's one of the vermin. Don't shoot!' he screams. 'It's the girl! We want her alive! We'll make her tell us everything.'

Richter!

I turn and run for my life. Down the road as fast as I can, then I leap back into the woods. I can't think about Anton or Raven or anyone else, this is just survival. I want to live; I want to get away from Richter and his men.

I pound through the forest, flying through the trees.

Monsieur Durance's words ring in my ears: '*Run, Coco, you can get away.*' I repeat them over and over in my head. They give me strength as I plunge on.

The rapid cracks of gunfire don't matter, even when I hear a bullet soar past my ear. I keep on running, faster, stronger, branches whipping my face, thorns tearing at my clothes.

Nothing else matters, I have to get away. But I can hear someone right at my heels.

Chapter Nineteen

Faster and faster I pump my legs. I will not be caught. I'm determined not to be caught. But the rucksack is thudding and thumping against my back, dragging me down, slowing me up. I keep on running. I can't drop this rucksack; people have risked their lives for me to have this rucksack packed with equipment.

Footsteps are thudding right behind me. I push myself, knowing there is not much more I can give. My legs, my chest, my neck, everything is burning with the pain of effort. Ahead of me the ground falls away. I have no idea if this is a small hill, a steep drop or a deep gorge. But I know I have to leap . . .

'Coco!'

I'm in the air, falling, when I hear the voice. It's not a Nazi, it's Raven! He's behind me. But before I can see it, I feel the ground rushing up to meet me.

Leaves ... please let there be lots of dried leaves ...

Smack!

For a moment I have no breath at all. A searing pain spreads out from my stomach. I pull myself up and sit gasping, wheezing, trying to make the air go in and out. I can hear a scrambling sound. I think Raven is coming down after me.

'Coco! Are you all right?' He's crouching over me, asking: Can I move my ankles? What about my wrists? Have I hit my head? He's so kind I want to cry.

'Can't ... breathe ...' I tell him, gasping for air.

'You're winded, maybe. Your diaphragm's in spasm. Just be calm and it will feel normal in a few minutes. We're not being chased any more.'

I lean my head on his shoulder and feel soothed. I remember now that he's a doctor. I think he must be a very nice and comforting doctor.

'Where's the Poet?' I ask, as soon as my breathing feels better.

'I don't know,' he replies, 'and I'm very worried about my wife.'

'We'll hide our rucksacks and go back and look for them.'

'Right.'

I'm glad he's agreed without any fuss. I thought he might try to make me hide and wait while he went back, but that would kill me. I need to know what's happening.

I need to know where Anton is.

Eyes and ears straining for any sign of our pursuers, we creep back towards the road. As we approach, we see headlights. Richter's car must still be there. I'm straining to hear dogs, but the animals must be in another part of the wood. Raven and I creep as close as we dare and try to understand what is happening.

As soon as I focus on the car, I see Anton. He's there, on the back seat, his head bowed down. He's been caught. They have him. They have him! There's an officer sitting beside him.

I dig Raven in the ribs and point frantically. I'm in panic. Once again, I'm fighting for breath.

Raven claps his hand over his mouth.

I point to the two other officers looking in ditches at the side of the road for anything we might have dropped. And Richter, standing in the full glare of the headlamps, ordering everyone around.

'*Weiter suchen! Macht weiten!*' he shouts. Keep looking.

'I'll have to distract them . . . and get rid of the guard in the back seat,' Raven whispers.

'No, I'll distract them.'

'But they'll catch you . . . how will you get away?'

I look at him. 'You can drive, can't you?' Stealing their car is a desperate plan and I know it. But we have to do something – now.

'Coco . . . too much could go wrong. We could all be caught . . .'

'We have to rescue him. Otherwise, he's going to be dead,' I insist. 'We've got to try! I'll distract them. You get rid of the guard in the car, then drive forwards, fast, and I'll catch up with you.'

I'm already off, creeping through the undergrowth so that I can jump out ahead of Richter and his men and take their eyes from the car. I don't worry about being within range of their guns, because I already know that the Kriminaldirektor wants me alive.

When I'm 200 metres away from Richter, I run into the road and scream. Immediately Richter and his men swivel round in my direction.

'There she is! Seize her!' Richter shouts. 'Don't shoot!'

I turn and run, on the road this time, so they can see me in the headlights of the car and follow me.

I'm terrified. My legs are shaking because I've already run so hard and so far tonight. The long-legged, super-fit soldiers are right behind me almost immediately. How did I outrun them before?

But then I hear the crack of a gun, the roar of the car engine and shouts of dismay. I keep sprinting. Shots ring out, then the car speeds past me. For a moment, I think Anton and Raven are leaving without me, but then the back door opens and I'm grabbed, hauled in and find myself in Anton's arms. We're showered with glass as the back window is shot out.

Raven stamps on the accelerator and shouts: 'Let's go!'

We speed up . . . we're getting away.

Chapter Twenty

We speed and swerve for only a few tense minutes before Raven outlines his plan. 'I have to drop you off, Poet . . . then Coco, then I have to abandon this car and escape.'

'I want to go with the Poet,' I say immediately. We've only exchanged a few words, but I can tell Anton is stunned by what's just happened.

'No, we have to split up,' Raven insists. 'I'll take Anton's rucksack and hide it. You need to try and make your way home without being seen. Or hide out tonight and get home tomorrow. Just do not get caught. They won't give up searching and we've no idea how many of us are already in their hands.' I think of Hope. Raven must be frantic with worry.

As the car slows and Anton prepares to jump out, I reach for his face and kiss him hard. 'See you soon . . . please,' I say, all my hope in those words.

'Take care,' he replies.

A few more bends in the road, then it's my turn.

'Good luck,' I tell Raven.

'You too. You were fantastic tonight.'

'You too. See you later.'

Then I'm outside in the freezing night air again, facing a stretch of woodland. I have no idea where I am. There are no stars and anyway I have only the vaguest clue about navigating by the stars. There's a North Star at the tip of the Plough, or something like that. I'm lost.

I'd better just go into the woods and hide until this terrible night is over, I decide. I step carefully, looking, listening. I don't want to fall again and I don't want to bump into a Nazi.

I've not gone far when I hear rustling. I freeze. I just know that I'm being watched. The hairs on the back of my neck stand up. Someone else is here. I don't know whether to run or to stay still. I hear the rustling again. I have to get out of here.

'Coco!'

I swivel round.

'Coco?'

The word is coming from a tangle of leaves and branches.

'Over here.'

I walk towards the branches, but can't see anyone. 'Where?' I ask.

'Here!' A hand suddenly appears from the pile, making me gasp with fright.

I move a few branches and see Hope's face, pale and scared. She doesn't want to come out; she wants me to come in. I scramble into the little hollow and we pull the branches and leaves over the opening once again.

'Oh, Coco,' she whispers and holds me tight in a hug. 'Have you seen—?' she begins.

'It's OK, Raven's OK, I saw him just a few minutes ago, we escaped together with the Poet.'

'Oh, thank goodness, thank goodness . . .' She is so relieved she begins to cry.

'How are you?' I ask. 'Have you had to run very far?'

'Yes, to get away from the dogs . . .' She shudders. 'I was with Plum . . .'

This is Padrice's stupid codename, I remember.

'He pulled me on. He helped me run faster than I ever could have alone. Then he helped me in here when I injured my ankle. I told him to run on, see if he could get back to Brussels with the supplies.'

I look down her leg and see the joint all stiff and swollen. 'Did you see the Owl?' I ask. 'Did he get away?'

She puts her hand over mine and squeezes. 'You know him, don't you? I mean, away from the Group.'

'He's my teacher at school . . . my best-ever teacher.'

'I think he stayed behind, Coco. He decided to put up a fight, to give us all time to get away.'

'Do you think he's dead?' I ask, feeling unbearably sad.

'I don't know,' she replies.

'I'm losing everyone,' I wail. 'First my papa, then La Belle, now Monsieur . . . Owl. We had to rescue the Poet from the soldiers, they captured my Poet, but I wouldn't let them take him.'

Hope squeezes her arms around me.

'Do you and Raven have children?' I ask.

Hope whispers, 'Yes. They are our treasure, our reason for being. We keep them guarded, very safe, in the country, with those we trust absolutely. We do this for our children, Coco.'

I have another question, but I don't know if she's allowed to answer. 'What are all the explosives for?'

She turns and searches my face. Maybe she's trying to decide if she can truly trust me.

'On the 23rd December, in the middle of the night, hundreds of Nazi soldiers are going to be allowed home on leave. They're putting on special trains to take them back to Germany and we're going to help the Hawk bomb the station.'

Chapter Twenty-One

Madame Morel opens the door. 'Nicole, what's going on?' she asks.

I wonder if she can even begin to imagine. To get here today, I've had to scramble out of my overnight den, wash my face and all the incriminating mud from my legs and clothes in a stream, replait my hair, help Hope limp to the roadside, hail a passing tractor, chat and lie to the farmer, chat and lie to all the checkpoint soldiers, make excuse after excuse to my mother and Grand-Mamie.

Now, finally, I'm here, desperate to know if Anton has made it home too. I can't wait; I have to know.

'Is Anton here?' I ask.

'Yes, he's upstairs, but—'

There's no stopping me. I dart past her, fly up the stairs and burst into his room. I throw myself across him.

At first I can't speak, it's so good to see him. I just hold him tight and bury my face into his rough woollen jumper which smells of mud and sweat. His heavy arms fold on top of me.

'Nico, you're safe,' he whispers.

'You too.'

I'm so glad, so relieved. We hold each other tight and I look right into his eyes and realize with a jolt of happiness that this is love. I'm in love with him.

He's in love with *me* too. I can read it in his face, just like he can read it in mine. There's no need to say a word. For a long moment we look at each other and understand. Then I have a rush of questions.

'Were you followed? How did you get back? Do you think anyone's suspicious?'

He shakes his head and kisses me gently on the forehead, the cheek and the lips. 'I can't stop thinking about being in the back of their car,' he says. 'They had me . . . I thought I was going to die.' A brief sob jerks from his chest, but just once. Then he pulls his mouth straight.

'I'm sorry,' I tell him, laying my head on his chest. 'I'd have killed them for you. I think Raven did kill one of them . . .'

Anton nods.

'I'd have done anything to get you away from them,' I add.

'Thank you,' he whispers. 'Thank you for saving my life.'

I try to make light of it and joke: 'Yeah, well, just make sure you repay the favour.'

'Nico . . .' He opens his fingers to let mine slide between them. Our hands grip tightly, laced together. 'You know I'd give up my life to save yours.'

'Please don't,' I whisper, not joking now, 'because if you're dead I won't want to be alive.'

At this, our mouths touch together. I taste him, I'm right here with him, longing for him, wanting to touch more, my heart beating right next to his.

When we break off, he holds my face in his hands and asks, 'Is everyone else all right?'

'I travelled into Brussels with Hope. She thinks Padrice escaped; hopefully Raven is still OK. We don't know about anyone else . . . the Owl, he stayed behind to hold the soldiers back. We don't think he . . . he . . .'

I find I can't finish the sentence because my throat is suddenly full of tight sobs.

'Oh, Nico,' Anton says and folds me up in his arms again. 'I'm sorry.'

'Have you heard what the explosives are for?' I ask when I find my voice.

'Obviously a big bomb, but I don't know more than that.'

'Hundreds of soldiers are going home for Christmas on special trains and—'

'Are we going to bomb the station?' Anton asks.

I nod.

'That's a huge mission,' he whispers. 'Very dangerous.'

I try to imagine being captured and what might happen afterwards, but find I can't. Maybe my mind just won't let me think about it. 'Do you remember before the war?' I ask Anton, running my fingers through his hair. 'Do you remember having daydreams and plans for the future?'

'That feels like a long time ago.'

I move my fingers to touch the side of his face tenderly and feel another rush of love. 'I wanted to get married and have lots of children,' I admit, thinking only, crazily, about being Anton's wife. 'Maybe four or five, and I thought it would be interesting to be a teacher.'

'You'd make a good teacher,' Anton says, then asks, 'Four or five children? Is that to make up for being an only child?'

'Maybe . . . but I never think about things like that now. I just think about Nazis, how to get rid of them and how to stay alive so I can fight them for as long as I can.'

Anton strokes my head. 'If we live through this, Nico, we have to make sure our lives are wonderful, for the sake of everyone who dies.'

'What are you going to do if you grow up?' I ask.

He smiles. 'When the war ends and we have food again, I'm going to own the best cake shop in the whole of Belgium. You can come in whenever you like and I'll always have your favourite.' He kisses my nose.

'What's my favourite? It's been so long I can't remember.'

'Easy. It's hot waffles with sour cherries and cream.'

'Yes it is,' I whisper, and I'm swept back years ago to a happy summer of sunshine, football, fresh waffles, cherry-picking and Anton, my best friend in the world. The boy I love. But I shake my head. 'No, you won't have a cake shop. You're going to be a writer, a poet. It's what you've always wanted to do and you're going to be wonderful.'

Softly he replies, 'Sometimes I think you might know me better than I know myself.'

Raven opens the door to the crypt that night with a grim expression on his face.

'I'm glad you're back,' I say, but he doesn't smile or make any reply.

I walk into the room, Anton following behind me, and see Hope, Padrice and Vivienne's brother, code-named the Torch. I look around once again and I'm frightened to see there's no Monsieur Durance.

Raven slams the door shut behind us. 'So who is it?' he demands. His face looks dark and furious.

'What?' I ask.

'Someone is talking.' His voice is menacing. 'Someone is leaking to the Nazis. Someone brought those soldiers and the police to the field last night and I want to know who it is.' He stands in front of me and glares into my face. Before I can say anything, he grabs hold of Anton. 'What about you?' he demands, shaking him by the shoulders. 'What were you saying to the officer in that car? They weren't beating you up, were they? They were talking to you.'

'No!' Anton answers, horrified. 'Of course not!'

'Have you made a deal with them?' Raven shouts.

'What are you doing?!' I burst out, pulling Raven from Anton. 'I'd trust him with my life.'

'Stop it, please stop it!' Hope cries. 'Everyone in this room has risked their lives and proved how absolutely loyal they are. We can't start tearing each other apart. Look around you,' she tells her husband. 'There's Coco, who turned back to rescue the Poet from the Nazis. Would she do that for someone she didn't trust absolutely? There's Plum, who slowed up to help me run faster, who found me shelter. There's Torch, who's already lost his brother and sister to them. Which one of these people don't you trust? I'd trust them all to carry my deepest secrets to the grave.'

Raven sighs and then collapses into a chair. He buries his face in his hands.

Hope immediately goes over to him, puts her arms around his shoulders and tells him, 'Last night was terrible. You're exhausted and you're not thinking straight.'

'We were ambushed,' he says from behind his hands. 'Someone must have told them where we were and it looks as if the Owl has died because of that.'

There's a breathless silence in the crypt as we take in his words. I don't want to believe it. There must still be a chance for the Owl. I still think I could walk into school and find the Owl there. Surely there's still a chance?

'There were two other groups working with us last night,' Hope reminds him. 'We can be sure of everyone here, but we can't be sure of the others.'

'We're planning a huge attack,' Raven reminds her. 'We need to know that we are safe and planning it in secret. We can't risk carrying out this mission if we think someone might be informing on us. We'll be walking into a trap.'

'Well then, we'll have to use only people from this group. We know we can trust everyone here, so we won't involve anyone else in the final plans,' Hope says. 'The first thing to find out is if they've moved the date the soldiers are leaving.'

'How are we going to do that without the Owl?' Raven asks. 'He was the contact. He's the only one who knows how to get in touch with the Hawk.'

'The Owl told me before last night that if anything happened to him, I was to lead the group . . .' Hope announces this with her usual quiet modesty and we all look at her, intrigued, including Raven. 'He absolutely loved and trusted you too,' she says, squeezing her husband's shoulder, 'but he hoped I'd still be here, because I'm always extra-careful. He told me how to contact the Hawk and he gave me the information for the mission.'

'He picked the right person,' Raven says, taking Hope's hand in his.

'Agreed,' I say.

'Absolutely . . . yes . . .' Padrice, Anton and La Belle's brother add.

'We have to plan every detail very, very carefully,' Hope says, her voice grave. 'It's going to be complicated and it's going to be very dangerous.'

Chapter Twenty-Two

'This is the station,' Hope says quietly as we round a corner in a part of Brussels I've never been to before and find a substantial red-brick building in front of us. 'They've picked this station for their troop trains in the hope that it will be quieter and attract less attention. Because they know about the plane landing, they're very worried about sabotage,' she adds, 'so they're taking as many precautions as they can.'

She fidgets nervously with her hair, with her coat collar, with the straps of her handbag, and the dark rings under her eyes show she hasn't been sleeping well. We're here so we can make an exact map of the station for the others and she can explain my part in the mission.

In a tense whisper she says, 'The Hawk has told me there are going to be six bombs, and even if they don't go off at exactly the same time they should still bring the roof down.'

I look at the solid tiled slopes of the station roof ahead of me and find this impossible to believe.

'The Hawk is going to plant six packages of explosives in the middle of the night, when the station is only guarded by one or two sentries. Our job will be to get the detonators into these packages just minutes before we want the explosions to happen.'

'The pencil detonators?' I ask. 'The ones the British gave us?' When the rucksacks were all brought back to the crypt, I managed to spend a little time working out how these clever metal devices operated.

Hope nods. 'Once they've been planted, they should give us a few minutes to get clear.'

It's my turn to nod. The detonators are supposed to be 'reasonably' reliable. But sometimes they go off early and sometimes they don't go off at all.

'It's best to put two or three in an explosive,' Hope says, 'to make sure, but I don't know if we'll have enough . . . Now, let's walk around the building and I'll explain what we're going to do. Look cheerful – there are bound to be soldiers around somewhere . . .'

So we walk, arm in arm, smiling and occasionally giggling as if we are having a lovely gossip.

'Two of us, probably the Torch and I, will use that

ventilation shaft to get the detonators into the bombs high up on the central supports of the roof,' Hope says, nodding her head in the direction of the shaft, rather than pointing. 'Raven and Plum are going to pose as painters – the Hawk has arranged special station permits for them – so they will be able to access the two columns at the back. That leaves two crucial columns at the front, in the central concourse – which is going to be busy.'

I swallow. This is no doubt where Anton and I come in.

'The Hawk has identified two columns. One has a postbox beside it; one is behind a small kiosk. He thinks he can hide explosives beside them both. So you and Anton will have to be in the main part of the station. Then, when the time comes, you put in the detonators without being noticed and leave as quickly as you can.'

'Sounds . . . straightforward,' I say. Although I know perfectly well the station is going to be swarming with German soldiers.

'We'll go in there now and take a look. We'll ask for some train times and I'll show you the columns,' she says.

As we walk towards the station, I remember something else. 'But Hope, this is happening in the middle of the night, to keep it all as hushed up as possible. How can Anton and I be there in the middle of the night? I mean . . . what excuse can we give? Why will Raven and Plum be painting? Or have you got us all soldiers' uniforms?

But how can I pass as a soldier? I'm too small . . .'

A deeply troubled look crosses Hope's face. 'There's been a change of plan,' she says. We walk on in silence for several paces before she can bring herself to explain: 'It's not happening at night any more. They've moved the time of the troop trains to coincide with the evening rush hour. They've decided they're safer mixing troops with civilians, because . . . well . . .'

I understand immediately. 'They think we won't attack the soldiers if there's a chance of killing civilians.'

'Exactly,' she whispers, and I can read the pain of the dilemma in her face. 'I don't want to do it now,' she admits, 'but the Hawk and others higher up in the chain of command think it's a unique opportunity to strike at so many soldiers.' A tear falls from the corner of her eye and she wipes it quickly away.

I'm bewildered and don't know what to say at first. None of us wants to kill civilians. It's wrong, and it gives our cause a bad name. But we have British explosives which poor Monsieur Durance paid for with his life. We can't hide these explosives for ever, and hundreds of soldiers gathered in the same place is obviously an opportunity.

'We'll have to talk to the group,' I tell her. 'No one can take part in a mission like this without being prepared.'

Chapter Twenty-Three

I wake up, open my eyes and know at once that it is 23rd December – the day of the station bombing. I hurry to the bathroom, then dress carefully, choosing my navy wool pleated skirt – too short now – warm tights and my cosy jumper. Grand-Mamie had got the jumper for me, via Violetta whose granddaughter had outgrown it. It's pale grey with a pretty patterned neckline. Apparently it was hand-knitted in the Shetland Islands, somewhere between Scotland and Norway. Pulling it over my head, I marvel at how it's come all the way to Brussels. Then I brush my hair and put it into two girlish plaits.

When I open the kitchen door, I am hit by the magical smell of warm cinnamon, gingery spices and baking. All at once it feels like Christmas; like Christmas as a little girl when there were only stockings, presents and gingerbread biscuits to think about.

'Good morning, Nicole.' Mama wipes her hands on her apron, then gives me a hug. 'Surprise!'

'You're baking, with real ingredients?'

'My darling, we would never let the Nazis get in the way of our Christmas baking,' Grand-Mamie says from her place at the table, where she is carefully rolling dough and using a battered little star-cutter to press out a pile of Christmas biscuits.

I kiss her cheek. 'It smells delicious in here. Where did you get proper white flour? And cinnamon? Even a vanilla pod and . . . oh my goodness!'

I can hardly believe my eyes: there in a little blue dish on the table is a pat of golden . . .

'*Butter!*'

Before anyone can stop me, I stick my finger in, scoop out a blob and put it into my mouth. The flavour is so intensely rich and delicious I have to close my eyes.

'We've been hustling,' Grand-Mamie says with a grin. 'We have been saving, swapping and scheming to get hold of all the little treats. Who knows, maybe somehow by some miracle we will even have George home for Christmas . . .'

Christmas without Papa is unthinkable. Sometimes I'm not just sad about him, I'm *angry*. If he's out there, free, couldn't he have got in touch by now? What about a short letter? Just a word, something . . . anything to let us breathe a sigh of relief for him.

I sit down at the table but don't dare to put my finger in the butter dish again. I might be tempted to wolf it all down at once.

'We can hope,' Mama says.

When I look at her, I see that her hair is growing greyer and her lines are deepening because the war has given her so many worries. I would love to stay with Mama and Grand-Mamie in this kitchen for the rest of the day, rolling dough, cutting out star shapes and inhaling cinnamon fumes as I wait for biscuits to bake. But the rucksack hidden in my room upstairs is urgent. In fact, the longer I sit here with a package of detonators under my bed, the more danger I put my family in.

'Wouldn't it be wonderful if we could all be together for Christmas?' Mama says.

I smile. I'm about to help plant six bombs in a railway station. If I survive unharmed, uncaptured, un-suspected, then maybe I can come home. The thought that tonight I might be on the run with those terrible dogs at my heels comes into my mind, but I try to push it away.

'Well, I'll be here for Christmas, I promise.' The words '*If I can*' I say very quietly to myself. I enjoy the happy smiles on the faces of the two women I love most in the world. 'So what's the news from Mass?' I ask, and for several happy minutes I hear Grand-Mamie tell all the latest gossip from St Peter's.

'Frieda has a white cat with a black patch between its ears and a little black splodge below its nose, so she's named it Adolf. And it's true: the cat does look like Hitler. We kill ourselves laughing at it. Also, I've started a graffiti wall near the church. I never knew breaking the rules could be so much fun,' Grand-Mamie confides.

'A graffiti wall?' I splutter. 'What do you write?!'

'"Nazi nitwits out!" "The Führer is a small man with a silly moustache", or "Grannies v Nazis". Something that makes people smile. As soon as we all realize what a joke these vandals are, then the game will be over. If you can laugh at something terrible, Nicole, then you can face it.'

'Adele, you take unbelievable risks,' Mama warns.

'Don't get caught,' I tell Grand-Mamie. 'They won't have any sympathy, not even for a granny of eighty-three.'

Several loud raps on the front door cause us all to look at one another anxiously.

'Are you expecting someone?' I ask.

'No,' Mama replies.

'Quick,' Grand-Mamie warns. 'We need to hide the forbidden food. Maybe someone has smelled biscuits baking and has called in the Gestapo. Oh my goodness, what a world we live in now.'

I grab the butter dish and shove it into the nearest

cupboard, but the beautiful white flour is all over the table and will not be so easily hidden.

'Go to the door,' I urge Mama, 'and we'll do what we can in here.'

Mama closes the kitchen door as Grand-Mamie and I dash about hiding dough in cupboards, opening the window to let the smell out into the bitterly cold air. We float a clean tablecloth right over the floury mess on the kitchen table and then hear laughter from the front hall.

'Don't panic,' Mama calls. 'It's Anton, Nicole, come to pick you up for whatever Red Cross adventure you're going on today. I just hope he's going to bring you home before the curfew for a change. Really, you two, try and think of it from my point of view.'

Anton, already! I glance at the clock. He's early. I've not eaten anything . . . and I've not put my letter in place.

His head appears round the kitchen door. 'What's going on in here? We have reports of illegal activities,' he jokes. 'I'll have to search this address.'

'If you mean, have we managed to get our hands on some butter and flour to do a little Christmas baking, then I'm afraid we're guilty,' Grand-Mamie says. 'What's the punishment for that these days? Beheading?'

Prrrrrrrrrrrrrrrrrr . . . prrrrrrrrrrrr . . . I hear my cat, Gaspar's, deep, rasping purr. He is stalking towards me so I bend down and throw my arms around him. Gaspar, a solid black cat, one of the few creatures not starving in Brussels this winter, leaps up onto my lap and for a moment or two I bury my face into his fur.

Part of me doesn't want to go now.

Part of me wants to stay in this warm kitchen and be safe with the people I love.

'Where are you two off to?' Mama asks.

'We're studying in the library,' I reply, wolfing down the rare egg and grey bread set out for me, 'then it's Red Cross in the afternoon: just packing boxes and loading lorries. We shouldn't be late.'

'Good,' Mama says.

I hug my grand-mamie, then Mama goodbye. I try not to cling, not to make it feel too serious or final. I don't want them to guess that something very different is happening today.

'All set?' Anton asks, trying to sound cheery and casual, but when I read the look in his eyes my heart jumps with nerves.

'I'll just get my bag.'

I run upstairs and pull my rucksack out from under the bed. I know I have everything I need; I've been over and over it all last night. I pull out the short letter that has taken me hours to write and place it inside my address book on top of my chest of drawers. This is where I know Mama will look, but only when she is worried enough.

I know the letter by heart. If I don't return, these are the words my family will read:

My darling Mama, darling Papa and darling Grand-Mamie,

Please know first of all that I love you. You've brought me up with love, wisdom, kindness and generosity, and I'm so very lucky to have been surrounded by such good people. I never wanted to hurt you and – Papa, I know you warned me not to get involved.

But I had to. If I can't grow up in a free Belgium, then I don't want to grow up at all.

I would do anything not to cause you pain, but in your hearts you must know I've made the right choice, and I hope you can always be proud of me for doing my duty for our country.

I love you. I'll do everything I can to get back to you. Everything. I promise.

Your Nicole

Chapter Twenty-Four

At 4.35 p.m., two streets away from the station, Anton and I know this is where we have to split up and make our way to our columns alone.

As we turn to wish each other goodbye and good luck, it feels very serious. I reach up to hold his face in my hands and he puts his hands over mine. When I look deep into his eyes, I suddenly feel afraid. What if I don't see him again? What if he doesn't make it out of here alive? What if we're both captured?

'Shhhhh,' he says, as if he can hear my questions. 'Courage is refusing to listen to your fears. It's very well-planned. It's a closely guarded secret. We have every chance.'

Chance. We are trusting our lives to a chance.

'I don't feel brave enough,' I admit.

'Yes you do,' he says, putting his arms around me and

pulling me close. 'You're the bravest girl I know. You're my fierce girl. You just have nerves. We all have nerves. Any performer will tell you nerves are good – they focus your mind, sharpen your performance. Just breathe and let your nerves work for you.'

I bury my face into his coat and feel with my fingers under his scarf for the soft skin of his neck. I need to touch him before I leave. His face reaches down to mine and we kiss intensely. I don't want to let him go.

But too soon he breaks off and tells me, '*Au revoir.*'

'*Au revoir,*' I repeat.

I kiss Anton again on the mouth and don't want to stop. *Au revoir* – to meet again – never have these words meant so much to me.

Today, we risk everything.

'Be brave,' Anton whispers into my ear. 'Our country needs us.'

His arms are still around my waist but he is ready to go. My brave and handsome Poet is ready to go. But I don't know if I'm ready yet.

'Anton?' I want to keep him here for just a little longer. The thought that this could be the last time I see him is making me feel crazy. I'm more scared of that than of detonating my bomb.

'If we get through this . . . let's do something mad . . . like . . .' I don't know, I can't think. 'Dance in the fountains or run away to the woods?'

'If we get through this, we'll be together, I promise,' he says and hugs me fiercely once again. 'I have something.' He reaches into the pocket of his coat. 'I made it for you . . .' He holds out a ring of plaited copper wire.

I pick it up, see how carefully the strands have been woven together, and I'm very moved.

'Thank you,' I tell him. It's so small and delicate it only fits onto my smallest finger. But that's perfect. I look deep into his eyes and tell him, 'I love you,' for the very first time. The words just spill out and they feel unspoiled and new, as if I'm the first person to ever say them.

'I've always loved you,' he replies without hesitation, taking hold of my hands. 'My first and best love.'

'Anton . . .'

I want to cry, but I can't because I can't really let myself believe this might be the last time . . . if I believed it, I wouldn't be able to let him go now. We have to be brave. Bold. Determined. We're both committed to a cause much bigger than the two of us and our little hopes and dreams.

'I need to give you something too,' I tell him. It feels urgently important and I know immediately what I'm going to do.

He shakes his head but I'm already unclipping the chain of the silver cross that has hung around my neck since my first communion.

'No, you don't have to . . .' he protests.

'I want to, please,' I insist.

As I fasten it round his neck, I see the soldier for the first time. He's standing in the street looking straight at us. He's watching our long goodbye, the rucksacks on our backs, and he looks suspicious. Any moment now, he's going to come over and ask to see our papers and maybe look into our bags.

'We have to go,' I tell Anton. 'Promise me we'll meet again.'

'Cross my heart,' he says and manages to smile.

'And hope to live,' I whisper.

We kiss quickly, one last brush of the lips, then turn and take our separate paths to the station.

I walk into the station building and have to remind myself to keep breathing. I've been told to move around slowly, casually, and to only glance occasionally at my column to check the explosives are there.

I can see them now. They're neat packages, red-brown to blend in with the brickwork, stacked between the column and the postbox beside it. When the station clock sounds the half-hour, I have to take out my detonator, break the glass tube inside it to start the chemical countdown, push it into the explosive and get out of the station as quickly as I can.

It's 5.09 p.m. So it's not time yet.

I see the high ladders up against columns five and six

at the back of the station where the troop trains are waiting. On top are Plum and Raven in white overalls, painting. Once they've planted their detonators, they know they may not have enough time to climb down the ladders and get out.

I've only once passed Anton, who is milling in the crowd like me, but we didn't even risk a smile.

Over and over, I've rehearsed what's going to happen next. At 5.29 p.m. I'm going to walk to the postbox beside my column. I'm going to drop the detonator on the ground, and as I bend down to pick it up I'll crush the end under my heel. I'm going to lean with my back to the column, make sure no one's watching and stick the detonator into the explosive. Gently . . . otherwise the force will detonate the bomb straight away.

Then I'll make straight for the exit. I'll keep walking for as long as I can, but as soon as I turn out of Station Road, I'll run for my life.

All around me, it looks almost too normal. Commuters are arriving to catch trains home from work, buying tickets, reading papers, sipping cups of ersatz coffee, having their bags and papers inspected by the handful of guards on duty. I try not to look at the civilians at all. We've all had to accept that some civilians will die in this act of sabotage, but this is war and winning will only come at a price.

The German soldiers start to file in at exactly the

time predicted by our network of informants. I think of Monsieur Durance gunned down in a green field trying to protect us, I think of La Belle, her beautiful face ruined with the filthy word 'traitor', and I can feel my courage rising.

The soldiers come in groups of tens and twenties, in their green and grey uniforms and overcoats, with their peaked caps or tin hats, their rucksacks packed for home. The noise level in the station rises. Soon there are hundreds of uniformed men jostling for space. For the first time, I look properly at the tall Christmas tree beside the ticket office, hung with simple decorations made from paper and straw. I wonder if the Nazis put it up, to make the station more festive for the big Christmas leave.

The troop train isn't due to leave until 5.45 p.m., but the Germans are famed for their punctuality, so the station is filling up almost to bursting. It's a good atmosphere. The soldiers are talking, laughing, and in high spirits. Some of them take off their hats and I see happy faces and boyish grins.

None of them look any older than Henri, Padrice or Anton. Maybe that's why the Nazis keep sending our teenagers away, because their boys are drafted as soon as they leave school.

I glance at the station clock. It's 5.24 p.m.

Then the soldiers do something no one could have

expected. I don't know how it begins, maybe with just one or two voices, but soon everyone is involved.

They begin to sing the famous German Christmas carol – *Stille Nacht*, 'Silent Night'. During the long months of the Nazi invasion I've learned to loathe German and everything about it. So it is eerie to hear this ugly language of oppression sound so beautiful. I'd forgotten how many lovely German words there are.

Hundreds of male voices are all joining in, making the air vibrate with the sound: '*Stille Nacht, Heilige Nacht . . .*' Silent night, holy night . . .

It's beautiful. This is the carol we've all sung every Christmas since we were small. People turn to watch the soldiers and we all share the ache, the longing for Christmas as it once was: with our families, with enough to eat . . . Christmas in *heavenly peace*.

The soldiers are waiting for the train home, thinking of their mothers, fathers, their brothers, sisters, girlfriends . . . no one looks old enough to have a wife or children. Most of the boys here are going home to Mama.

All over Germany star-shaped cinnamon biscuits are being baked for boys on their way home. My eyes begin to blur with tears.

'*Schlaf in himmlischer Ruh . . .*' Sleep in heavenly peace. *Ding-a-ding-dong.*

Distracted by the singing, I'm startled to hear the clock begin to sound the half-hour. I rush over to the postbox beside my column and fumble the detonator out of my coat pocket. I drop it to the ground, grind the glass end under my heel and crouch down to pick it up.

When I straighten, I suddenly don't know if I can do this. All around me are boys, singing, longing for home. There's an old lady struggling with a suitcase . . . a tired-looking man hurrying to the platform. I'm about to detonate a bomb in their midst and destroy hundreds of lives. Not just the lives here, but the lives of the families waiting for all these travellers to come home.

I look around desperately, the detonator stick trickling into life in my hands, and I panic. I don't know what to do . . .

Then I'm looking at Anton. He's still some distance away but I look right into his eyes. He's walking towards me and we can read each other's thoughts. He has planted his detonator and he's here to help me plant mine.

'Come on,' he's telling me, 'we can do this. We *need* to do this. It's almost impossibly difficult and we're risking everything, but our cause is greater than all of us.'

'Thank you,' I whisper. Then I lean back and slowly slide the stick in between the packages of explosive.

We've arranged to leave by different exits, but as our paths cross, we brush our hands against each other and I surge with hope. Within minutes, we could be out of here, down the streets, heading safely towards our agreed meeting point. We'll get away. We're getting away!

If I just keep going, this will all be over. I push through the crowd, but more soldiers are pouring in through the main door. I'm trying to swim upstream against the tide.

'Excuse me . . . sorry . . . just trying to get through . . .'

Soldier after soldier comes in, but there are civilians too. I try not to notice, not to look as they hurry into the station towards their destruction.

Just as I make it out, that's when I pass those I most can't bear to see. A mother, harassed, distracted, is pushing a pram with one hand, pulling a little girl along with the other. She passes right beside me.

Innocent people will die. This is the price of freedom and we will have to accept it.

That's what we were told and now I find I can't accept it at all. I can't let a little girl, barely four years old, be crushed to death by a falling roof. Why should she die in a bomb attack on Nazi soldiers?

I turn back. There can only be seconds left to get them out. 'Madame, excuse me, I have a message for you!' I put my hand on the woman's shoulder. 'You're needed outside, now! There's a message. It's urgent!' I insist. I'm pulling at her. I want us all to get out. Now! There is no time left.

The woman turns. She's very pretty with wide green

eyes and a harried, harassed look across her face, as if she's late.

'*Ja? Was ist los? Was wollen Sie?*'

She's German! But I see the tiny baby boy in the pram. He's not a soldier, nor is the little girl, nor is this woman.

I do what I have to do to get her out of the station. I grab the hand of the little girl and tug. 'Follow me,' I hiss to the woman. 'Follow me out. It's not safe.'

'*Was machen Sie?!*' What are you doing? Her voice is rising.

'There's a bomb . . .' I hiss under my breath.

'*Eine Bombe?!*' she shrieks.

I've made a terrible mistake.

Heads swivel towards her. I scoop up the little girl and begin to run.

'*EINE BOMBE!?*' she screams. I think she's turned the pram. I think she's running after me.

The word 'bomb . . . *bombe*' is being repeated all around the station. There are shouts, cries.

I am running desperately to get away. I will put the little girl down just as soon as it's safe and run for my life.

Then there is just noise, heat, and a terrible, deafening roar.

Chapter Twenty-Five

I fly forward. I'm swimming in waves of hot air. Finally, I land with a crash. My face slams into pavement, my body thrown down harder than I've ever imagined. The wind, the sense, for a moment everything is punched out of me.

When I open my eyes, I see the street slanting away from me, feet rushing in all directions. There is movement underneath my chest. It is a huge effort to prise myself up onto my elbows, but when I do I realize the little girl is there. I've fallen on top of her, but maybe because I had my arms around her she doesn't seem to have come to any harm.

'Are you OK? *Alles gut?*' I ask.

She looks at me, eyes wide with shock; it takes a moment, but then her face crumples and she cries out: 'Mama!'

I put my arms around her again, murmur, 'Shhhhh,' and try to make sense of what is going on around me.

The air is dark with dust; already I can hear sirens in the distance and shouting, while soldiers race towards the building. Also, I can hear the terrible wailing and howls of pain coming from the station. I want to block my ears against it.

The building looks just as it did, except all the windows are shattered and the large tiled roof, the imposing grey slopes that crowned the red-brick walls, are gone. They have completely collapsed inwards and swirling, choking dust fills the air. Everyone around me who isn't running is staring at the building in horror.

Jeeps packed with soldiers are pulling up at the station. I don't know if they've been summoned or if these are more soldiers expecting to catch a train home for Christmas. There's so much shouting, shrieking and running, it's hard to make sense of anything.

I ache everywhere. My head is ringing, my cheek feels raw and swollen, my hands, knees, elbows, shoulders – everything that slammed against the ground – hurts.

I have to get out of here. I just need to get the little girl back to her mother and then I can go. I stagger to my feet and look around. There are so many people here now, shouting, screaming. Some have come wandering out of the station, splattered with blood.

Then I see the mother, still with the pram. Just as I

begin to walk towards her, the little girl in my arms, she spots me too. She doesn't smile; instead she grabs at the nearest soldier, points to me and shouts: '*Da ist sie! Sie hat es gewusst! Da ist sie!*' There she is. She knew. There she is!

As I let go of the girl and watch her run, arms wide towards her mama, two soldiers appear at either side of me. They grab my arms, they ram a gun into my back and they march me towards a waiting van.

The police station is packed and there is an intense round of paperwork: name, address, date of birth, occupation, papers please. I am Eglantine DuPont. Eglantine DuPont. I must remember that.

Every time I'm asked a question, I protest my innocence. I say I don't know why I'm here. I was leaving the station, I was hit by it too, I don't know what it's about and of course, I repeat my phrase, the one which rescued me the last time: '*Ich bin ein Einzelkind, ich muss nach Hause.*'

But I am ignored.

'*Ruhe hier!*' Silence, one policeman shouts at me.

My bag is taken from me and my fake papers. Then I have to change into a rough blue and white nightdress and they take away my clothes. I'm left with nothing but the nightdress, my shoes, my woollen socks, my underwear and my copper pinkie ring.

Then I'm marched by grim-faced female guards along endless corridors until we reach a door. It's unlocked for me and I understand I'm to go in.

The door slams shut behind me and when I hear the key turn in the lock, when I see the wretched space with its scratched walls, bare bed, stool, toilet bucket and tiny window covered with a grille, I can no longer be strong. I'm gripped with panic and despair.

Sitting on the bare mattress, I cover my face with my hands and begin to sob. I cry for myself. I'm scared. I don't know what they are going to do to me, but if I'm suspected of Resistance, I will be tortured. Maybe I will have 'traitor' sliced into my face too before I am beaten to the verge of death. Poor La Belle, poor, poor La Belle.

I cry for Mama and Grand-Mamie, who will be so frantically worried. I cry for my papa because he went through this before me. Papa — where are you? Why don't you come back and help us?

Then I think of the group. I wonder if they got away before the roof fell down. And what about you, Anton? Did you escape?

Chapter Twenty-Six

At the moment when I wake but don't yet have my eyes open, I feel a huge sense of relief. The station bombing, being arrested, being thrown into a cell . . . it didn't happen. It was a dream! It wasn't true!

But when I see the bare, scratched walls of my cell in the weak light of a December dawn, I can't express my wretched despair.

Having a moment of hope makes the reality seem even worse.

I look at the scratches and see that they are in fact words, names and numbers. Little lines have been made and crossed through to mark the passing of days and weeks in this cell.

'Louisa Hubert 14.10.40,' I read. She has scratched out twenty-nine days and written the simple word: 'Hope.'

I am about to try and decipher some of the other

names and words when the heating pipe beside my bed begins to bang. It attaches to a little grille where warm air might come out if our captors heated our freezing cells.

I'm stunned to hear a faint voice floating out from the grille. 'Hello in cell number 252, can you hear me?'

I don't reply. Does this mean me? I was in too much of a state to notice the number on my door last night.

'Hello, you were brought in after the bombing? Can you hear me? I'm in the cell above.'

'Hello,' I say hesitantly, my face to the grille.

'Hello. Were you at the station?'

'I was there, but I had nothing to do with the bomb,' I say because I realize immediately this could be someone who has been planted to spy on me.

'It must have been marvellous. Hundreds of them have died, hundreds. Richter's nineteen-year-old son was travelling home for Christmas and they think he's one of the dead. So, good work.'

'It wasn't anything to do with me,' I repeat.

I let my head fall back on the mattress. If Richter's son has died in the bombing, there is going to be a terrible price to pay.

The key turns in the lock and the door is opened by a warden who barks: 'DuPont, *raus!*' She wants me to come out.

Hours have passed since I first woke up. In that time I have used the horrible toilet bucket and washed myself from head to toe using a greying flannel and the water in the other bucket. I have eaten breakfast, passed to me through a slot in the door: a cup of truly awful coffee and almost inedible bread. Since then I have waited and fretted and wondered what is going to happen next.

Over and over in my mind I have rehearsed what I'm going to say. I need to keep my story straight and simple. No matter what they do, I can't tell them anything about anyone. If they believe I have any involvement, they will never let me go.

Two wardens walk me along the corridors. Then I'm shown into a little white room. There's a small desk with a chair on either side, right beside a wall. I'm asked to sit down.

After a few minutes, a Gestapo officer in a spotless grey uniform and gleaming peaked cap comes in and sits in the chair opposite me.

'Eglantine DuPont?' he asks, putting papers I recognize as my own down on the desk.

'Yes,' I reply. I wonder how long it will take them to check out my false identity. We were promised safe houses and identities that would stand up to investigation. But it's another reason to be frightened.

He asks for my address and my date of birth. I reply with the answers which are in front of him.

'Why were you at the station last night?'

I'm about to tell him I had just visited a friend and was travelling home when I realize he will ask which friend; he will maybe even want to find her.

So instead I say, 'I was looking for tobacco for my . . . uncle.'

He looks at me coldly. 'You live three kilometres away from that station. Do you expect me to believe that you travelled all that way in search of tobacco?'

'I made a trip out of town to buy vegetables. So I was passing the station,' I reply. 'I lost my bag of vegetables in the chaos.'

'Six very professional bombs were planted in the station yesterday which exploded between 17.32 p.m. and 17.33 p.m. You ran out of the station before the first explosion and told another traveller that she needed to get out because there was a bomb.'

I widen my eyes. 'That's impossible,' I say.

'*Ja*. We have a witness statement here from Sabine Fischer.'

He pulls a sheet of paper from the pile and I feel flickers of deep fear.

'Perhaps you'd like to read it? Frau Fischer was rushing to the station with her children to meet her husband, Hauptmann Fischer, so she could board the 17.45 p.m. train to Frankfurt with him. Her husband's body has not yet been recovered from the mess.'

He leans forward. His clean-shaven face is almost touching mine.

'So, let us try again, Mademoiselle DuPont. What were you doing at the station last night?'

'I was looking for tobacco . . .'

WHAM!

For a moment I don't understand what has happened. One side of my head is burning, while the other is reeling with crashing pain.

WHAM!

It happens again. For several seconds, I see nothing, just a red-tinged darkness. I open my eyes and try to focus. My brain is scrambling to make sense of this.

He has hit me. He has struck me hard on the cheek and my head has bounced against the wall. I'm so shocked I burst into tears.

'Why did you do that?' I ask. 'I'm trying to tell you what I know. Now I can't think . . .'

WHAM!

'I don't want you to think. I don't want a clever concoction of lies. I want you to talk. I want you to tell me everything,' he demands.

My head is spinning. The pain is closing in from both sides. I can even feel a trickle of wetness. The force of the wall against my cheekbone has broken the skin.

'I can't talk like this.' At first it comes out like a

whimper. But when I repeat it, I sound stronger. 'I can't talk if you do this.'

I realize I can make a choice. I can be silent. Then he won't know if I'm silent because I am guilty or if I'm silent because he is beating me.

'I won't say anything if you hit me,' I insist. I grit my teeth, ball my hands into fists and try to prepare myself for the next blow. I want to put my arms around my head but that would be cowardly. Although I'm very scared, I don't want him to know. So somehow I try to steel myself inside. I look at the officer's face. He seems to be clenching his jaw.

'Why were you at the station?'

'I had been buying vegetables. I passed the station and I wanted to see if I could buy tobacco for my uncle at the kiosk there.'

'So you didn't speak to Frau Fischer?'

I'm not sure what is best to say here. Will they bring Frau Fischer in? They will never believe me over her. If I say I spoke to her, I will have to make up what I said, then I will have to remember what I've made up.

'No,' I say, then ball my fists and try to prepare for the blow.

'So is Frau Fischer a liar? Frau Fischer, whose husband is dead. Is she a liar?' He sounds furious and clenches and unclenches his jaw muscle.

'I didn't say that. I just said that I didn't speak to her.'

'So she was mistaken? It wasn't you who told her there was a bomb in the station, it was another Belgian teenager described here as' – he picks up the statement – 'small, only about one-point-five metres tall, with brown hair, shoulder-length, and a pale face, dressed in a blue woollen coat. That sounds just like you,' he adds.

'It sounds like lots of girls,' I say gently. I do not want to be cheeky and risk another smack to the side of my head.

'Are you a member of the Resistance Group K?'

I make a huge effort not to let my shock at these words show on my face. They know about Group K . . . this is terrible news. What do they know? Have they caught other members? Have they already tortured information from them?

'No! I'm not a member of any Resistance group.'

I feel like Judas. I think of Monsieur Durance, Raven, Hope, Anton and the others, and blink to stop the tears forming in my eyes. It would be much worse to tell this officer that I know them. But it feels terrible to deny knowing them.

'We have information that a fifteen-year-old girl, codename Coco, is with Resistance Group K, which blew up the station. Are you Coco?'

'I don't know what you are talking about,' I insist. 'I know nothing about any of this. *Ich bin ein Einzelkind, und ich muss nach Hause.*'

The officer looks at me. I think he is trying to decide whether he is going to hit me again or not.

'Christmas in solitary confinement,' he says finally. 'That might make you a little more talkative.'

I had forgotten that tomorrow is Christmas Day.

Chapter Twenty-Seven

Christmas Day, Boxing Day, the next day, the day after that . . . I spend them all in my bare cell.

Each day is exactly the same as the last: I wake early at first light and for a beautiful moment think I'm waking from a bad dream; then I realize I really am here and my heart is heavier than lead.

My three meals a day, one as bad as the next, come through the slot in my door. I'm shown out of my cell to change my toilet bucket and my water bucket once a day. Then the rest of the endless hours I must somehow fill.

I scratch a calendar onto the wall with my nail. I now know the names, dates and lengths of stay of all the others who have written on the walls. There has been no more communication from the heating grille, but at night there is crying and shouting from the cells as darkness falls and people slip into despair. Sometimes if there is too much noise, the guards go in and silence prisoners with a beating.

I do not cry or wail because I have fallen into a deep silence. I have nothing I want to say to anyone. My pain inside can't be expressed. And every word I might say to one of the devils is like a little trap I might spring for myself.

I have chosen silence.

There is nothing I want to say. I don't want to defend myself; I don't want to incriminate anyone. I don't want to beg for mercy or sympathy. I am mourning the loss of everything I once had: a loving family, a comfortable home, good friends, a boy who loved me and hope for the future.

Now I have nothing. Now I am prisoner number 30698, Eglantine DuPont, a girl without a real name or address: a girl in a rough linen nightdress who scratches words and lines onto a wall, slowly, to fill the long, silent hours.

'Silence,' I scratch with infinite care into the peeling paint, gouging the plaster so that my word will remain here. A trace of me.

'DuPont, *raus*,' the warden shouts from the door on the morning after my fourth day alone.

They march me along the maze of corridors and

down the stairs, so I know I am headed for the interview room again. I'm numb. The silence has settled on me like snow and it won't be broken.

Inside the silence I am safe.

This interview room is bigger than the last. There is a narrow desk with two chairs, right beside a wall again, so I know what that's for. This time, there is also a long, low table. When I take my seat, I move it as far from the wall as I can without being obvious. Every centimetre I can move away from the wall will mean less force when the devil slams into my face.

The same Gestapo officer comes in, but two younger, lower-rank men follow him in this time. The officer sits down opposite me, while the other two remain standing behind him, arms folded over their chests, looking at me from beneath their caps.

'Eglantine DuPont: that's not your real name, is it?'

I consider his question. I decide it is not worth breaking my safe silence for this. So I say nothing.

'That's not your real name,' he repeats, louder this time.

I say nothing.

'Tell me your name!'

Nothing.

WHAM!

Just when I thought I wasn't going to be treated like this again, his hand jumps out and slaps me hard, though

I don't bounce against the wall with quite so much force as the last time. Or maybe I've got used to this a little.

'You are Codename Coco, you work for Resistance Group K and you helped to bomb the station on December 23rd, causing the death of one hundred and eighteen soldiers and twenty-three civilians,' the officer states, his voice firm and loud.

One hundred and eighteen soldiers. Twenty-three civilians. The bomb killed 141 people.

I think about that and say nothing. Silence feels safer.

'You'd better talk to me now or I will leave you in this room with these men and they will do what they want with you. Do you understand?' The officer glares at me furiously.

I look past him at the two soldiers, their arms folded, their faces expressionless. I do not want to be left with them. I'm very frightened about what they might do to me. But I do not want to talk. A single word could make things worse for everyone I love.

'What is your real name? Come on, that's an easy question to answer.'

I ball my hands into fists and realize I'm shaking, waiting for his blow to fall.

A long moment passes. Then the officer pushes back his chair, gets up, barks an order to the soldiers in German and storms out of the room, slamming the door shut.

The devils dive onto me like dogs. I'm dragged from the chair and pushed down onto the table. I kick and struggle, I flail and scratch. They curse and shout at me, calling me a murderer. I don't say a word, but I sob, tears running down my face.

They strip off my nightdress although I struggle against it for as long as I can, but there are two of them holding my arms, pinning down my legs. Then they pull off my underwear. I won't lie still, I refuse to just lie on my back and let them use me. I refuse. I am crying hard, sobbing, but I won't beg them for mercy.

After several terrible minutes of sobbing, struggling, refusing, they shout to one another, then push me over so I am face down on the table, pinned down, dreading what's going to happen next.

That's when I feel the first terrible blow.

Something thin, hard, hot as lightning swipes my legs: again, then again. Across my naked legs, my bottom and my back, over and over, terrible red stripes of pain are being beaten into me. The soldiers have canes or maybe belts or batons and they are beating me ferociously.

I close my eyes and hear a terrible groaning, wailing sound. I realize that it's me; I am making that noise.

The red-hot swipe lands again. I think of the 141 dead at the station . . . maybe I deserve to be beaten for what I have done. Again and again the blows land, tearing into my flesh.

But then there is a momentary pause, I breathe, I try to collect myself, I suddenly remember Hope's words: 'You can endure pain as long as you know it will end.'

It will end.

They can't go on beating me for ever.

I will either die and the pain will stop, or they will grow tired, put down their sticks and the pain will stop.

The pain will stop.

Swish.

Swipe.

My agonized gasping and groaning continues. But it is a different part of me making that sound. Not the part that it is sitting tight, still and silent, deep inside. This part of me knows that if I can just endure for a little longer, the pain will stop.

Swish.

Swipe.

Slash.

I can feel blood trickling from my wounds. I can endure.

Just a little longer.

One. Two. Three more heavy blows are landed; then, cursing even more, the soldiers leave the room.

I cannot move. My entire body is on fire.

The door opens and I manage to turn my head to see the senior Gestapo officer walking in once again. A woman in a white uniform follows. A nurse? He's bringing a nurse in to see me? This is illogical madness. First they beat me to a pulp, then they bring in a nurse, in smartly pressed white, to treat me.

The woman throws a towel over my body. She helps me to sit up on the table and wraps me up snugly. She even holds her arm around me. 'I'm sorry this had to happen,' she tells me as the officer sits down in the chair nearest to me.

The door opens once more and an orderly brings in a trolley. There is a coffee pot on top, china cups and a plate with a large slab of fruit cake. Now I really can't believe my eyes. After treating me like an animal, they are going to serve me coffee and cake? *Kaffee und Kuchen?*

The officer pours out two cups of coffee with milk. He puts one into my hands, which are shaking so violently that hot coffee spills out over my fingers. 'Take a few sips, it will help,' he suggests in a voice that is not friendly, but is no longer so cold.

Maybe he is impressed I said nothing even when two guards were beating me to smithereens. I'm impressed I said nothing. I'm hugely impressed. In fact, I'm flooded with relief. I was beaten to a point way beyond agony and I remained silent. My biggest fear – whether or not I could bear torture without giving anyone away – has been faced. I've survived round one and said nothing. Maybe they will stop now . . . maybe they will even let me go.

I find myself smiling at the thought. I'm so relieved, so happy, almost excited. I sip and let warm, proper coffee filled with real creamy milk flood down my throat and into my stomach. It glows with heat and feels deeply comforting. I'm passed a slice of cake on a china plate and I cram big bites into my mouth, then pour down more delicious coffee after it.

The officer smiles at me, I smile back. I'm so relieved, *so* relieved, so warm. The cake is beautiful, one of the best I've ever tasted.

'Now come on, my brave girl, you're not really Eglantine, are you?'

His voice pours over me like treacle and I just want to talk. I want to tell him that no, I'm Nicole. Nicole de Wilde. I have Papa, Mama and Grand-Mamie. I have Anton and Hope, the Raven, Padrice, even Monsieur Durance, even Aurelie. I'm so happy, so content, I'm even feeling fond of Aurelie right now. I'd love to see them all again. Even the Hawk, especially the Hawk. I'd like to shake his hand and say, how clever, how very, very clever to bring down a whole station roof with just a few boxes of explosive . . . brought to us by the British Lysander – that was the name of the plane, wasn't it?

We have been so clever and so brave. And especially me. I've endured the worst ordeal ever and I've not said a word. Am I not the bravest Resistance fighter ever? I swallow down my cake, take another sip of coffee and

I'm ready to start. I want to get it all off my chest. Wrapped up here in this cosy towel, eating cake, drinking creamy coffee. This is the place to confide and make a fresh start.

'You're right,' I begin. 'I'm . . . I'm . . .'

The officer leans forward.

I'm shaking with relief . . . I'm longing to talk. Babble. Tell him everything. Because I'm so clever: I endured the torture, I can endure anything.

'You are . . . ?' He leans even closer, his face friendly, encouraging, confiding.

And that's when I realize I've been played.

I thought people gave away their secrets under duress, to make the pain stop. Maybe some of them do. But I see now that I'm about to give everything away because I've survived the pain and I'm so happy. I just want to talk, confess, confide. I've been in self-imposed silence for four days and I'm desperate to talk.

'I'm . . . *ich bin ein Einzelkind und ich muss nach Hause*,' I declare.

The officer roars with frustration, slaps me so hard in the face that the coffee cup flies from my hand and splashes all over his trousers.

'Back to her cell,' he shouts. 'Next time she sees Richter!'

Chapter Twenty-Eight

'DuPont, *RAUS!*'

I'm lying face down on my mattress. I am too sore and swollen to lie on my back. All night I've hardly been able to sleep because of the pain, and this morning my breakfast went untouched because I couldn't even bear to hobble to the door.

'I can't move,' I tell the bully in the hideous grey outfit at the door. My wounds have swollen, crusted over and become excruciatingly painful.

'*RAUS!*' the witch repeats.

I stagger to my feet and limp towards her. Every step is agony. Every step makes me feel as if the skin on my legs, bottom and back is tearing open and hissing fire. My blood-caked nightdress is coming unstuck from my legs, ripping scabs off as I walk.

I shuffle alongside the guards through the corridor

and down the dreaded steps. There's no doubt that I'm being taken for another 'interview'.

I don't want to be hurt again. I really, really don't want to be hurt again. But I also know that I'm not so afraid this time. I'm still afraid of the pain, but I know they can't make me talk. I will go back into my safe silent place deep within myself, and I will stay there until this is over.

Will I be handed over to Richter, like the officer threatened?

I wonder if Richter's son was really killed in the bombing, like the disembodied voice in the heating system said. If it's true, Richter will be wild. He will want to take a terrible revenge on us all.

I would give anything for news of the others. Are any of the group in this prison with me? Is anyone else being tortured? Did anyone get away? I am desperate to know.

I am also desperate to give word to my family. They can have no idea what has happened to me. Even if they've contacted the police, there will be no record of Nicole de Wilde at the prison. I wonder if my mother has searched my room yet and found my letter. If she has, maybe she'll realize she must not go to the police.

As I hobble along, wincing, even groaning with the pain sometimes, a man in uniform approaches. We stand aside to let him pass and I make a point of looking under the peaked cap right into his face because I want these devils to know they are doing this to us, to real Belgian girls.

As I stare, he looks at me too. Our eyes hold one another's and, to my shock, I see that I am looking at Monsieur Van Roy, Aurelie's father.

'Good morning,' I say tartly, shoulders back, because I may be in prison in a filthy bloodstained nightdress, but at least I am not a collabo without a conscience reduced to working for the Gestapo. 'And how are you?' The guards take me roughly by the shoulders and push me along, but not before I've managed to say: 'Give my love to your daughter, Aurelie – I hope she's well.'

Good. I hope that will stain his Gestapo record, having a daughter who is friends with someone sus-pected of Resistance. I glance back to see M. Van Roy still looking at me. His mouth is open and I'm pleased to see he looks shocked. I hope he sees the back of my dress with its multiple streaks of blood from my flogging. Only as I walk away do I consider that he might tell someone my real name.

Too soon, we come to the interview room. This one is even bigger than the last. Several chairs are lined up in front of a table. There is a lamp on the table, papers and pens. In the corner of the room there is a cast-iron stove with a fire already lit, and beside the stove there is a table with . . . implements.

I look quickly away. I think I may have seen metal pliers there. I don't want to think about that . . . the Gestapo are known to remove fingernails. I don't want to think about it. My knees buckle a little with fear.

I am led to a chair and pushed roughly down. I gasp with pain as my wounded flesh hits the seat. My arms are pulled behind my back and tied tightly behind me. I've begun to pant with anxiety, so I make an effort to inhale deeply and slow my breathing down. I can get through this. If I can just get through this, then there will be nothing left to fear. They will let me go, I tell myself. They have no evidence, so they will let me go.

Or kill me, comes the horrible thought, creeping into my mind like a creature from the deep. I try to push it back down again. They will let me go. They have no evidence.

Frau Fischer . . . but what about Frau Fischer?

Shhhhh.

If I had let Frau Fischer and her two children walk into the station, I might have escaped. But I would never have been able to forgive myself. I may have helped to kill 141 people, but the fact that I saved the little girl and the baby in the pram lets me believe that I am really a good person.

If I can get through this interrogation and say nothing, they will let me go.

There are more guards at the door now, and they are

leading in another prisoner; she is hobbling forward on her bare heels, her feet wrapped in bloodstained bandages which suggest that her toenails have been removed.

My eyes travel up from her feet, past her bloodied dress to her face, and I realize with a lurch that beyond the bruises, the split lip and the awful, broken nose, I am looking at Hope.

I want to cry out to her; I want to shout, 'Hello, my darling friend, be brave, find your courage, they have no evidence, we will get through this and they will let us go.' But instead I look at her and know I must not give any sign of recognition. Our eyes meet. We hold the look and I try to tell her all the things I would like to say with just a look.

I think she tries to do the same.

She is tied into the chair beside me. She turns to me and whispers, 'Be strong.'

'You too,' I whisper back.

Her hand feels for mine, she squeezes it tightly and I squeeze hers back.

'Give them nothing,' she says. It's a tiny sound, I can hardly hear it, but I nod.

'We'll get out,' I reply.

There's no time to say anything else. The door flies open and the officer I've been questioned by before marches in. There are two others behind, but I don't know if these are the men who beat me. Underneath their peaked caps with their pale, expressionless faces, these devils all look the same.

The officer asks the same questions: what are our real names? Why were we at the station? Are we in Group K?

We are held by our hair, slapped in the face and at one point I am punched in the stomach.

We groan and we grunt with pain, but neither of us says a word.

'You are stubborn. You are a pair of stubborn sluts,' the officer shouts, 'but don't you worry. We're going to get you talking. Just you wait and see what we have lined up for you.' He barks instructions at one of the men who goes over to the stove. I don't dare to look, but I can hear the clank of metal on metal. I have a horrible suspicion that something is being heated up to use on us.

The officer starts on Hope again. He punches her face hard. It's worse than being hurt myself. I don't know what to do. I can't bear to look, but I can't bear to close my eyes, so I try to fix my gaze on the white wall and make my mind white and empty too.

Then the door opens and immediately the officer jumps into a salute. 'Heil Hitler,' he says, shooting out his arm and clicking his heels.

What a sad joke they are, these Nazi puppets.

'Heil Hitler,' *click-click* comes the reply.

From the corner of my swollen eye I see Richter enter the room. I immediately hang my head, letting my damp, sweaty hair fall over my face. I've met him too often before, and I'm in danger of being recognized.

He sweeps in, his face ashen but filled with a concentrated fury. I believe it now that he has lost his son. He wears a look of pure vengeance.

'I have everything I need, Schultz, you may stand down. Or stay and watch if you like. If your stomach is strong.'

Slowly, terribly, Richter walks up to us. 'So, according to your papers, which are probably faked, you are Eglantine DuPont.' He looks at me. 'But this is really Marie Boegart.' He looks at Hope now. 'For some reason, she carries her real papers. Maybe she's careless. Maybe she thought she'd never get caught. You both helped to transport weapons and explosives from a British Lysander on the night of the eleventh of December when we executed your comrade Nicholas Durance.'

It is terrible to hear. Poor Monsieur Durance. My wisest friend. Executed.

'On December the twenty-third at 17.30 p.m. you both helped to bomb the commuter station, when one hundred and eighteen soldiers, off-duty, going home for Christmas, were murdered . . . IN COLD BLOOD!' He shouts these last words, his face turning red, spittle flying onto our faces. 'Prepare to talk, you witches! And prepare to die! *Ja!* . . .' He turns to the junior men waiting at the door. '*Bringen Sie die Kinder herein.*'

The children? I look up, wondering if I have misunderstood.

Then two soldiers walk in. One is carrying a little toddler girl, maybe three or so. She is curious and calm. The other is pushing forward a boy, who looks tearful and reluctant. He is tall and fair-haired, maybe ten or eleven years old. Fear rises in my throat like bile.

'There's Mama. Don't be afraid, go and say hello,' Richter says in an attempt at a gentle voice, but it doesn't work. He sounds mean and crafty.

Hope lifts her head and makes the most terrible, agonized cry I've ever heard. 'Oh no . . . oh no . . .' she cries. 'Pascal . . . oh no . . . oh no, my baby . . . Odile, oh no . . .'

'Mama?' the boy asks. He sounds unsure and so frightened. He maybe doesn't recognize her with her bruised and bloodied face.

'Oh, Pascal, I love you, I love you . . . oh no . . .' She sounds so frightened, I begin to panic too. My breath is rasping in and out of my chest. What's going to happen? What are they going to do?

We've killed Richter's son. His fury will know no bounds.

Hope starts to rock in her chair. 'Why the children? Why are they here? They are innocent, *I* am innocent,' she pleads. 'I know nothing about any plane or the station, nothing about the bomb. I was travelling home . . .'

Richter is sitting on the desk. He looks relaxed, as if he's enjoying the scene.

'Whimper as much as you like, Madame Boegart,' he says. 'I'm not going to make any changes to my plan until you stop lying to me. And what about you, girl?' He turns to look at me. 'Codename Coco, aren't you? We know you helped to blow up a bridge as well as the station. Are you ready to start telling me the truth? It will go so much easier for you if you do. We could let you go . . . If you just give us some names, addresses and information, we could thank you and let you go.'

I am shivering with fear now. He knows. He knows us. He knows Hope's real name and he has her children. There is no escape.

'I'm innocent,' Hope cries. 'Don't you think if I knew anything, anything at all, I would tell you? You've got my children, for pity's sake!'

'Well, let's see, shall we? Let's see how far you're prepared to go. Let's see how far I'm prepared to go.' He speaks to the soldier fast in German. I don't catch the instructions.

But Pascal is pushed across the room to the stove.

'No, no, no!' Hope cries.

'No,' I join in, finding my voice, breaking my self-imposed silence. '*Das ist noch ein Kind.*' That is a child.

'Oh, you *can* talk, can you? Well, start talking!' Richter snaps. 'I want your real name . . . I want to know about everyone involved . . .'

Pascal's shirt is pulled down so that his pale neck and shoulders are revealed.

'*NO!*' Hope and I scream together.

Behind Pascal is the stove and one soldier is using a thick leather glove to pick up a red-hot poker, while the other soldier holds the trembling, crying boy tightly in his grip.

'Did you bomb the station?' Richter shrieks.

'*NO!!*' we scream in reply.

'Who is in Group K? This is your last chance. Start talking. Quickly!'

The poker is moving towards the back of Pascal's neck and he is crying out with fear.

'*NO! NO! NO! WE KNOW NOTHING!*' Hope screams.

I can't think of anything to do, anything that will help. I want to comfort Pascal, I want to tell him that we love him, but we have to remain silent; we cannot give Richter answers even to save Pascal from this terrible pain, otherwise not one of us, not even baby Odile will leave here alive.

Suddenly: '*Dodo, l'enfant do—*'

The lullaby my mama used to sing to me bursts from my mouth. The lullaby I've heard so many other mothers sing to their children too.

'L'enfant dormira bien vite,
Dodo, l'enfant do,
L'enfant dormira bientôt.'

I'm singing, even though I'm crying. Hope joins in . . . Good, she knows it, so Pascal must know it too. We sing loudly.

'Tout le monde est sage,
Dans le voisinage,
Il est l'heure d'aller dormir,
Le sommeil va bientôt venir.'

'What are you doing? Start talking!' Richter demands. He walks right up to me. He grabs my chin and forces me to look at him. Into his pitiless eyes.

My hands are behind my back, I'm completely at his mercy, but I want him to know I'll never give in. I defy him. I despise him. I will never, ever stop hating and fighting him and everything he stands for.

I gather up what little saliva I can from my parched, frightened mouth and I spit into his face.

Chapter Twenty-Nine

Never give in.

It has taken me almost two days to scratch these words onto the wall beside my pillow so that I can look at them whenever I lie down.

I have repeated them to myself so often their meaning has swum and blurred in my mind, like when we did lines at school.

School . . . it seems so long ago, in my safe and distant past in a Brussels which no longer exists.

Never give in.

Didn't Sir Winston promise that if we just persevered we would overcome our enemies? Sometimes his words make sense and give me strength. But sometimes I lie on my bare mattress and sob tears of helplessness because I'm so small and insignificant. What can I do that will make any difference at all?

Why did I even try?

Why am I not at home with my family?

But even in these darkest moments I know I have followed the right path. How could any of us have even pretended to be happy at home this Christmas when the Nazis are in charge? When Papa is missing? When I could be sent to a work camp at any moment? When there is no coal? When Grand-Mamie risks her life every morning for a newspaper? When Mama is trying to make us food out of weeds?

As well as the deep wounds scabbing up all over my buttocks, back and legs, I have the vicious burn that Richter branded into my arm after I spat at him. Everything is regularly doused by the nurse in biting, caustic iodine.

There are also itchy bumps all over my body and face. When I first realized that the mattress in my cell was infested with bed bugs, I was disgusted. I spent several hours after the discovery sitting on the stool as far away from the bed as I could, itching, scratching, tormented by the horror of the situation.

But somehow I am adapting to everything around me. Now, I almost feel quite friendly towards the little brown bugs, the size of raisins, which on some days are the only other living creatures I see.

Sometimes, I collect a few of them and race them against each other across my stool. It passes the time and

I am desperate to distract myself from my bleakest, darkest thoughts. I've even caught myself giggling at the silly bugs, just for a forgetful moment or two. But then usually there is a cry or a bang at the door, something to remind me that I am still here, in prison, at their mercy.

For three days, I've not spoken to a soul. The slot in the door has been opened and closed to let my meal trays in and out. The door has been opened once a day to let me bring out my buckets. But I've not said a word and apart from my name and '*Raus!*' being shouted at me, there has been no contact.

In the deep silence, I feel safer.

Although I don't want to, I can't help replaying the last interrogation over and over again in my mind. They threatened Pascal three times with the poker. Hope and I sang. We also cried, screamed and dripped with sweat in our terror. It was the worst thing I've ever, ever had to endure. Surely it will be the worst? Surely they can't have anything worse planned for us?

Finally they let Pascal, screaming with fright, run to his mother. But they didn't loosen her arms, so she couldn't even hold him. By then his little sister was crying wildly too. But Hope wasn't allowed to hold her either.

When they took her children away, she cried like a wounded animal – fierce, desperate howling. All she wanted to do was be with her children, hold them, comfort them, but the beasts didn't just deny her, they seemed to enjoy denying her.

Then they took me away. I'm frightened they might have worked on Hope some more, threatening her children, desperate to make her talk. But as nothing has happened for three whole days, I think she must have remained strong. As she told me on my very first visit to Group K, if the Nazis think you know anything, you and everyone you know are lost.

The slot in my door slides up, which surprises me. It is maybe about three in the afternoon, not a meal-time, so I don't know why the slot would open.

A piece of crisp white paper slides in and floats to the floor. It seems to be typewritten, so I pounce on it, desperate to have something to read, desperate for information about anything at all.

At the top is the address of the main court building in Brussels, yesterday's date (I think . . . I am no longer so confident of the days, although I keep marking them down on the wall) and then, with a start, I read my false name, Eglantine DuPont, my false address and date of birth. Despite my encounter with Monsieur Van Roy, my false identity is holding.

With a tingling sensation I read on. Here is my crime: *murder*. The date: *December 23rd*; then the full address of the railway station.

When I read that I have been tried and sentenced in

my absence, the hairs on the back of my neck stand up.

According to this sheet of paper, I have been found guilty.

I read on with a sick sensation growing in my stomach. I have already been sentenced. I look up at the bare walls of my cells. I need to take a breath, stop for a moment, because I already know what I am going to read on this slip of paper. This typewritten page contains my horrible fate.

How can this have happened without me? Why was I not allowed to be there? Whey couldn't I at least have looked into the faces of my accusers? Has even that right been taken away from us now?

I look back down at the page. It is shaking a little in my hands.

```
Sentence: death.
Eglantine DuPont will be taken to a place
of execution and hanged by the neck until
she is dead.
```

Hanged? *Hanged?*

This is an ugly shock. In my darkest hours, I have imagined a firing squad. Being blindfolded and listening to the commander shout, 'Take aim, fire!' It would be over in moments.

Hanging frightens me much more. I picture myself

standing on the scaffold, with my hands tied behind my back, feeling them put the rough rope of the noose around my neck . . . adjusting it, my necklace of death.

It's barbaric and terrible to imagine.

I wonder if I will be calm and accept my fate? Or if I will want to shout out against the Nazis to the last.

Not until I have read the page over and over again do I realize that more words are written on the back. With a jolt, I see that I already have an execution date: February 7th, 1941.

Suddenly I need to rush to the bucket and be sick.

Chapter Thirty

It is after the slice of bread and bowl of grey cabbage soup have been eaten and taken away that I hear keys jangling outside my cell door.

I think it's maybe 6 p.m. or so as the daylight has faded and I am faced with long hours of darkness before I can fall into a restless, nightmare-troubled sleep.

According to my wall calendar, I am three days away from my execution date. All my pleas to the women bringing my meals that I would like to write a letter to a friend or even talk to the prison chaplain have been in vain.

I've not been allowed to see anyone.

The cell door opens and, huddled on my little stool, I cringe to see an officer enter. Maybe I am going to be tortured one last time, to see if I will reveal anything now that I know I am going to die.

'I've brought someone to see you, Nicole.'

I'm startled to hear my real name, but now I recognize the voice and the face under the terrible peaked cap.

It is Monsieur Van Roy, Aurelie's father.

I don't make any reply because I'm so surprised to see who is coming into my cell behind him. She's in a smart blue coat, belted over a checked skirt and red jumper. Her hair is curled out under her beret and her lipstick is a dark, polished crimson.

It's Aurelie.

Despite everything, I can't help feeling pleased to see her. I smile and she rushes over to throw her arms around me.

'Oh, Nicole, you look terrible,' she cries, enveloping me in a perfumed hug. She kisses me on both cheeks and I wonder if she's left lipstick marks.

Monsieur Van Roy leaves the cell and locks the door behind him. Aurelie looks around with undisguised horror.

I stand up and offer her my stool. 'I'll sit on the mattress, I'm used to the bed bugs,' I tell her.

She shudders and doesn't even sit on the stool. For several moments we just stare at each other. She is clearly distraught at what she can see and I feel a burst of anger.

'Your friends run a nice hotel: no sheets, a bucket for a toilet, regular torture . . .'

'Please don't!' Aurelie protests. 'It's awful – I had no idea how awful it was going to be.'

'Have you seen my family? Is everything OK with them?' I'm desperate to know.

'I haven't seen them . . . I mean, I haven't been to your street . . . I've not heard that anything has happened.'

Again I feel furious with her: how can she come here and not have this vital information for me?

'Please tell them where I am,' I manage. 'They don't know. Maybe they could visit . . . if I gave you the name I use now. Maybe there's still time . . .'

'Before what?'

I look right into her face. I want her to feel the full horror of this. I want her to know what her Nazi friends are really like. 'Before I'm executed, of course.'

Her eyes widen and she puts her girlish hand with its bright red nails over her mouth. 'No!' she gasps, like some silly film heroine.

'Why are you here, Aurelie? Have you come to look at my wounds?' I pull up the sleeve of my nightdress and show her my ugly burn, still seeping fluid. I stand up and turn, lifting my dress so she can see the scabbing lash marks on my legs. 'Or are you supposed to try and get some information out of me with some laughable promise that if I just name a few names, I can run home free?' I ask.

Aurelie has the decency to look embarrassed. I try to remember why we were such good friends. I used to think she was fun and clever, with a daring streak like me. Now, I think she's just a deluded fool.

'I don't know anything. I'm innocent,' I tell her. 'I wasn't even at my own trial. They're going to hang me on Friday.'

'No,' she says, but it's a whisper now. 'Nicole, you have to do something. Just give them something and they will let you go. I promise, I'll make sure it happens. Tell them something about Monsieur Durance. How can it hurt? He's already dead.'

I ball my hands into fists and squeeze to stop myself from slapping her. How dare she even say his name?

'I don't know anything,' I repeat.

'Of course you do! You were picked up at the station right after the bomb. Tell them they forced you into it. Tell them you didn't know what you were doing. You're still at school, for goodness' sake!'

'That hasn't stopped them sentencing me to death.'

'Please stop it, please stop talking about it, I can't bear it,' she cries.

'Oh, I'm so sorry. Is this a little too depressing? I'll try to think of something more cheery. How's your boyfriend?'

I will her to say something about Anton. She must

know I'm desperate for news about him, but I can't ask first. I don't want to give away any hint that he might have been involved. There's still a chance that he escaped.

'I'm trying to help you,' she says. 'I have influence. My father's an important—'

'Collabo.'

'It's over, Nicole; the Germans are in charge of Belgium.' Something in her face hardens as she says this. 'The sooner we all get on with creating the New Order in Belgium, the better. People like you are just standing in the way of progress.'

'Oh, really?!' I can feel the blood racing to my cheeks. I want to hit her, but instead I say as calmly as I can manage: 'Well, as long as I'm standing in the way of thugs who torture children – yes, I've seen it with my own eyes – thugs who terrorize old ladies, who lock up fathers, shoot innocent people and send teenagers to work as slaves, then that's just fine. I'm more than happy to be standing in their way.' I glare furiously at her.

Luckily she doesn't say anything. One more stupid comment and I will hit her.

'I think you'd better go,' I say. 'I would say *au revoir*, but that's not going to happen.'

She goes to the door, knocks frantically, and within moments it's unlocked and she's gone.

I lie on my mattress and watch the sky grow dark. I twist the little copper ring on my finger and wonder where Anton is. In a cell? Already dead? Or out there, free, plotting another attack against the enemy?

More than anything, I just wish he was with me.

Chapter Thirty-One

When it's completely dark in the cell, I again hear keys in the door. This has never happened before; I've never been taken out at night. I sit up, my heart thudding with fright.

The door opens, then closes; I can make out a uniformed officer at the foot of my bed.

'Nicole, you need to come with me.'

Once again, I recognize Monsieur Van Roy's voice.

'I'm Eglantine DuPont,' I say. 'I'm innocent. I've been tried in my absence.'

'Yes, I understand. But you need to come with me now.'

I wonder why he's whispering. I used to enjoy M. Van Roy's company when I visited Aurelie's house. He had an excellent sense of humour, though I imagine there isn't much call for it in his new job.

'Why?' I ask, suspecting one last burst of torture is in store.

'A group of women leave for a work camp in Germany within the hour,' he says, his voice low. 'I could put you with them . . . it's not a release, but at least you won't be executed.'

I'm astonished. 'But why?' I ask.

'Because you're the same age as Aurelie . . . and because she begged me to help you.'

'A work camp . . .' I repeat, trying to take this in. I've been so focused on preparing for death that I can hardly register this change of plan. Not that a work camp is much of an alternative to execution. Henri's stories from the camp were terrible: the boys had to work for fourteen hours a day. They were beaten constantly; those who didn't work hard enough were even beaten to death. There was never enough food; there was illness and disease. It sounded like hell on earth.

But it is still a chance at life. If I don't take it, the hangman's noose will be around my neck on Friday.

This is my one and only chance.

I have to take it, and maybe somewhere on the way to the work camp I can escape. You read about it all the time in the Resistance papers, people who smuggle saws on board the wooden carriages, make holes in the floor and get away. Isn't my own papa supposed to have escaped during a transfer?

'I'll go to the camp,' I tell him, 'but can you please try and get word to my family?'

'I'll try. You need to come now.'

'Won't you get into trouble?'

'I'll say there was a paperwork error. They will try to track you down, but if you're in Germany it will take a long time. Come on.'

It seems ridiculous, but for a moment I'm startled at the prospect of leaving this room unexpectedly, knowing I will never come back. I glance around, as if there's something I might take with me, but of course I have only the clothes I am wearing and Anton's wire ring on my finger.

'I'm ready.'

He puts his hand on my shoulder and leads me out. He stops to lock the door and nods brusquely at the guard.

'DuPont to be transported,' he says. The guard nods back.

I'm led through the prison and into a large waiting room, packed with women of all ages, all wearing the same grubby prison dress as I am. Monsieur Van Roy speaks to the policemen entering names into a ledger, and all at once I am Anita Groote.

He doesn't say anything else to me, just leaves me here in this silent, subdued crowd where I scan anxiously for the face of anyone I know. I half want to see Hope, but then feel relieved when I don't. Maybe, somehow, she has made it home, along with her beloved children.

It is at least thirty-six hours later when the sliding wooden door on our railway truck is pulled open.

I have survived a journey into the depths of hell. Packed into a wooden cattle truck, we have rattled on and on through the cold and the darkness with nothing to eat, nothing to drink, nowhere to sit, hardly any space to stand and only a filthy bucket in the centre of the truck to relieve ourselves.

To cope with the wailing and the hysterical sobbing all around me, I have dug down into my silent place once again. I didn't want to talk or to listen to another lost soul on board. There are no words to express the pain and the horror of this journey. Even cows in a cattle truck would be fed, watered and given enough space. Because someone would care if the cows came out alive at the other end. No one cared whether we lived or died on this journey.

'*RAUS!*'

'*RAUS!*' a guard shouts at us from the blinding flood of light where the door has been pulled away.

We hobble, shuffle and stumble towards the exit. Once we are all out and our eyes have adjusted to this dazzling new light, I see that there are hundreds of us, maybe thousands. It's a huge train: many more trucks have been added as we've made our way through Belgium, then Germany. Now we are all standing bewildered and exhausted, armed guards every few metres training their guns on us.

Behind the guards is a vast wire fence, three or four metres high, with rolls of ugly, glinting razor wire on top. Beyond the fence are low grey buildings with corrugated metal roofs stretching as far as the eye can see.

A harsh voice is shouting through a megaphone at us. His words reverberate through the air. He talks in German, then in French:

'You have arrived at Ravensbrück concentration camp. None of you will ever go home. You will never see your families again. You are here to work until you die.'

Chapter Thirty-Two

I have been stripped, searched and washed, out in the open, with icy water, in February. They've taken my little copper ring, despite my protests, and my lovely hair. My thick brown-blonde curls that fell below my shoulders have been roughly chopped off with a blunt pair of scissors, but at least I was not shaved like so many others.

I'm still wearing my lace-up shoes and my woollen socks, the last trace of my old life, and another striped prison dress, which has not been washed since its last inhabitant stopped wearing it. No underwear: they have taken that away, leaving me freezing cold and exposed.

I'm struggling to make sense of this place. It's huge: grey, vast and colourless. Between the endless low huts there is a bare, broad street which we new prisoners are marched along. We pass hundreds of other women prisoners, all grey, dirty, haggard. There are even children here, ragged and starving, walking or sitting listlessly in the muddy earth. When I look at any other face I see only the despair I know must be written across my own.

I'm given a bowl and I queue for a ladleful of grey watery soup. I can identify only chunks of boiled parsnip and some potato peelings. I'm not hungry but I eat the soup and my chunk of mouldy bread because I know I need to eat to be strong for the work that is coming. If I'm not strong, then like the boys I've heard about from Henri, I will be beaten to death.

When we are marched into the dormitory, we are greeted with plaintive cries in many different languages.

'Is anyone from Paris?' 'Amsterdam?' '*Polska?*' '*Ist hier jemand von Berlin?*'

I walk past rough wooden bunks three beds high, packed with faces peering down at us – thin, grey faces, desperate for news: news of the war, news of their cities, news from home, or even hoping against hope to hear of their families . . .

I am listening for the cry that will let me know I have found others like me.

'Is anyone from Brussels?' I hear at last.

'Yes!' I answer, and hands reach down to lift me up. I'm hauled into a top bunk, full of straw, and from up here I can see how many beds there are in this shed, how many countless women, how many faces. The three scrawny women up here are Belgian and desperate to pump me for news.

'What's your name?' I'm asked.

Who am I? Nicole? Coco? Eglantine? Or Anita? Or the new identity I've been given today: number 427790. It's printed on the label sewn onto the front of my dress. Apparently we are 'lucky' – at other camps, they tattoo the numbers onto the arms of the prisoners.

'Nicole,' I decide. The guards are only ever going to refer to me by number, so what does it matter if these women know my real name?

I'm bombarded with questions. How is Brussels? How is the war going? Has Britain been invaded? I answer as best I can. I try to be honest, but I don't want to plunge everyone in this desperate situation even further into despair. I don't want to tell them that it looks hopeless and the Germans are winning everything.

There is no need for them to ask why I am here; I have a big red triangle badge sewn onto my dress, which marks me as a political prisoner.

'How did you get caught?' one woman asks, pointing to my badge.

Even here, I instinctively answer, 'I can't talk about that.' I'm determined to preserve my silence to the end.

Then come more particular questions: which area of Brussels do I come from? Which church and school did I attend? They are trying to find out if I could possibly know anything about their relatives or their friends.

Another woman approaches the bunk; she shuffles along the dirt floor and looks up at me. Her face is withered and sunken. From the yellow star sewn onto her dress, I can tell she is a Jewish lady.

'St Teresa's School?' she croaks up at me. She must have heard my reply.

'Yes.'

'You look about the same age as my Lottie.' The words are said slowly and with great sadness.

The only Lottie I knew was my friend, the Jewish girl in my class who disappeared on the day of the Occupation. I always hoped she and her family had managed to escape.

'Lottie Rosen?' I ask, but with terrible foreboding.

'Yes, my Lottie. Did you know her?'

The woman looks up at me with a spark of enthusiasm. I realize I am looking at Madame Rosen and I cannot really believe it. To find her here, so far away from Belgium, so long after she and her daughters disappeared. It seems almost incredible and yet have I not witnessed all kinds of strange reunions going on in this terrible barracks?

'Madame Rosen?' I ask uncertainly. I've met her before, but she looked nothing like this aged grandmother figure standing in front of me. I remember shining black hair, a bright tweed suit and smart jewellery.

But in a prison dress, starving and filthy, with only a few inches of hair left, we are all unrecognizable.

She nods slowly.

'I'm Nicole, Lottie's friend. She sat next to me in class. Monsieur Durance was our teacher.'

'Oh, Monsieur Durance! Now there is a gentleman. A wise and cultured gentleman.'

At these words, a tight, pained sob builds up in my chest.

'And . . . Lottie?' I'm frightened of the reply.

'She died a month ago,' Madame Rosen says, and shakes her head. 'But I'm glad,' she whispers. 'Anywhere is better than here.'

The sob that began in my chest at the mention of Monsieur Durance wants to burst out, but I swallow it down.

'Ettie is here,' Madame Rosen adds. 'Come and share our bunk.'

'Esther?' I ask. 'Lottie's little sister?' She nods.

I clamber down and let her lead me to the corner of this nightmarish dormitory where she lives. There are many other Belgians here, mainly Jewish, but we share news and street names and ask questions to see if we have any friends in common.

No one has heard any word of Hope or Anton or any of my comrades.

Finally, the few lamps dimly illuminating our shed are

turned off and we are ordered to be quiet by the prisoner guards – the Kapos – who run this barracks.

Of course, I do not have my own bed. I have to share with Madame Rosen, another thinner, even frailer woman and Ettie, who is now nine, dressed in a ragged nightshirt, with huge eyes and a bald head, but she can't stop grinning at me and making cheerful little jokes. We all huddle together, embarrassingly close, and pull up the blanket. I cannot sleep like this; I cannot even close my eyes. With every part of my being, I just want to get out of here.

I touch the place on my finger where Anton's ring used to be, and for the first time in my life I wonder if it might be better to be dead instead of alive.

'Shhhhh.' Madame Rosen strokes my shorn head. 'Try to sleep. Hard labour is coming tomorrow.'

Chapter Thirty-Three

It is still pitch dark and bone-achingly cold when I am roused from what feels like just moments of sleep by shouts and bangs.

'Time to get up. Time for roll call,' Madame Rosen tells me. I lace on my shoes, which on her advice I have kept under my head because desperate prisoners steal good shoes. In the camp, anyone without shoes can't walk, can't work and will quickly be killed.

We hurry down from the bunk and queue for the pit that serves as a toilet. Hundreds of women are already behind us and the smell . . . I blink back the tears in my eyes. I don't know if I can live like this. We are being asked to sacrifice our humanity and live like animals.

Further proof, as if I needed it, is the terrible scrabble for food. Baskets full of bread and a huge pail of soup are doled out. Every prisoner has a tin bowl for the slop of soup, and we hold our bread in our hands. I see some women just snatch bread out of the hands of other weaker women. Some swap soup for bread or bread for soup. The ravenous glint in everyone's eye as they guard their food is horrible.

Once I've been served, Ettie appears at my elbow. 'Enjoying your delicious breakfast?' she jokes.

'Potato peel and dishwater, my favourite.'

'Can I have your bread? You're still new, so you won't be as hungry as me yet.'

I hand it over without protest. She falls on it and munches it down with total concentration, then carefully licks the crumbs from her filthy palms so as not to miss a single morsel.

'How long have you been here?' I ask.

She shrugs. 'I don't know. But I'm a Jew, so I belong in prison.'

'No. You don't belong in prison,' I insist.

'If I get out, I'm going to eat all the food I want, all day long,' Ettie says. 'I'm going to be a very smart, grown-up lady, like we used to see in Berlin, in a lovely dress with a beautiful hat. I'm going to have a special long handbag, and do you know what I'll keep in it?'

'No?'

'A baguette,' she replies. 'A warm, freshly cooked baguette. So I'll be able to eat some whenever I want, whenever I get even a tiny bit hungry.'

'Good idea,' I tell her. I smile and my face feels all tight and unused to smiling. I probably haven't smiled since I last saw Anton. The despair of never knowing what has happened to him washes over me.

'I'll look for you later,' Ettie says, heading off.

'I'll look for you too.'

Then I'm following the mass of women out into the barren broad street. We line up and stand to attention. It is still dark and cold, maybe only four or five o'clock in the morning, and it has begun to rain.

We stand and we stand and we stand in our rows like a regiment of scarecrow women soldiers. I wonder where Ettie is. Does she have to line up too? Does she have to work? Or do the beasts let the children peck about the camp during the day?

Soon the rain has made my face numb with cold; it penetrates the rough material of my dress and I am soaked and freezing. But we stand, stock-still and silent, while women guards roam up and down, counting us, checking numbers, making sure every single one of us is here.

I don't dare to even turn my head, but I swivel my eyes around. Old women, weak women, young women, girls younger than me, all kinds are here, lined up in flimsy nightshirts, facing forwards, hands by their sides in the raw rain before dawn. Even the bodies of the women who died in the night have been carried out, so they can be ticked off the list.

Everyone who staggers or sways is shouted at, punched or hit with sticks. I try not to look or to listen. It's not that I don't feel sympathy; I feel so much sympathy that I fear it will burst out of me. I will shout at the demons and they will beat me to death.

As dawn begins to break, trucks drive into the camp. Men jump out and begin to walk up and down the rows of us latest inmates. We are asked to roll up our sleeves, pull up our dresses. They want to see our muscles and how fit we are. So we display ourselves just like slaves at the market hundreds of years ago.

I'm quickly chosen and marched with many others towards one of the trucks. When it's full, the canvas coverings are closed and we are driven out of the camp.

Although I'm in the back of a truck, probably headed for a factory for a fourteen-hour work shift, an amazing sense of elation hits me as, peering through a tiny tear in the canvas, I see us pass through the gates of the camp.

There is a way out.

If there is any chance to escape, no matter how slight, then I have to take it because I know that to stay here is to die.

I endure the day. I sit at a conveyor belt for hours and hours and hours doing a simple repetitive task, filling shells with gunpowder.

There is one break in the twelve hours we work

when we are allowed to use a toilet pit, eat a chunk of bread and drink a cup of water.

One of the foremen – who works for the factory, not the camp or the Nazis – walks up and down among us, explaining what we must do and gently improving errors. He has both a kind voice and kind eyes. I can tell that he is desperately sorry for us. When one woman fainted onto the conveyor and was beaten until she came round, I could see him wincing in horror.

All I'm able to think about all day long as my hands pick up little shells and stuff them with gunpowder is how to escape. I know that I will need to use all my cunning, all my intelligence and all my bravery to get out of here. But if I am clever, maybe it can be done.

Most important of all, I will need some clothes. There is no point trying to escape in my striped dress as I'll be recognized and re-arrested as soon as I'm seen.

I stuff cases and try to think. Soon I am so tired that I am straining to keep my eyes open and my hands working. Everything keeps blurring in front of me.

WHAM!

A blow to the side of my head makes me reel with pain and shock. '*Weiter arbeiten!*' the woman guard screams. I know this means 'carry on working', because I've heard it all day long.

When we get back to the camp, it's already dark. We endure an hour or so of roll call, then we are marched back to our barracks. I'm astonished to realize that we are getting no more food. Even the dreadful grey plateful of parsnip and potato would have been welcome. I have been awake since 4 a.m., I have worked for at least twelve hours, I am so tired I cannot stand any more, and now I am to have no more food until tomorrow.

How can we be expected to last for more than a few months with this treatment? No wonder there are dead and dying women everywhere. Some die overnight in the bunks, some die during roll call, some simply drop dead on the march in and out of the barracks. No one acts surprised or sorry or even dares to pause. We are just expected to carry on . . . to step over the dying if we have to. It's unbearable, yet somehow, if I want to live, I must bear it.

Madame Rosen hugs me as I climb into the bunk. 'You went out to the factory?' she asks.

'Yes.'

'Is it better there?'

'I don't think it's any better, no.'

She touches my cheekbone, which feels bruised and swollen. 'Did they hit you?'

'Only twice. What do you do all day?'

'I sew uniforms as quickly as I can and I watch them punish people who are too tired, too weak, too wretched to sew any more. One day I will be carried out and thrown away too. I stay alive to watch over Ettie for as long as I can.'

Ettie and the other woman who share this bunk with us are already asleep, so it's safe to whisper into Madame Rosen's ear. 'I'm making a plan. I'm going to escape from a lorry and get back to Belgium. I'm going to make sure you're all rescued. I just need to get some ordinary clothes . . . the foreman at the factory seems sympathetic . . . maybe I can get to know him . . . maybe he can . . .'

Madame pats my hand and looks into my eyes. 'Perhaps . . .' she says.

We lie down on the straw too. After a little while, she says, 'One girl jumped from the back of a lorry on the way to the factory . . . but they found her and hanged her. We all had to watch.'

Chapter Thirty-Four

When I arrive back at the camp after my second day in the factory I am burning to escape. There must be a way of making friends with the foreman; I have to get out of here as soon as I can.

Already I'm exhausted and weak, losing my courage and my hope. Soon I am going to be like the women who have been here for months: grey, thin as skeletons and without hope. Then I will drop dead or be beaten to death or be shuffled off to the hospital wing to die.

New women arrive here every day to replace the ones too weak to work. With an endless supply of slave labour from all over Europe, no one even wants us to live. They can barely house or feed us all.

If I want to get out and somehow get back to Belgium, back to my family, my love, my friends, my country again, it must be as soon as possible, while I still have the strength and the will.

Inside the dormitory, I find Ettie at the bunk, waiting for me. She slips her spindly hand into mine. 'Come to the children's corner for a while,' she invites me. 'We're eating dream food tonight.'

I have no idea what she means, but I follow her to a different part of this huge, stinking barn. We find a bunk bed shared by a group of girls and boys who look aged between eight and thirteen, although it's hard to tell because they are all so pale and so thin.

'This is my friend,' Ettie tells the others.

'I'm Nicole, from Brussels,' I say.

'We're eating dream food,' Ettie repeats. 'It's lovely, Nicole, you'll like it.'

The oldest girl signals for me to climb into the bunk with them, so then we are all huddled together in the straw.

'I'll go first,' says Ettie. 'I'm trying to think of one we haven't done before.' She closes her eyes and then begins to tell us: 'In the summer, when it's lovely and warm outside, Mummy likes to make a cold supper. Potato salad with tiny little potatoes, covered in mayonnaise and sprinkled with chives and parsley. Sometimes there are slices of pickled beetroot and I like to chop the beetroot up and put it with the potatoes, because it makes everything purple.'

I look at the other children; they have their eyes closed to savour every morsel of this imaginary meal.

'Sometimes we have pickled herring with the potato salad,' Ettie adds. 'It's one of my favourites.'

'And maybe a crunchy gherkin,' the little girl beside Ettie whispers.

'For pudding, there is a lovely fruit fool: boiled gooseberries mixed up with cream and sugar,' Ettie says.

'Oh yes, we've not had gooseberry fool here before,' says one of the boys.

'You go.' Ettie opens her eyes and looks at me. 'Tell us about one of your favourite meals.'

I try to think, but my mind fills up with grey parsnip soup and terrible concoctions of cabbage and nettle. It's been so long since I had a delicious meal, I'm not sure if I can remember anything as good as Ettie's gooseberry fool.

'How about a delicious breakfast?' I begin finally. 'With real bread, a fat brown loaf, cut into thick slices, warm, not long out of the oven, and onto my bread I'm going to put creamy yellow butter . . .'

'Oh yes!' Ettie exclaims. 'Butter! Remember butter?'

'And over my butter comes a layer of Grand-Mamie's sour cherry jam, which is sweet but with a perfect tang . . .'

Suddenly I'm ten, high up in a cherry tree with Anton. We're picking sour cherries in the bright summer sun while Grand-Mamie directs us from below: 'To the left, Nicole, there's a big bunch just to the left.'

I have to go home. I have to be with them. The yearning is so powerful I can hardly breathe. This is what it is to be homesick. I've never been away long enough to know it before. I am desperate for my mama and papa, my grand-mamie, even Gaspar. I want to be home, and I don't care if I have to eat cabbage and nettle soup every day for the rest of my life, I just want to be home. And I want to find Anton. I worry about him endlessly. Where is he? What's happened to him?

'It's OK,' Ettie says gently. She pats my arm. 'We were all upset when we started this game too . . . but you get used to it. It becomes fun to try and remember.'

A little later, Ettie and I go back to the bunk with Madame Rosen and the other women. The lamps will be extinguished soon, and the Kapos will demand silence.

When I lie in the straw beside her, Madame Rosen whispers: 'All day long, with my friends, I have made a plan for you . . .'

'What do you mean?' I whisper back.

'To escape. I've been thinking about it; I didn't sleep at all last night for thinking about it. We're going to sew you some clothes and sneak them out of the workshop. The girl who was caught, she was wearing a prison dress, so she was too easy to find.'

'You'll sew me clothes?' I'm astonished by the generosity of her offer and at last I feel the slimmest ray of hope.

'You and Ettie have to come with me,' I tell her. 'I'll find a way to get you onto the lorry and we can make the jump together. Don't you want to go home?'

Madame looks at me very gravely, her eyes swimming in their hollow sockets. 'My home is gone, my husband too and my eldest daughter. Ettie is all I have left. I can't jump from a lorry with her and risk the tiny chance of life she has. We have to hang on here and hope that one day soon we will be rescued. Somehow . . .'

'I want to go home,' I say, burning with the wish. 'If I can get home, I'll tell everyone that you need to be rescued.'

Chapter Thirty-Five

The next night when I crawl back into my bunk, starving and exhausted, Madame Rosen is there and I can see at once that she has something to tell me. Her face has a look I've not seen before; something close to excitement is playing over the thin lips and grey cheeks.

'Look under the straw,' she whispers.

I dig down and see grey material. My heart jolts.

'Trousers,' Madame whispers, 'and a tunic. We made them for you and got them out. There's a pocket in the trousers filled with our bread. When it's dark, put the clothes on under your nightdress. Then you will be ready to go tomorrow.'

Tomorrow. My head reels. Tomorrow? It's too soon. I'm overwhelmed now with how enormous this task will be.

'But how will I find my way back to Belgium?' I ask

her. Even if I make it out of the camp, I'll be alone, in the middle of Germany, an escaped prisoner without a map or a single penny.

'Do you know how to find the North Star?' Madame whispers.

'Follow the stars at the end of the Plough to the tip of the Little Bear . . . is that right?'

'Yes. If the North Star is on your right-hand side, then you know you are heading west.'

'But what if it's cloudy?'

'Then you must walk towards the sunset.'

All night long, I lie awake and try to make a plan. When we wake up, I'll give Madame Rosen and Ettie the only gift I can: my woollen socks.

During roll call I stand with my nightdress over my tunic and trousers, and despite the cold I sweat with the fear of being discovered. I've rolled the trousers up as high as I can, in tight folds, but if they unroll when I walk towards the truck, the guards will see and I will be killed. Maybe Madame Rosen and the other women who sewed the clothes will be killed too.

But I get to the truck and as it drives out of the camp to the factory, I don't take my eyes from the slit in the canvas, trying to work out where will be best to jump out. It will be dark when we head home, but I need a place where I can roll into the bushes as quickly as possible.

Just thinking about jumping out makes me feel sick. How will it work? Surely the truck following behind will see me. They will stop and shoot me . . . or worse.

This could be my last day on earth.

I try to stop these thoughts and just concentrate on finding a good place to make the jump. The road is not wide and there are bushes and trees all around. Surely if I can just jump out and get off the road, I have a good chance. I have every chance.

All day long at the conveyor belt in the factory we work in silence. I add the chunk of bread from midday to the three other chunks in my trouser pocket. These are my only supplies for however long it may take to walk to Belgium.

I try to imagine the distance. Someone has told me that Ravensbrück is north of Berlin. I know that Berlin is about 760 kilometres from Brussels. Could I walk twenty-five kilometres a day?

Even if I could, even if I was always going in the right direction, it would still take thirty days. A whole month of living on my wits in Nazi Germany without any money . . . it's impossible. But the chances of surviving here for more than a few months are impossible too.

I poke some gunpowder into the shell casing in front of me and tell myself not to think ahead. First of all, I need to get out of the lorry and away from the guards.

This impossible journey must be made one impossible step at a time.

Then an important-looking senior officer holding a clipboard comes into the room. The conveyor belt stops and all one hundred or so of us at work here look up at him.

'*Die suchen jemanden!*' he says calmly, but loud enough for us all to hear.

I look at the women on either side of me for an explanation.

'They are looking for someone,' one whispers.

'Eglantine DuPont,' the officer shouts.

All the hairs on the back of my neck stand up. Monsieur Van Roy's re-shuffle of the paperwork hasn't kept me hidden for long.

'*Ist Eglantine DuPont hier?*' the officer asks. He looks around with an almost pleasant expression, but I'm not going to be fooled.

I glance at the women beside me and try to remember if I could have used the name Eglantine to them. I don't think I've had the chance to speak to anyone today for longer than a few moments. I don't think names have been exchanged.

'*Eglantine DuPont melden Sie sich!*'

There is silence. I don't reply and no one else says anything. The women around me are looking down; no one wants to attract any attention to themselves. I look down too. My heart is hammering in my chest.

Richter has tracked me down all the way to a factory in the middle of Germany!

'*Alle von Brüssel, aufstehen!*' the officer commands.

Several women with a B marked on their dresses stand up. I have a B for Belgium too, so I stand up. The officer looks at the eight of us dotted across the factory floor. He approaches the girl nearest to him and asks: '*Wie alt sind Sie?*'

When she doesn't reply, he tries again in our language: 'Your age?'

'Seventeen,' the girl murmurs.

'Name?' he asks as well.

'Madeleine Huppert.'

He looks at his clipboard and makes a mark. Then he moves on to the next person. I can feel blood pounding in my ears . . . what is the name I came to the camp under? All I can think of is Eglantine DuPont, but that isn't right. Monsieur Van Roy gave me another name.

The officer has already checked two girls off, then three, then four. He is coming nearer. Eglantine . . . no. It began with an A . . . now I can only think of Aurelie.

The broad chest, gleaming with war medals and decorations, is opposite my face now. The officer is looking down at me with almost a smile as if he wants me to believe that if I just admit who I am, it will be OK.

'And how old are you?' he asks.

'Seventeen.' I risk the lie. If I admit I'm fifteen, then surely he will guess I'm Eglantine.

'Your name?'

A heartbeat of a pause . . . then I remember.

'Anita Groote.'

He looks at me for only moment or two, then makes another tick on his list. He checks the names and ages of the three remaining women and finally tells us to carry on with our work.

I sit down, the conveyor belt starts up again and I grab an empty cartridge. I hope no one notices that my hands are trembling. Richter is tracking me down. His son is dead because of me. He wants revenge and he's going to keep on looking until he finds me.

For a moment, as I push gunpowder into a shell casing, I wonder what his son was like. Maybe a merciless thug like his father . . . maybe not. I set off one of those station bombs and I will have to live − or die − with the consequences. Anita Groote will not keep me safe for long.

I have to jump tonight. It's my only hope.

Chapter Thirty-Six

When the shift is finally over, I feel no relief – just sudden, intense fear. As soon as the truck gets onto the road, I'm going to have to take my life into my hands and jump.

As we walk out into the yard, I suddenly have to bend over and retch. If there was any food in my stomach, I would be sick with fright, but because hours and hours have gone by since I've eaten anything solid, just a small mouthful of clear liquid appears.

Then comes the shocking thud of a stick over my back. The guards won't let us stop even for a moment, so I quickly stand up and walk on. Our numbers are checked as we climb into our trucks, just to make sure that no one is missing. There will be a check at the end of the journey too.

I know I'll have to jump from the truck as soon as I

can, as far from the camp as possible, so they can't come after me too quickly. They are certain to come after me . . . I think back to the night in the forest with the dogs and shudder.

I judge my place in the queue and end up as close to the tarpaulin flaps at the back of the truck as I can. The canvas covers are rarely tied and no one wants to be near the back because we have to stand and when the truck is packed full and lurching along the road, whenever it brakes, there is a danger of falling out.

If I'm caught after I jump, this is going to be my one hope of defence; I'll say I fell. But I'm not going to think about getting caught. I'm going to find my courage and think only about escape.

I'm going home. The journey is about to begin.

I stand on the edge of the crowd of exhausted scarecrows and watch the road begin to move beneath the wheels as we move off. It's dark; that's good. The truck behind us is not far away, but because of the blackout its headlights are dimmed.

We begin to roll down the road. There is a low murmur of talk in the truck, but most of the women are too tired to speak. I stare through the gap in the tarpaulin at the road. We slow to turn a sharp corner, I can't see the headlights of the truck behind, so this is it, this is my chance.

'Make no sound,' I call out to the others, because if

they scream and cause the driver to stop, I will be lost. This is it.

No time to think. Time to act.

Anton's voice is in my head: *'Jump, my fierce girl, jump!'*

I vault from the back of the truck, thump onto the road and curl into a pained, winded ball. I hurl myself to the side. Grass and spiky bush branches rake my body, so I roll with force, hoping I can cover myself in time.

The roar of wheels passes by just inches away from me as the next truck goes past.

Desperately, I scramble through the bushes, clawing my way forward, branches scratching at my face, then suddenly there is no more ground and I am falling through the darkness.

Chapter Thirty-Seven

The impact is crushingly hard. Pain shoots up from my feet through my legs and into my body. I put out my hands and immediately feel my left hand crunch forward into the ground, followed by my body and then my head.

The pain is severe. I want to pass out. I want to be sick. My head bounces up then down again. My eyes are open but I can only see blackness. I lie fighting for breath. I want to sleep; I want this to be over. Maybe it would be OK to die. Anything would be better than lying here in the blackness feeling nothing but excruciating pain.

I close my eyes and breathe in and out slowly. My ribs hurt with every breath. Maybe I've cracked or even broken them. Beneath my fingers is the soft mossy grass which has saved my life . . . for a little longer.

I lie still and try to work out the extent of my injuries. I turn my ankles. They feel sore and rusty but they still turn. I bend my knees. It's the same sort of feeling, very sore and rusty, but they still bend.

My right hand and wrist both seem fine, but my left hand is throbbing with pain and doesn't want to move much. My head is aching too. I lift it up from the grass and feel a rush of pressure.

But slowly I get up.

I see the prison dress on my arms and a great burst of adrenaline pumps through me. I've escaped! I have to get out of here. I have to get as far away from here as possible.

I've escaped! I'm out!

I no longer care how much I hurt; I have to get away. I have to make sure no one can ever take me back there.

Using just my right hand I strip the dress off as quickly as I can. My eyes are adjusting to the dark; I'm in woodland, at the base of a sheer hillside. I find a dense bush and shove my prison dress right underneath it, hoping it will be hidden enough. I unroll my trouser legs, gobble down one of the pieces of hard bread inside my pocket and, despite my bruised and swollen ankles and knees, I begin to run.

I have no idea which direction I'm going in, but I know the road to the camp is behind me and I have to keep running. I often stumble and trip, and I'm quickly exhausted, but whenever the pain in my chest and in my ribs becomes too much, I just think of the terrible guards, the unspeakable camp, the untold horror inside, and I keep running.

I have all night, I tell myself; if I can run and run all night long, I will be away from the camp. If I can just keep on running, I will be far enough away.

The woodland is growing thicker, with more trees. Good, I think; just keep running, forward, onwards. The thicker the wood, the less chance of them ever being able to find me again. I run on, one foot in front of the next, my ears straining for the sound of dogs, or shouts, or vehicles. It doesn't matter that my legs are aching, my breath is rasping in and out of my chest, my ribs are burning with pain and my left hand is throbbing uselessly at the end of my arm. I must just keep on running.

With every step I am further away from them and their terrible camp. Every step takes me closer to home.

Sometimes I have to slow to walking pace, just to catch my breath. The months now that I've spent in the Gestapo prison and then the camp have severely weakened me. My arms and legs are spindly thin; my muscles have wasted away. Patches of my hair have fallen out and I'm sure my skin is just as grey and lifeless as that of the other inmates. But as soon as my breath is back, I start running again as fast as I can, deeper and deeper into the heart of this wood.

Sometimes I hear the rustle or cries of animals, but that doesn't frighten me. No animal on earth could ever be as frightening as a Nazi or a Nazi attack dog.

All night long I push myself on. I eat my way through all the bread in my pockets. I stop for a minute or two when I hear rushing water and take several handfuls of water from a stream. I know that running water is the safest to drink.

Only when I see the very first greyness of the breaking dawn and feel the deep chill in the air that comes just before the light do I decide that it's time to stop and rest and hide. I'm alone in enemy territory now.

Just like Hope did that night in the forest after the airdrop, I need to make a den, a place where I can be safe and hidden during the day.

I search around until I find a small hollow; then, with the last of my strength, I drag as many fallen branches as I can find towards it. I scoop up handfuls of dry leaves and cover the branches as thoroughly as I can.

In the dark, it's easy to imagine that this is a secret, well-hidden place, but in the daylight, everything will look totally different and I could be exposed. I look around once again, to make sure I am safe here. It is just forest. There is no sign of a house or any wood-cutting going on here. There is nothing built by human hands within sight.

Finally satisfied that it's a good hiding place, I climb

into my little den, pull the branches right over the opening, burrow down into the leaves and litter of the forest floor and curl into a ball. Although it's very cold and I have no blanket, I feel nothing but relief. I am alone. I am not sharing a filthy straw bed with frail women waiting to die. I am in a place where, at least for now, I am safe.

I am no longer Anita or Eglantine. I am Nicole de Wilde.

'Nicole de Wilde,' I whisper to myself. 'Nicole,' I repeat, drawing strength from my name, my real identity.

I'm going home.

Suddenly I remember the phrase: '*Ich bin ein Einzelkind und ich muss nach Hause.*' I am an only child and I have to go home.

'*Ich muss nach Hause,*' I repeat.

'*Nicole de Wilde muss nach Hause.*'

I fall into a deep and dreamless sleep.

Chapter Thirty-Eight

When I open my eyes and see blurred branches in front of my face, I remember with a surge of excitement that I have escaped. The journey ahead may be almost impossibly difficult, but I am free and I am on my way home.

I uncurl my body as much as I can in this cramped space. My legs feel bruised and sore, and my ribs still hurt, but most of the pain is concentrated in my left hand, which has swollen dramatically. Several of my fingers won't wiggle, but my thumb works . . . maybe this is just a bad sprain, not a break.

I peer through the branches. When it's a little darker, I'll get out and start running again. Today, I need to see the sunset; I need to know that I'm now heading in the right direction. Maybe I can run again all night. Maybe I can cover more than twenty-five kilometres a day.

Maybe I will be home sooner than I can even imagine.

In the glint of the last red rays of the sun, I push the branches aside and haul my stiff body out of the hollow. I brush the leaves from my clothes and run my fingers through my tufts of hair. But I haven't a hope of making myself look normal. I must be filthy. I haven't been allowed to wash ever since I arrived in Germany. I'm wearing a comical outfit sewn out of pieces of army-uniform material and my hair's been shorn off with blunt scissors. If anyone sees me, they'll know immediately I'm a prisoner on the run.

I begin to walk, my ears and eyes keenly alert. I listen for water as I'm ragingly thirsty after my long sleep. I also need to find something to eat. But I'm so used to the feeling of gnawing hunger pains in my stomach that I can ignore these more easily.

I begin to jog west and it's glorious to have the last embers of daylight ahead of me, so I know which way to go. Every step west takes me one step closer to Brussels.

When the light has faded almost completely, I reach the edge of the forest. I knew it was coming, because the trees had begun to thin out and I passed stacks of felled wood, chopped logs and the small brick buildings used for making charcoal. Now there is grass, fences, open countryside and, in the distance, a farmyard ahead of me. The prospect of a farmyard is enticing. Could I find something to eat there?

With my eyes darting left, right and ahead, my ears pricked for any sound, I creep over the dark field towards the farmyard. It's obviously a smallholding; there's a squat farmhouse with several sheds and barns behind it. I know I need to be on guard for animals giving me away. Even cows will low if they are suspicious . . .

I realize Anton told me that. Once again, he comes striding into my head, jacket collar up, his scarf round his neck and his eyes looking right into mine as he stoops to kiss me.

'Hi,' I whisper, pretending he's right beside me. 'Courage is refusing to listen to your fears, right?'

I'm glad he's in my head as I sneak towards the barn. I always feel safer when Anton is with me. I look very carefully around. There is no one here. I can see lights on in the farmhouse, so hopefully the family have retired for the night. There is a large wooden sliding door on the barn, so I inch it open, then squeeze myself in through the gap.

For a moment, all I can smell is dusty floor mixed with the tang of tractor oil. It is deepest dark and my eyes can't make anything out. I listen. There is no sound of animals. No breathing, no scratching or pecking. I think I'm alone in this shed. I sniff carefully; alongside the dusty, oily smell, there is something I recognize. Earthy still but . . .

Mushrooms!

Yes, I can smell mushrooms. This must be one of those barns where mushrooms are grown in the dark. I creep forwards, feeling my way, and my foot kicks against something solid and lumpy.

With my hands, I can make out a sack. I unfold the top and my fingers find the smooth roundness of potatoes. I hurriedly stuff as many potatoes as will fit into my trouser pockets. Then I grope further into the darkness. My hands touch damp earth and I move my fingers along and feel the first smooth mushroom. I break it off, wipe it and stuff it into my mouth. It tastes crunchy, juicy and like fresh earth. I feel for another one, then another, then another.

I'm cramming mushrooms into my mouth as quickly as I can, wolfing them down. But once the first, sharp edge of my hunger has dimmed, I know I must stop. I've been starved for so long that any kind of over-indulgence is going to make me ill.

I take another handful of mushrooms and squash them into my pockets along with the potatoes. Then I turn back towards the gap in the shed door. Just as I reach it, I see the back door of the farmhouse open and a large dog come bounding out of it.

As quickly but as quietly as I can, I push the shed door closed, then I creep backwards into the shadows, crouch down beside the wall and make myself as small as I possibly can. But the dog has already started to bark and he's heading for the shed. I grope about; beside me is a small pile of rough sacking: the potato bags. I pick one up and throw it over me, then, crouched down with the earthy, rough material over my face, I wait.

The dog is barking at the shed door, I can even hear the scratching of its claws against the wood. A man calls out and the dog keeps barking. Now comes the *clump*, *clump* of the man's footsteps approaching the barn. I begin to tremble. If the man lets the dog into the shed, then surely I will be found.

The shed door rumbles as it's pulled open. I hug my arms tightly around me. Through the sacking I can see the beam of a torch pass quickly around the shed. I can hear the dog whining because the farmer must be holding him by his collar.

I don't dare to breathe.

Then the door rumbles shut again.

'*Komm jetzt!*'

I strain to listen. I think both the man and the dog are walking back towards the house. I hear the farmhouse door shut and I listen and listen, desperately trying to work out if it is safe to leave.

Only when long, long silent minutes have passed do I dare to get up and tiptoe towards the barn door. Once I'm out, I creep as quickly as I can over the field away from the farmyard. When I come across a cattle trough filled with water, I take several handfuls to drink. I wash my filthy face and hands, then I carefully clean my potatoes, taking care not to drop a single precious one into the murky depths.

It's a clear night, so I find my North Star and try to keep west, munching on mouthfuls of raw potato and mushroom as I go. I try to jog, but more often than not I slow to walking pace.

I have grown so weak. Lack of food, lack of sleep and the hours of work and worry have sapped my strength. The pain and swelling in my left hand is almost a minor problem compared to the great aching tiredness in my body.

But still I walk on.

Every step, I keep telling myself, every single step takes me closer to home. I must keep going.

Over and over as I walk, I repeat the words Grand-Mamie and I heard on the radio so long ago now. Sir Winston's words: 'Never, never, never, never give in.'

Chapter Thirty-Nine

I wake.

The first moments of waking are always the hardest. My troubled dreams are filled with home, my mama and Anton, or interrogation, beatings, the terrible camp, and I never know where I am when I first open my eyes.

I see branches in front of my face and realize I'm in Germany, alone, still trying to stay free and get home.

The exhilaration of escape has long gone. I have walked for five nights now. Always towards the sunset, with the North Star on my right, but I have no idea where I am. I have crept past villages, but their names on the signposts mean nothing to me. I could be closer to Brussels, or I could be even further away than when I started.

It's already sunset. I'm growing so tired and weak that I sleep from dawn till dusk without stirring. My cramping stomach lets me know that I need to get out of this den. I part the branches and look around carefully. I'm back in the forest, but I take great care. I know now that German forests are busy places, full of tree-fellers, charcoal-makers and children. I know how well trained German children are to report anything suspicious, so being spotted by a child would be fatal.

There is no one around, so I come out and quickly find a place to squat. Horrible cramps rack my body. I know I'm ill. I feel hot to the touch, but I shiver and ache with cold. My diet of raw vegetables, cattle water and dandelion leaves is doing me no good at all.

My left hand is still swollen and now an angry blue-black. To add insult to injury, three of my teeth have fallen out over the last two days and several feel loose and wobbly in my swollen gums. The thought that I might die alone, unknown, unmourned, somewhere in these woods, is worming its way into my mind. I try to keep it at bay. I try to think of home, of Anton, even of Sir Winston . . . but the black thoughts of curling up and waiting to die are lurking at the edges.

I look towards the golden rays of the sunset and try to find inspiration. Brussels is just over there . . . keep walking west. But I'm a child chasing the pot of gold at the end of the rainbow.

One step in front of the last. One step in front of the last.

Hours have passed. I have walked and walked into the dark gloom of the German countryside. I have to squat every half an hour or so to pass crampy trickles of fluid. I'm shivering and shaking. I need clean water, medicine, rest in a calm, clean bed and a bowl of hot vegetable soup.

Images of soup and my bed at home keep floating into my head. I wonder if I'm delirious. I stumble on. The North Star is always on my right. If I wasn't so tired and confused, I would be grateful that I've had such a run of clear nights.

I walk onwards. But soon I know it's no use. I'm not going to be able to walk any further tonight. I need to dig myself a hollow, find the strength to cover it with branches and I need to rest. I see a small huddle of trees ahead. Maybe I can find a place to lie down there.

As soon as I enter the woodland, I sense the danger. Although I'm hot and I'm ill, I can pick up something different. There is a heightened silence, no stirring of animals. I'm not alone; there are other people in this wood. I look around quickly, trying to decide where's best to hide. Just a few metres away is a thick tree trunk. I need to get behind it and work out what to do.

I step as quickly as I can towards the tree, hating the crack and snap of the tiniest branches beneath my feet. I feel for the trunk and edge behind it. As I round it,

I come face to face with a teenager: his white face is smeared with mud, there's a helmet on his head and he looks even more startled than me.

It takes me a moment to understand – the helmet, the camouflage on his face – he's a cadet! Maybe on training . . . the wood must be full of them . . . I'm in serious danger here.

It takes him a moment longer to work out what I am.

As I turn to run away, he screams: '*Achtung! Feind!*' Attention! Enemy!

And the wood seems to burst into life.

I don't pause to look back. I plunge forward. But now there are many, many people running after me. I only have moments. I'm small and very weak. This is a group of super-fit, super-strong German teenagers, kids who've been in Hitler Youth groups since they were toddlers. Kids who have guns and know how to use them, kids who are going to hunt me down and either kill me here in the woods or drag me to their superiors.

'*Da!*' '*Da ist sie!*' '*Fangt sie!*' they're shouting: *There! There she is!* and *Chase!* Urging each other on with yells and whoops.

I hurl myself through the trees. There's a wooden fence ahead . . . using the last of my strength, I vault over it, right hand only, my left still sore and useless at my side.

On the other side I lose my balance, fall over and roll down a steep embankment. I gasp with pain as I roll over my damaged left hand. The cadets are right behind, they're piling over the fence . . .

There's another sound, a low, clanking rumble. I recognize it, of course; it's a train approaching. I've rolled down an embankment towards a railway track. I look now and see the silver tracks, glinting in the moonlight, just twenty metres or so ahead.

Now the train is coming into view. Not fast – it's moving sedately as if preparing to come to a stop. But it's bearing down on us, huge and vast, billowing black steam. I race towards the tracks. If I'm quick enough, maybe I can put the moving train between me and my pursuers.

I slip and stumble over the rails and the sleepers, the metal beast looming towards me. I'm enveloped in the cloud of thick hot steam. I can't see if anyone has followed me over the tracks or not.

The train is slowing right down, but it hasn't stopped. I run beside it, desperate to try and make out what kind of train it is.

Cattle trucks, packed with people, headed for a camp? A soldier transport, rammed with Nazis who will shoot me dead in an instant?

Through the darkness and the billowing clouds, I think I can see metal-sided containers. I can also hear voices. A handful of the cadets are over the tracks, they are on my side of the train . . . searching in the steam for me.

Knowing it's my last hope, I slip between the moving metal wheels and feel desperately against the sides of the containers for a ladder. I know if these are coal wagons, there will be a ladder at the side. As soon as my hand touches the slim metal rail, I can feel the train start to pick up speed again.

The whistle sounds as I grab for the rail. I only have one hand I can use . . . I cling to the ladder and heave myself up. With huge effort, I wedge my left elbow over a rung so my body is held. Then I cast about with my foot for more rungs. For several wild seconds, I swing . . . the train getting faster, the burning pain of effort shooting through my arms and shoulders.

Then my foot finds the rung and I'm there, I can hold on . . . I can scramble up, one hand, two feet, and launch myself over the edge. I fall hard, deep down into the solid metal belly of an empty coal truck. For a moment, I lie there, a wounded, winded heap of bones at the bottom, inhaling coal dust, feeling nothing but pain and nausea. Then as the train gathers speed and I leave the cadets behind, for the first time in days, I feel the surge of hope welling up in me again.

I get to my feet and walk to the back of the truck. There, I crouch down in a corner so I am resting a little but not inhaling dust and able to watch the starry sky above me. My North Star stays to my right, this train is moving west. I am OK. I can stay on board.

I listen to the roar of the wheels on the rails as the metal beast picks up speed. The wind tears at my hair and my face, making tears rush from the corner of my eyes. But I am smiling, grinning . . . I even begin to laugh. I am travelling home at speed.

'*Ich muss nach Hause!*' I shout into the wind.

I don't know how long I've been travelling: maybe two or three hours, but there is still no sign of dawn when I suddenly realize that the star has moved. It is no longer on my right; it's now behind me. We've turned and the train is now rattling me south. I'm speeding in the wrong direction.

The realization is awful. How long have we been heading this way? Why did I not notice? Have I been asleep in the back of this truck? It feels as if I have to wait an age before the train slows. But as soon as it does, I climb the internal ladder, gripping tightly with my good hand, then swing my leg and find the footholds on the other side. As I begin to climb down, the train gives a deafening whistle and pulls to a stop. I can see a manned signal box ahead, so I rush down the ladder, drop onto the tracks and scramble out from between the wheels before I can be spotted.

Only when I am back in the safety of the embankment bushes do I realize there is wetness all over my face. I've split the skin on my cheek and it's bleeding freely. I lie down in the tangle of hedge and grass and try to rest for a moment.

The fright and stress of running from the cadets and riding the train has made me forget for a few hours how weak and ill I am. But now, lying here, I know I am in deep trouble. My left hand is completely numb. The rest of my body feels raging hot to touch, but I'm shivering with cold. For the first time since the Gestapo officers took hold of me at the bombed station, I realize that I can't survive on my own. All my strength, all my spirit and all my resistance are used up.

Somehow, here in enemy territory, I will have to try and find help or I am going to die.

Chapter Forty

I stagger to my feet and wipe the trickling blood from my face. I walk out of the bushes and towards the one thing I have avoided so far on my journey: a road.

But roads lead somewhere. Roads lead to towns, villages and people, and I need this road to lead to someone who will help me. I do not have the strength left to walk far.

Just as the sky begins to grey with the first light of the morning, I round the corner and see a small country village. It's as pretty as a village in a fairy-tale book with plaster and wood houses, a duck pond and a small stone church.

Maybe because I am feverish and growing delirious, I tell myself that this village looks peaceful and friendly. I walk slowly towards it and wonder which person I will meet first. How can I ask for help without landing myself back in the camp?

I pass two or three houses which still look asleep, although it is hard to tell with the blackout curtains tightly closed. I wonder if the bakery is open yet . . . and if I dare to step inside and try to speak to the baker. Then I pass in front of the gateway to the church, it's Catholic; and it's called St Agnes's just like the church in Brussels used by Group K.

I take this as a sign. This is where I have to go.

I know that the Nazis don't like Catholic priests. So maybe Catholic priests don't like the Nazis?

The gate makes a loud creak on its hinges when I push it open. The church looks closed up and silent. But tucked in behind it is the small house with arched windows where I'm certain the priest lives.

I'm not ready to knock on the door. It's still too early and I don't know yet if I dare. I see a bench tucked into a corner of the graveyard, close to a tall yew hedge, and I think it's safe to go and sit there for a few minutes.

I shiver and wait. Sometimes I close my eyes and doze for a few moments, then I wake with a start and shiver again. When the sunrise is well underway and the sounds of the village coming to life drift over the hedge, I decide to shuffle over to the door of the house. I stand there, looking at the peeling black paint, my hand raised to knock, and again I'm not sure. I could be surrendering my freedom. I could be back in custody within the hour. Everything I have fought so hard to win could be taken away from me.

I don't know what to do.

Then a fresh wave of dizzy nausea washes over me and I tap weakly at the door.

If I can't find help, I will be lost.

When I hear the sound of someone coming to the door, I am once again frightened and all set to run away. I'll pretend to be dumb, a mute, so they can't guess I'm not German . . . I'll say nothing – I'll just hope he can give me a morsel of food and let me be on my way . . .

A key turns in the lock, the door swings open and I am looking into the face of a man hardly any taller than me. An elderly man, with a ring of fluffy white hair which sticks up in a semi-circle around his otherwise bald head. He's already dressed in his black suit and shirt with the white collar insert at the neck.

The priest is not wearing glasses, so I can look straight into his face. Beyond the surprised and questioning look, I see kindness and compassion. I look into this man's eyes and I see a human being. A man who is moved by my plight. He extends his hand to me, and when I offer him mine, he takes hold of it with both hands to grasp it in a warm greeting.

'*Was ist los, mein Kind?*' he asks. What is it, my child?

'*Ich bin ein Einzelkind und ich muss nach Hause*,' I whisper.

He gestures for me to come inside and closes the door behind us.

'Pfarrer Becker,' he says and I think he is introducing himself.

I wonder what to call myself. I don't know if any of my names are safe any more.

'Elisabeth,' I say, deciding to name myself after my mother.

I follow him through the entrance hall into a small sitting room. There is a time when I would have found this room sparsely decorated with its white paint, faded green armchairs, desk, and wooden crucifix on the wall, but after months of imprisonment this looks like the most sumptuous comfort and so dazzlingly clean.

I'm painfully aware of how filthy, wretched and stinking I must be.

But Pfarrer Becker says kindly, '*Setzen Sie sich.*' He gestures towards an armchair and I sink gratefully down. He pulls a chair up opposite mine. '*Was ist passiert, Elisabeth, mein Kind?*' He looks at me with his kind eyes. I don't know what he has asked, but once again he is calling me 'my child', and as he waits for an answer with patience and understanding, I think I can risk telling him that I am not German.

'I am from Belgium,' I say. 'Brussels.' I point to my chest.

'Ah! *Nicht Deutsch?*' Not German.

I shake my head. How am I going to make myself understood? '*Arbeiten,*' I say, I'm not likely to forget the German for work. '*Arbeiten, arbeiten in einem . . .*' What did they call it? I strain to remember. '*Konzentrationslager?*'

Pfarrer Becker's face grows serious. '*Ein Konzentrationslager?*' he repeats and shakes his head. '*Ja. Ich habe davon gehört. Ganz schlimm. Ganz, ganz schlimm. Kriminell.*'

Something is bad, very bad . . . criminal, even.

'*Ich muss nach Hause.*' I repeat my phrase with determination; I need to show him I really mean it. '*Mama, Papa, ich muss nach Hause.*'

'*Wie alt?*' Pfarrer Becker asks me, and this time I understand because the officer asked it too. How old am I?

I hold up fingers to show one, then five.

He shakes his head once again and gives a deep sigh. Then he leans towards me and reaches for my face which he holds in his soft hands. He peers at the wound on my cheek, which I have forgotten about. Then he presses the back of his hand against my neck.

'*Heiss?*' he says. Hot. '*Wasser?*' he asks. Water.

I nod. He leaves the room and I slump back in the chair. I rest my head and let my eyes close. Although I still feel completely on guard, I think I can allow myself

302

to trust Pfarrer Becker. I think he will keep me safe, at least for the next few hours.

When he returns, he is holding a glass of water in one hand and in the other a small white plate. When I see a bread roll, a real wheaten bread roll spread with butter, and beside it a little piece of yellow cheese, I'm tearfully grateful.

'Thank you, you are a very kind man,' I tell him.

It doesn't take me long to eat my roll and cheese and gulp down my water.

'*Sie müssen schlafen,*' Pfarrer Becker tells me when I have finished. I think he means I need to sleep.

'*Ja,*' I agree. Just a few hours of rest, I could do that . . . somewhere comfortable and safe. By tonight I will be better and I'll be on my way again.

'*Kommen Sie bitte mit,*' he says, gesturing for me to follow him.

I wonder why he says *Kommen*, instead of barking *Komm* like the guards do, and I realize he is using the polite form, the way we would talk to strangers in French.

He walks up the little wooden staircase until we come to a door, which he pushes open. Beyond is a tiny bedroom, all white with a scrubbed wood floor. A single bed is made up with white sheets and a snowy eiderdown. On the wall is another crucifix. This room looks pristine and untouched. Not his room, but surely a spare for visitors.

'Oh . . . *danke,*' I say. Thank you. But I stand at the threshold, unwilling to enter such a perfectly clean haven while I'm so filthy.

'*Waschen?*' I ask, wondering if I have the right words for washing.

'*Natürlich.*'

He smiles and points to a bathroom on the landing. It is plain and white with a small bathtub. '*Wollen Sie baden?*' he asks and puts his hand on the bathtub to show me what he means. Do I want a bath?

'*Oh! Ja, bitte!*' I say. Yes, please! Even though I know I must go to sleep, I must rest and recover from whatever illness or poison is racking my system, the thought of being clean is too wonderful to resist.

'*Und dann schlafen . . .*' he says. Then sleep.

'*Schlafen . . .*' Sleep. I repeat the word and try to breathe my gratitude into it. 'Pfarrer Becker?' I stretch out my hand to him. He takes it and holds it with both of his. '*Danke,*' I say: thank you. '*Bitte, keine Polizei, keine Gestapo . . .*' Please. No police, no Gestapo.

I begin to cry, I wish I didn't, but I can't help myself. I'm so tired, I'm so desperate to rest, but I'm so afraid to lose my freedom.

'*Ich muss nach Hause,*' I repeat. I need to go home.

He nods solemnly: '*Keine Polizei,*' he repeats. Then with a smile he turns back down the stairs and I let myself into the bathroom.

I marvel at the steaming water running from the tap, as if I've never seen such a thing before. Above the sink, there is a mirror. Carefully, preparing myself for a shock, I look into it.

What I see makes me recoil in horror. A filthy, pinched face, smeared with dirt, coal dust and blood is peering back at me. I'm amazed now that Pfarrer Becker let me into his house. I look like a street beggar. My eyes are hollow and sunken just like all the other eyes that stared back at me in that terrible place.

My hair . . . oh, my tufty clumps of hair and the bald patches, they are shocking to see.

I open my mouth and stare at the ugly gaps where my teeth are missing and the oozing swollen gums where the others are loose. Not wanting to look any more, I take off my grey clothes, caked with dirt and lower my strange spindly body, marked with filth and scars, into the bath. The hot water washes over me, warming and comforting. Finally the deep aching chill in my bones is soothed.

I turn the tap on again, making the bath hotter and deeper. I hope Pfarrer Becker doesn't mind. But this is the first wash I've had since Belgium and I am going to revel in it.

Once I have soaked my body through, warmed it and turned my grey skin pink, I lie back and wet my hair, then my face, making the gash on my cheek burn. There is a bar of soap and a scrubbing brush, so I begin at my battered and blistered feet and work my way thoroughly up. When I finally get out of the bath, the water is dark brown and scummy. Although I'm exhausted now, I clean the empty bath as best I can.

In the bedroom, there is a simple nightshirt hanging behind the door, so I take it down and slip it over my clean body. Then I pull back the eiderdown and the crisp white sheet and get into bed.

I'm in a German bed, and I'm still on the run, but somehow I have to let down my defences and take the huge risk of going to sleep.

Chapter Forty-One

The fever takes hold of me. Intense heat and pain rack my body; my mind whirls with confusion. I'm tossed and turned on a nightmarish sea. When I dream in incredible detail that I'm waking up in the camp and my escape was just imagined, tears of horror stream down my face.

Then I'm at home, in my bedroom – Mama has redecorated in pure white while I was away.

Then Anton is here. He really is. He kneels beside my bed and puts cool hands, cool cloths onto my head, my neck, my wrists and my ankles.

'Shhhhh,' he soothes me. 'It's OK, Nico, I'm going to look after you now.' He spoons cool water into my mouth.

I cling onto his arm as he leans over me, putting another cool cloth onto my head.

'What's happened to your wrist?' he asks. He takes hold of my left hand and the stabbing pain pushes me back into darkness.

The Nazis are pursuing me right into my dreams, chasing me in my sleep, trying to rob me of my secrets even when I'm not awake to defend myself.

'Hope!'

Have I called for her out loud? I'm tossing and turning, burning with heat and pain. I do not know if my secrets are safe any more.

'Help!' I call out. 'I need to go home. Help me!'

Another cool cloth is laid over my burning face. 'Shhhhh.'

'Anton, are you there? Is it you?'

My eyes open. It's daylight, and for a long time I look at the bright white wall in front of me, decorated only with a crucifix.

I wonder if I'm in hospital . . . then I wonder if I'm dead and this is some sort of waiting room for Heaven. I look around and can remember nothing about this place. There are no clues. It is completely white with only this little bed, the crucifix and an empty wooden chair.

I raise my hand in front of my face and try to read some clues from it. It looks clean, but still dirty under the jagged nails. My other hand is still under the white covers and I struggle to bring it out.

As soon as I set eyes on it, the bruised and swollen fingers sticking out from a tight new bandage, I remember everything. I am in Pfarrer Becker's house. But how long have I been here? Sunlight is filtering in through the filmy curtains. I arrived here in the morning . . . is it later the same day? Or is it already the next day?

I wriggle up into a sitting position. I need to move on. I'm still on the run. I'm still trying to escape.

I push back the cover, step out of the bed and immediately collapse in a heap onto the floor. What's the matter with me? My legs feel wobbly and useless. I try to pick myself up and find I haven't the strength. The door opens and Pfarrer Becker rushes over to help me to my feet.

'*Sie müssen im Bett bleiben.*'

I think he's telling me to stay in bed.

'*Sie haben Fieber und ihren*' – he points to my wrist – '*Handgelenk gebrochen. Es ist wirklich schlimm. Sie müssen im Bett bleiben.*'

Fever and something about my wrist . . . could I have broken it? I climb back into bed obediently, but still I tell him that I want to go home, I need to go home to Belgium.

He nods his head and looks at me with total understanding.

'*In zwei Tagen wird das Rote Kreuz einen Lastwagen nach Belgien schicken.*'

I don't make out much of this.

'*Zwei Tagen*,' he says, holding out two fingers. '*Lastwagen nach Belgien*.'

He goes over to the crucifix and points. '*Rot*,' he says. '*Rot*.'

And suddenly I understand: he's pointing at the cross and saying 'red'. The Red Cross has a truck going to Belgium in two days.

'*Ich?*' Me, I say, pointing to myself. '*Ich in Lastwagen?*' Me in the lorry?

His face splits into a grin and he nods.

'*Keine Papiere*,' I say: no papers. I want to make it clear I can't just ride in the front of a lorry; I'm an escaped prisoner.

'*Versteckt?*' he says, and covers his head with his arms to demonstrate 'hidden' for me.

'*Ja, versteckt*,' I repeat.

'*Essen!*' he declares. Eat! And he hurries out of the room.

I lie in the peaceful whiteness and try to imagine going home. There are still untold hurdles. Can I hide in a lorry all the way to Belgium? Can I cross the border? What will happen then? I'll still be a long way from Brussels with no papers and no money. Even if I make it to Brussels, can I go home? Am I still unsuspected? Safe behind my false name? Or would I land my family in deadly trouble?

But home . . .

It already feels closer than ever. Close enough to be possible.

'Anton?' I whisper, as if he might be hiding somewhere in this room. Of course, it must have been Pfarrer Becker putting cold cloths onto me as I burned with fever, but Anton felt so real and so close.

There's no reply. Instead, Pfarrer Becker comes into the room with a bowl of barley and vegetable soup so good I can't speak at all as I eat my way through it.

'*Sehr gut,*' he says with satisfaction as he takes the empty bowl away from me.

'*Danke. Danke für alles,*' I tell him. Thank you for everything.

'*Wir helfen viele: Soldaten, Gefangenen, den Hilflosen.*'

I shake my head; I understand very little of what he's just said.

'*Latinum?*' he asks.

I nod. And we realize we can perhaps communicate in the oldest European language: Latin.

He comes and sits on the edge of my bed, takes my right, unbandaged hand in his and looks deep into my eyes.

Once again I'm struck by his overwhelming kindness. Love just seems to radiate from him. I realize once again why I can trust him, because I can tell he is a truly good person.

'*Esurivi enim et dedistis mihi manducare. Sitivi et dedistis mihi bibere. Hospes eram et collexistis me,*' he says gently.

I recognize it. It's from the New Testament, Matthew: *For I was hungry and you gave me something to eat. I was thirsty and you gave me something to drink. I was a stranger and you invited me in.*

I nod. I was a stranger and Pfarrer Becker did invite me in and I will always be truly grateful.

So I reply as best I can: '*Quamdiu fecistis uni de his fratribus meis minimis mihi fecistis.*' Whatever you do for the least of my brothers, you do for me.

Chapter Forty-Two

I will never, ever forget Pfarrer Becker of St Agnes. One day, when the war is over, I will come back to his village and thank him all over again.

I'll bring him a basket of fruit and vegetables and a selection of Belgian cheeses and beautiful loaves of real bread, to thank him for opening his door to an escaped prisoner. For sharing his little allowance of food, for the use of his bathtub and his spare room and, of course, to thank him for handing me over to the two Red Cross drivers who have hidden me in a cardboard box in the back of their truck which is now heading for Belgium.

We will drive all day long and cross the border near the German town of Aachen.

It's a big box and I am quite comfortable in it at first, but then sitting in the same position for hours becomes more difficult. But I tell myself that every cramped kilometre I travel is bringing me closer to home. In just two days, I've recovered much of my strength and all of my determination.

I'm certain I'm going to get home now. I'm not going to let anything or anyone stop me.

After a short sleep, I'm suddenly jolted awake by the loud bang of the driver, then passenger doors slamming shut. The truck has stopped. I sit in the blackness of the box and wait, straining my ears, hardly daring to breathe.

'Good afternoon, papers please.'

We are at a checkpoint. My heart racing with excitement, I realize that the guard has spoken in French. Surely we must be at the border? If everything goes smoothly, I will be in Belgium within minutes.

If everything goes smoothly . . . I hug my arms around my knees and breathe as quietly as I dare.

'We're heading for Liège,' the Red Cross driver explains, 'with medicine, bandages and supplies.'

'And you have the package for us?' the guard asks in a much lower voice.

'Yes, we have the package.'

I hear the back doors of the truck opening up. Then comes the sound of boxes being moved and lifted. With a growing sense of panic, I curl up and keep my breathing as quiet as I can.

A package? What package would the Red Cross have for the border guards? And why have I not been told?

Shouldn't they have warned me about this? I didn't want Pfarrer Becker to even tell the drivers about me; I just wanted to be delivered to the Red Cross depot like a parcel. But he insisted that a person couldn't travel in a truck without the drivers being informed. He promised I didn't need to worry.

They are moving the boxes right beside mine now and I can feel sweat begin to trickle down my sides.

'There, that's it, the big one in the corner.' It's the driver's voice.

Now, to my horror, my box begins to move. I'm shuffled towards the doors, then my box is lifted up and placed with a bump on the ground.

'Careful,' the driver warns.

'Don't worry, we know what to do,' replies a voice that must belong to one of the guards.

My stomach clenches with dread. They know . . . they know I'm in here. I ball up my fists and curse myself for being so trusting and naïve. I'm being handed over to collabos, to guards who may speak French but who still work for the Nazis. How could I be so stupid! I know I'm a wanted person! I know Richter is after me. I was sentenced to die for my part in the station bombing and I escaped from a concentration camp. I am wanted. I'm on the run. How could I be so stupid!

I don't know what to do. I don't know whether to sit

still or try to break out. Should I try to talk them out of this handover? I don't know what to do.

The box is lifted up and carried.

Two men are involved; I can hear one on either side of me.

'Gently,' one warns.

I'm carried for a little distance, then tipped up as I'm taken down a flight of stairs. With every step I want to shout out: leave me alone! Let me go! I've been through enough!

I'm set down on the ground.

'I need to go back up there,' one of the voices says.

'OK, I won't be long.'

I hear the turn of keys in a lock. One of the men is still in this room with me. He is approaching the box. I am about to be discovered.

Chapter Forty-Three

I ball my hand into a fist. If I hit him square in the face, maybe that will give me enough time to get out of here.

The cardboard flap lifts and a face peers down at me: a young man wearing the cap of the border police.

I launch my fist at him with all my might. He jerks his head out of the way and I just manage a glancing blow on his jaw that makes his teeth snap shut.

'What are you doing?' he hisses. 'I'm on your side.'

He makes the mistake of leaning back into the box. I let fly at him again and this time connect with his cheekbone and eye socket.

'Owww!' he says, staggering back.

I jump out of the box and run for the door. The key is dangling in the lock, but before I can get to it strong hands grab hold of my arms.

'Stop right there.' The guard is behind me.

I kick back hard, making contact with his shins. I've come all this way; I have no intention of being handed back to the Nazis now.

'Ow! Please stop, you little idiot. *I'm on your side!*' He gives me a shake, as if he's trying to bring me to my senses. 'You can't go out there. Only two of us are Resisters – the rest of them are collabos and Nazis.'

'How do I know I can trust you?' I ask desperately.

'Because your friends in the Red Cross have given you to me,' the man replies. 'They know I'm a border guard by day, but a Resistance worker by night.'

He's still got a tight hold of me and I'm considering launching another kick. I believe nothing and I trust no one.

'Why should I believe you?' I ask.

'My friend, drawings of you are on posters all over Belgium. If I was a collabo, I would have claimed my handsome reward by phoning for Richter himself to unload you from the van. Welcome home, Coco.'

Coco.

It's at once strange and yet a huge relief to be called by that name again. I finally think I can believe him.

He lets go of me and I turn to take a proper look at him. He's broad and muscular with a lively face: amused brown eyes, dark hair, dark eyebrows and a mouth on the verge of a grin. Oh, and there's a big red mark where I've punched him.

He extends his hand: 'It's an honour to meet you.'

'I don't know about that . . .' I say, but I hold out my hand to shake his.

'Jacques Janssens at your service. The drivers were the ones who thought it must be you. You don't look anything like the girl on the posters, by the way. Are you sure you're Coco?'

'The hairdressers at the work camp . . .' I touch my head.

'Obviously know nothing about the latest styles,' Jacques says.

And for the first time in weeks, maybe even months, I begin to laugh. It's just such an overwhelming relief to be here, to be back in Belgium with a fellow Resister who's going to help me. I can hardly believe it.

'Shhhh!' he urges, but he's laughing too: playful, boyish laughter that reminds me painfully of Anton. 'There are other guards upstairs. I have to go back up.'

'I'm here!' I whisper. 'I'm really in Belgium . . . you can't know how amazing this is!'

'Welcome home, comrade,' he says, and to my surprise he takes hold of my shoulders and gives me a quick kiss on each cheek. This convinces me more than anything he's said that Jacques is on my side.

I'm startled by the unexpected feel of stubble against my skin, the warm grip on my shoulders. Anton . . . I want to be held and kissed by you.

'Thanks . . .' I manage. 'So what happens now?'

I'm desperate to be home. I feel as if I could run straight to Brussels without pausing for breath. Mama, Grand-Mamie, Papa . . . I long to see them.

'You stay here in the basement until tonight, when Fabian and I will help you organize safe passage to Brussels. I'll try to bring you some food and water. But you must wait now and be very, very quiet.'

Chapter Forty-Four

Much later, Jacques comes down to the cellar to tell me it's safe to come up. I follow him up two flights of stairs to a cramped sitting room where I meet Fabian: younger and perhaps a little more serious than Jacques.

The windows are blacked out, and as Fabian stands guard beside the closed and locked door, Jacques goes round the room – behind books, inside a trunk, under chair cushions – until he has several pieces of a simple radio set in his hands. He quickly assembles the set and puts it onto the little table.

As they usher me into a chair in front of the radio, I try to be calm. I can't believe I'm here, in Belgium, out of Germany, away from the camp. But I'm still wanted, still in an occupied country, and it's too early to let go of the feeling that I'm going to be caught.

Also . . . I look at the radio dial and realize, desperate

as I am to speak to Group K after all this time, that I'm frightened to learn the truth.

What if there is no one left?

Fabian passes me an ersatz coffee and says he'll go downstairs as lookout: 'Radio detector cars everywhere . . . we have to be very careful.'

'We're only a small group,' I tell Jacques. 'I don't know if anyone will be on air.'

'It's a good time to try.' He glances at his watch. 'The BBC broadcast finished five minutes ago, so the airwaves will be pulsing with Resistance chit-chat. Just be very careful. Use your codes for everything important.'

'Do you have some paper and a pencil?'

Once I have them, I think back to the simple code, inspired by Shakespeare's *Henry V*. If I say 'princes' to whoever answers, the next word in the play begins with 't', so they'll know my code alphabet will start with 't' for 'a', 'u' for 'b' and so on. I write the two alphabets out on the sheet of paper.

'Just make sure you rip that into very small pieces afterwards . . . or eat it,' Jacques says with a smile.

I smile back, but I'm sick with nerves. I put the headphones over my ears and start to tune the dial to the Group K frequency; gently, gently, millimetre by millimetre, until I think I've found the channel. I've remembered the code-words of greeting – but what I can't know is if there is going to be anyone left at the church to hear me.

Crackling, whistling sounds fill my ears: radio waves
. . . radio silence . . .

'Hello? Hello?' I say uncertainly. I'm speaking into a
void. Nothing but crackling and whistling comes back.
'Hello . . . any news from the henhouse?' I ask.

I feel incredibly silly saying this, but dear old
Monsieur Durance wanted us to have some humour in
our lives when everything around us was so life-or-death
serious. I catch Jacques' eye and he smiles and nods at me
encouragingly.

Still nothing but crackles, whistles and strange radio
noises coming back.

'Hello, my friends . . . can you hear me? Is there any
news from the henhouse?'

There is just radio noise. I wait several minutes, then
I repeat the question.

Nothing.

'Maybe they're not switched on tonight . . .' I say to
Jacques. But my heart is heavy. Maybe they're all dead.

'Try a little longer,' he encourages me.

'Hello, any news from the henhouse?'

There's a long pause, then I think I hear just the
faintest of whispers . . . just a single word, barely audible,
but it makes me tingle with recognition:

'*Hello.*'

'Any news from the henhouse?' I shout down the
line.

The whisper comes back, a little stronger now: 'The chickens are laying.'

Oh! The chickens are laying. It's the right words, it's the right voice . . . 'Is it you?!' I cry, my voice cracking at the sound of hers. I can hardly believe it's Hope. The last time I saw her there was hardly any hope for either of us.

'Who is this?' she asks, 'Do I know you?'

'It's . . .' Then I remember about the code. 'Start from "princes". It's me: V-h-v-h,' I spell for her.

I can hear nothing but the whistling noise now. Maybe the connection has gone . . . but then at last she says: 'No. It's not possible.'

'*Yes!* It's possible! It's me. I've come back, I'm near—' Jacques treats me to a sharp dig in the ribs. Obviously I must not mention our location, in case we're overheard.

'Can it be true?' Hope's voice still sounds faint and disbelieving, then cautiously she asks: 'What was the Owl's favourite colour?'

Almost laughing, I remember the answer: 'Romeo and Juliet.'

There is a pause, then Hope asks: 'What was La Belle wearing the first night you came to us?'

Oh no, I can't remember this. I grope back in my mind, all the way back to that first night in the crypt, a lifetime ago. When we were all together and full of courage. Now I'm so much older and broken in ways I will never be able to explain to anyone.

'A rose,' I say, as the memory of La Belle's outfit comes flooding back. 'She was wearing a pink rose on her little hat.'

'Oh, is it really you?!'

'Yes, it's me! I'm so glad to hear you.'

And then, whatever has been interfering with our transmission clears and I can hear Hope's beautiful voice as clearly as if she were standing next to me.

'You've come back,' she says. 'Oh, my darling, you've made it back.'

'Yes. How are you? Are you really OK?'

'Yes. I'm OK.'

'And . . . the children?' I ask first, although I am now desperate to rush through the names, to hear how everyone is and to find out about Anton. Finally, I am going to learn and I don't know if I can bear to know.

'Oh . . .' She gulps, holding back her sobs, and my stomach tightens. 'He has the children. K–b–v–a–m–x–k.' Using my paper, I translate. Richter.

'He has them?' I repeat, horrified.

'But they will be returned to me soon, if my innocence is "maintained".'

I wonder why she is manning the radio, if all she holds dear in life is at stake? But of course I know why, because this is the most important fight and she does it for her children.

'What about K-t-o-x-g?' I ask, my voice small and frightened now. Raven.

'He's OK. He wasn't held.'

I have to rush on, I have to ask: 'And I-e-n-f?' Plum, I mean Padrice. I ask about him first, because I have to work up to asking about Anton, find my courage. My voice sounds wobbly and a little wild.

'He's fine. He's still with the group.'

My heart lifts: Hope is there, Raven and Padrice too; there's still a group. Maybe everything is going to be OK.

'And the H-p-e?' I'm asking after the Owl. Richter told us he was dead, but maybe, maybe there is just the smallest chance that this was a lie.

'His body was returned and we buried him,' Hope replies. 'A-t-p-d escaped. He is still working with us.' I scribble out the letters, H-a-w-k, and understand.

Then there's a pause. I listen to the crackling, like a small wind howling down the line. And I know. If there was good news, she would tell me. She would rush to tell me. So the news is not good.

But still I have to ask, my voice shaking: 'And my boy?'

I close my eyes. I don't want to hear . . . I have let myself believe all this time that I will see him again, that I must see him again.

'Sent to a camp in Germany. I am so sorry.'

A sob bursts out of me.

No. Not to a camp.

Not to a camp. Not Anton. Please, not Anton.

I sob down the line. I can't help it. I want Anton. I've made it back all this way. I've fought for survival, I've somehow managed to endure so that I can be with my family and be with him.

But he's been sent to a camp. I'm too late.

'I'm so sorry, my darling. I'm so very sorry.' She pauses, then adds, 'We were betrayed. They knew about you and the boy. They knew about the plane.'

'Who?' The word bursts from me with a terrible anger.

'You mustn't blame him. He thought it was for the best. He thought he was making a deal to save you all.'

'Who?' My mind is racing, trying to fill in this missing piece of the puzzle. Who would do this to us? Who would cause Monsieur Durance to be killed? Have Anton and me sent to the camps?

'It was your boy's brother.'

Henri! Henri betrayed us?

I can't believe it. For several moments I'm too overcome. 'But why?' I manage finally.

'They must have suspected your boy, then they went to his brother in the camp and offered him a deal for more information.'

'How could he?!' My hands ball into fists and I'm helpless with grief and fury.

'Maybe they told him his brother would be killed if he didn't agree. Don't be angry with him. He's dead now.'

'Dead?' Henri is dead, even though he betrayed us?

'He was hanged.'

I groan with sorrow and lay my head on my hands. I find myself thinking of Madame Morel; her two beautiful boys, both gone. I can feel Jacques's hand on my back, as he tries to comfort me.

Hope's voice is gentle in my ears. 'Where are you, darling? How can I help you?'

My eyes full of tears, I turn to Jacques. 'Where am I?' I ask.

He scribbles the name of this little village down on a piece of paper and says: 'In code, only in code.'

I spell out the name of the village in letters.

'I'll send A-t-p-d to come and get you,' Hope says, spelling out the Hawk's name. 'He'll need to sort out papers. It will take a little time, so please, stay safe until he comes.'

Jacques and Fabian are very kind. They share their casserole supper with me; Jacques even sits beside me, cradles my head and spoons some of the food into my mouth when I say I can't eat any more.

'You need to get your strength back,' he encourages me, 'and it'll make your hair grow.'

I try to smile.

'We pretend to be collabos because the food is so much better,' Fabian jokes.

'After supper, I'm going to polish your shoes,' Jacques says. 'Look at them – they've carried you halfway across Germany, they deserve some respect.'

I glance at my battered brown brogues. They're filthy and hard with mud, but still amazingly intact, although the soles feel paper-thin. Again, I try to smile, to repay their kindness and hospitality. But my heart is breaking; the news about Anton is endlessly painful and I just want to lie down, abandon myself to tears and hope that in my dreams I will be able to see him again.

'Some people return from the camps,' Jacques reminds me. '*You* returned from the camps.'

I just shake my head and cry harder. I know how very, very lucky I've been. I know how impossible it is to escape. In a men's camp, life is probably even harsher, and I can't bear to think about Anton there. I don't want to, but I keep seeing him grey, exhausted, haggard, with a hollow, hopeless look in his eyes.

All night long on my makeshift bed back down in the cellar, I cry or doze, trying to find Anton in my dreams, but there are only guards and officers with guns and whips, determined to hunt me down.

Early in the morning, Jacques brings me hot milk and two slices of bread. He sits beside me to make sure I finish them both.

'In the village, there's a bakery and the baker is a friend of ours. One of *us*,' he says significantly. 'You might need to know that later.' He seems pale and a little nervous, twitchy even.

'What's up?' I ask.

'I can't tell you,' he says, his dark eyes meeting mine. 'You've picked a strange day to arrive, comrade Coco. We have plans, something we've been preparing for weeks, but I really can't tell you. I need to keep you safe.'

'From what?'

'Look, you can't ask, you know how it is,' he insists. 'I don't want to lock you into this room, because I might not be able to let you out, but' – he takes a key from his pocket – 'will you lock yourself in? And will you promise me that whatever happens, whatever you hear, you won't come out until you're sure it's safe?'

I stare at him with wide eyes. I'm trying to respect his need for secrecy, but this is a lot to ask. He wants me to stay locked away, no matter what?

'But can't I help?' I blurt out. 'I've been useful before. I've been a lookout, a courier, I've detonated bombs – and I've even learned to shoot.'

This last part is stretching the truth. Anton – the memory surfaces, so sharp it has jagged edges: in

330

the woods when he tried to teach me how to use the German soldier's handgun. He fell about with laughter when I accidentally killed the pigeon. He had giggling, musical, unquenchable laughter. And it was always so unexpected, bursting from such a serious boy. There won't be any laughter where he is now, I think grimly.

'You detonated a bomb? What kind of detonator did you use?' Jacques asks.

'Pencil detonators from Britain.' I trust him enough to tell him. 'You crush the end, release liquid from one chamber into another, and it sets off a chemical reaction . . .'

'We're going to have to use bullets to detonate ours.'

'That should work. If you're a good shot.'

'You need to stay here,' Jacques says firmly. He takes my plate and my cup, then hands me the key. 'Please lock yourself in and stay hidden.'

We look at one another. 'Please let me help you?' I ask once more.

'No. You need to stay here, out of the way. If none of us makes it, you need to go to the baker and tell everyone in the village to flee. There will be reprisals. The Nazis will kill four or five villagers for every one of their men that dies.'

I swallow. 'OK.' I hold out my hand for him to shake. 'Good luck, Jacques.'

He takes it and gives it a long, double-handed grip.

He looks into my eyes sincerely. 'Thanks,' he says, 'we'll need it.'

I suddenly feel very sorry that I may never have the chance to get to know Jacques better. 'Thanks for polishing my shoes,' I tell him, because I want to lighten the moment, give him courage and hope for what lies ahead.

'No problem, next time you're passing I'll be happy to clean them again.' He smiles.

Now it's my turn to take hold of his shoulders and kiss him on each cheek. 'Be brave.'

An unfamiliar voice calls out: '*Janssens?* Are you in the cellar?'

'Just coming,' he replies. He darts out of the door, gesturing for me to lock it behind him.

I turn the key and look around my little prison. This cellar storeroom is small and dark, but some light comes in from a perforated metal grille at the top of one of the walls. If I climb up to it, I can maybe unscrew it and watch what is going on outside.

As quietly as I can, I move several boxes marked 'tinned tomatoes' over to the wall underneath the grille. Then I step up. When my face is against the grille, I am eye level with the road at the front of the checkpoint. I can see the boots of the border guards as they man their checkpoint stations, watching the road beyond.

The grille is tightly screwed on. But with the help of

the door key, I begin to work away at one of the screws. It's slow work, but I finally loosen two enough so that they fall out into my hand; then the grille slips away, leaving a much bigger slot for my curious eyes.

I watch only the occasional vehicle arrive and depart; this seems to be a quiet checkpoint on a not very busy route. Black leather boots walk forward and return to the post. But I sense the growing nervousness. The pair of boots I can see best are tapping at the ground restlessly. Something is about to happen.

Fat black tyres move slowly towards the checkpoint, the impatient tapping stops and instead, the boots walk towards the vehicle.

I can hear faint laughter and talk. Car doors open and close. More boots – highly polished, fine and black – have joined the scene.

'Is that real coffee?' I hear someone ask.

'But of course, we've been saving it for your visit, sir.' I'm sure this is Jacques replying.

'Bring us all a cup.'

Another car door opens and closes. Another set of feet joins the throng. There is something different about the way these feet work. The boots are black and polished just like the others, but one of the feet is slow, heavy, dragging . . .

The boot turns and I see the elaborate metal spurs of a former cavalry officer . . . one with a wooden leg.

Chapter Forty-Five

I should be looking around this tiny cellar for somewhere to hide. I should be jamming heavy objects against the door and wedging the key tightly in the lock so that no one can force it out and open the door from the outside.

I should be doing everything I can to barricade myself against my enemy, but instead, my eyes are glued to the boots. I can't stop staring at them and I'm straining to hear his voice, to make sure I have identified him correctly.

No one has betrayed me, I'm sure. This is a planned Resistance attack on Richter and his men. Planned for weeks, and by some stroke of fate I'm locked up in a cellar beneath it.

The boots are all standing in a circle now, but still I see the pair, dusted with earth from the road, tapping, restlessly tapping.

Something is about to kick off.

'So you've not uncovered anything interesting for us in months. What's going on over here? You've not turned traitor on us, have you?'

The words sail over clearly. He's pretending to joke, but really he's sneering. It's the thing he does best. Always mocking people, always making fun, always lording it over them, making clear he's the boss, the one with the ultimate power.

Richter.

My fists are clenching and unclenching. I'm burning to do something, desperate to know what's going to happen now.

Then all of a sudden, as they stand chatting, sipping at their cups of coffee, the gunfire begins. It's as shockingly loud as it is unexpected. It seems to come from all directions. Shots ring out; shells bounce ferociously to the ground. I pull back from the grille, worried I'm going to be hit.

But I still try to look out, jaw clenched, nerves racked.

There are cries of surprise, cries of pain. A body crumples to the ground. Now there's machine-gun fire in return. Richter's soldiers are fighting back. Shouts, screams . . . a heavy car door slams shut. Has Richter got into the car? Is he about to be driven away from this scene? Is he about to escape?

My blood boils at the thought. I won't let it happen. He can't get away.

Another body falls, landing not more than a metre from my grille. I see Fabian's face, splattered with blood, and I can't wait down here any longer. I rush towards the door, picking up whatever solid, heavy objects I can on the way. I race up the stairs towards the gunfight. Approaching the open front door of the checkpoint office, I try to work out what I can do to help. There's a soldier only four metres or so away from the open door, aiming his gun at someone I can't see. I lob one of the cans in my hand at his head. Momentarily distracted, he's shot and falls to the ground.

I crouch down in the doorway; I have two cans left, so I choose my targets carefully and fire. The second can earns me a bullet in return, which misses my head and slams into the wall.

The Gestapo men surround the car now, firing in all directions, protecting Richter who's in the back. There's a driver at the wheel and Richter is shouting at him. Maybe urging him to drive off . . . maybe I have only moments to stop them.

I look desperately around, wondering what I can use, and then I see the handgun. The soldier who has fallen in front of me must have dropped it as it's lying close to his hand.

If I can just dart out . . .

I don't think about it, I just go: out, lunge for the gun, spin round, rush back to the doorway; my fingers now bleeding where they have been grazed by a bullet.

But I have it in my hands: the gun — a big, clunky army pistol, not unlike the one Anton used to teach me . . .

A blaze of fury rushes over me. This is no time to be careful. This is time to take revenge. I'm going to stop Richter. For Anton, for Hope's screaming son, for my papa, for La Belle, for Monsieur Durance. I raise the pistol, cock it and from the doorway I try to fire straight at Richter. The car window shatters into smithereens, but I see him cower and carry on shouting. I've missed my target.

I duck back into the doorway as one of the Gestapo officers marches straight towards me, machine gun at the ready. Jacques breaks cover, runs across the road, takes down the officer heading for me and fires several times at the tall grain silo behind Richter's car. The bullets bounce off the brick walls.

Then a burst of machine-gun fire brings Jacques down.

'*NO!*' I roar.

The engine revs and the car is about to drive off, carrying my enemy away. The two remaining guards jump on board, one on either side of him.

'RICHTER!' I scream, and step out of my doorway into plain view.

All four men in the car swivel their heads towards me. Richter looks at me and I look right back at him. I hope that's recognition across his face. I want him to know it's me.

'I'm codename Coco,' I scream. 'I'm here to kill you!'

The guards dive across him and a burst of machine-gun fire stutters out. But this time I don't aim for Richter's head, because Monsieur Durance's words flash into my mind: '*We are fighting men without mercy, men without any human feeling. To fight them, you'll have to become like them . . .*'

So I look down the barrel of the gun, the way my love taught me to do. I know this could kill every one of us: me, Richter, Jacques, all the men around us – Nazis and Resisters – but that can't distract me from my mission now. I'm ready to die and I'm ready to kill, so long as I take Richter with me.

I look down the barrel of the gun: straight down the barrel but keeping it low. Then I fire over and over again at the small window in the grain silo.

I know what Jacques was trying to do. He didn't have a detonator for his bomb, so he was trying to use bullets.

The third shot rings true and the silo bursts inside out. Once again, just like at the station, I am running in the air, swimming through boiling waves, deafened by blasting sound. Behind me there is just a ball of heat and flame.

Richter, his car and his guards are swallowed up in the inferno.

Chapter Forty-Six

I run and run. I keep on running. As soon as I get to the village, I run straight towards the bakery. It's still early in the day and the shop is crowded with women on their daily hunt for food.

I rush in and realize I must look and sound like a lunatic, but I need everyone to know the terrible news.

'The Resistance!' I shout, gasping for breath. 'They've killed six or seven Gestapo men – including the Kriminaldirektor – down at the checkpoint. Everyone has to leave. Get out! Hide, as quickly as you can. Reinforcements will be here within the hour. They'll want reprisals. They'll take revenge on you all.'

At first no one reacts. Maybe no one can believe me. But then the baker comes to my aid.

'She's right,' he insists. 'If Gestapo have been killed

down there, others will come to the village for revenge. We need to leave.'

This provokes a reaction. Cries of horror greet the news; cries of shock. Some of the women begin to weep and wail.

'Just leave now,' the baker urges them. 'Take the bread, take whatever's here. You can pay me later. Just leave, find your children. Get out of the village, hide in the woods. You know it's true. You know they'll kill eight, ten Belgians for every German who's dead.'

Within minutes, the shop is empty but I am still standing there, not sure what to do. The baker's staring at me. I'll have to get used to people staring at me. With my cropped head, missing teeth, skeletal frame and pinched face, no doubt now covered in blood and dirt and whatever else, I'm a harbinger of doom. Plus, I see I'm still clutching my clunky army pistol.

'Jacques? Fabian?' he asks frantically. 'The others? Do you know what's happened to them?'

'I don't know. We have to go back and help them, but I had to warn everyone first.'

He nods. He strips off his white apron and from a shelf pulls down what looks like a battered old doctor's bag. I hope it's the first-aid supplies Jacques and the others will need . . . if somehow they're still alive.

'You're the wanted girl, aren't you?' he asks. 'I was

supposed to come and find you in the cellar when it was over.'

I nod.

'We need to go back,' I insist. 'There are injured men. They need help.'

'Not you,' he says. 'You have to hide. I have instructions – someone is coming to collect you and they've been told where you will be. So follow me now. Then I'll go back and see if I can help anyone.'

We hurry down the stairs to another cellar, this one much smaller and darker than the last. The baker brings out a gun from its hiding place and tells me: 'Sorry, I'm going to take this one.'

'Don't worry – you'll need it.'

Again I'm given a key and told to lock the door from the inside. I'm shown how to place the cupboard in front of the door; shown where the bottles of water and dried fruit are kept, the toilet bucket.

'This is your hiding place. Please, share it with me when you come back,' I tell the baker. 'I don't want to deprive you.'

The baker shakes his head. 'I'll go to my mother's after I've been to the checkpoint. She'll need help to hide. No one is too old for a Nazi reprisal.'

We wish each other good luck and then he's gone. I lock the door, slip the key into the deep bread pocket of my camp-made trousers, then I begin to wrestle the heavy oak cupboard in front of the door. When the job is done, I find some sacking and try to make myself comfortable in the darkness.

I don't know how long I wait for. I try to guess what's going on in the village above my head. At first there's the noise of vehicles – people leaving, I think . . . then for an hour or so, quiet. Eerie quiet.

When they come, there's no mistaking the German vehicles. Roaring army trucks, blasts of gunfire, and when no one can be found because everyone has already left, the ominous smoke and crackle of fires. Through the small grille of this cellar, I see several houses ablaze. But maybe because the weather is cold and damp, the fires extinguish and do not spread.

I don't feel any fear as I wait in the cellar. At last, I know that I must accept my fate. I think about all the people I know who have already been lost. I wonder if Jacques and Fabian died today. In fact, it is almost strange that I am not one of the dead. I have been too lucky for too long.

But I've killed Kriminaldirektor Johann Richter. This is the most important thing. This is perhaps the task I was set upon the earth to do. Without Richter, the hunt for me will be over because no one else will care so much. Surely Hope will get her children back now. Maybe even Anton will somehow be allowed home?

So I sit in the cellar, in the dark, listening to the Nazis

unleash frustrated chaos on the village above, furious that someone has raised the alarm and everyone has fled.

After hours of shouting, firing and destruction, the vehicles finally leave. In the exhausted quiet they leave behind, I lean against the sacking and finally manage to fall into a half-hearted sleep.

My last waking thought, as it will be for a very, very long time, is of Anton. Tonight, I choose the memory of rushing upstairs to find him after I thought he'd been captured. I run into his room and throw myself on top of him. My cheek is against his scratchy woollen jumper, his heavy arms hug around my back.

I revel in the memory. I relive every beautiful detail of it, even as it makes tears slide noiselessly down my face. Is there any hope that I will be with him again?

It's pitch-black when I'm woken from troubled dreams. I'm sure I've heard something. I listen in the blackness, trying to remember where I am when the sound comes again: *tap-tap*, *tap-tap*, *tap-tap*, *tap-tap*, *tap-tap*.

The smell of sacking beside my head panics me. For a moment, I think I'm in the shed, waiting for the guard dog to find me with my mushrooms and potatoes on that first night of freedom.

Tap-tap, tap-tap, tap-tap, tap-tap, tap-tap.

Where am I? I stand up and grope about ... I remember the explosion that killed Richter. I

344

remember running to the village . . . then I remember I'm in the baker's cellar.

The string of taps comes again and at last I realize it's the Group K knock. It's Monsieur Durance's iambic pentameter. The heartbeat of the poets. Someone from Group K is trying to get to me. Could it be the Hawk?

I grope about in the darkness for the cupboard. My eyes have adjusted just enough to make out its dark outline. I haul it out of the way and stand in front of the door, my fingers on the key. All at once, I'm not sure. I've been safe in here, protected from everything going on above ground. What if I open the door now and it's the wrong person waiting there for me? What if I've been tricked? Henri betrayed us . . . what if this is someone very clever from the Gestapo trying to find me?

'What is Monsieur Durance's favourite colour?' I say to the door.

Without hesitation comes the muffled reply: 'Romeo and Juliet.'

I search my mind for another question, something that only the Hawk could know. 'Where do you keep your jam jars?'

'In the bottom left-hand cupboard in the fourth shed down from the Rue du Moulin.'

At these words, a huge wave of dizzy relief crashes over me. A grin breaks out over my filthy, exhausted face. I know this voice! Oh, this dear voice . . . I haven't heard it for so long I can't wait to turn the key in the lock. I rush to pull open the door. I already know who this is and I cannot wait another moment to see his face.

The Hawk, the skilled bomb-maker, the best-kept secret of Group K and one of the bravest men to serve the Resistance: it's my papa!

Chapter Forty-Seven

I fall into his arms.

I cling as tightly as I can to my beloved father. It's overwhelming to see him. I can't talk, I can't cry, I'm so overcome.

For a long time, I hold tight, I hold on for dear life. When at last I can speak, I sob out: 'Papa . . . it's you.'

He releases his hold so that he can look at me. Past the shorn hair, past the thin and dirty face, he looks straight into my eyes and recognizes me.

'Oh, Nicole,' he gasps. He looks as astonished to see me as I am to see him. 'Nicole. You've come back to us . . .' he says, his voice cracked and scratchy. 'It's not possible.'

I grip him tightly again and bury my face into his coat, my lovely papa. 'Please tell me that Mama and Grand-Mamie . . .' I begin, my voice choked with sobs.

'They're at home,' he says.

It feels like a miracle. My papa is here, Mama and Grand-Mamie are safely at home.

'Oh, thank goodness . . .'

Finally, we pull away from our embrace again so we can look at one another. My father seems much older, much more serious and deeply tired. On his face I can read his joy at seeing me, but it's mixed with horror at my appearance.

'It's OK,' I try to reassure him. 'I'm well.'

'Oh, Nicole, what have they done to you?' He tenderly touches the raw ends of my hair, the bald spots on my head, the healing gash on my cheek, and then he begins to cry.

I cry too because no one can bear to see their father cry.

'You've come back from the dead,' he whispers.

'I was so frightened you were dead too,' I tell him, when I'm wrapped up safely in his arms once again. 'Where have you been?'

'I escaped when they moved us from Brussels. I've been in hiding, working for Group K . . . I had no idea you worked for us too. I always kept an eye on you, Mama and Grand-Mamie from a distance, and when I realized you were missing I risked my only visit home. That's when I found out you'd been arrested and I read your beautiful letter, but I didn't know you were Coco until now.'

He runs his hand over my hair once again.

'We were sure you were going to be executed and it didn't seem much better when Aurelie told your mother you'd been sent to a camp.'

'Poor Mama,' I say. 'Poor, poor Mama. Please tell me she and Grand-Mamie are OK?'

'I've not been able to talk to them much. They're surviving. But every day without you is very difficult for them. They're Resisters too now; they deliver *Le Libre* and help as they can. They do it for you.' He pulls me close again.

'You're the Hawk,' I whisper, 'and I never knew!'

'And you're Coco. Why did I not guess the night you rewired my detonator on the train tracks?'

For several minutes, we just hold on, tears streaming down our faces. I could have gone to my death, not knowing the very best and bravest thing about my father.

'I'm so proud of you,' my papa says.

'I'm so proud of you too.'

'I thought . . .' His voice cracks. 'I thought I would never see you again.'

'The same,' I reply, and hold my hand against his rough cheek. I can't stop my tears.

'It's all right, I'm here,' he says, running his hand soothingly over my back. 'You're going to come home.'

I need to tell him why I'm still desperately sad. 'Papa, there's a boy, Anton Morel . . .'

'Yes, I remember Anton. He's a fine boy.'

'He was in the group too. He's very special to me, very special . . . and they've sent him to a camp. The camps are terrible, Papa. We have to tell everyone how terrible they are.'

Then I have to cry hard into the shoulder I've leaned on so many times in my life. My papa lays soothing hands on my face and kisses my split cheek. I'm a little comforted by his sympathy.

'People come back. You've proved it to me, beyond a doubt. Remain hopeful,' he says. 'Now, I have a little food in my rucksack, even a flask of coffee. I think we'll be safe to bed down here in the cellar tonight, and in the morning I'll take you home, to Mama and Grand-Mamie. I'm frightened they're going to die with happiness to see you again.'

Chapter Forty-Eight

We talk late into the night, sharing all our news, bursting with happiness to see one another again. At first light, we leave the deserted village and hitch a lift with a farmer taking milk to the town of Eupen, where we can catch a train to Brussels.

Papa has brought my real papers, Nicole de Wilde's papers. He was so convinced I was dead he was going to give codename Coco my identity card in the hope that it would get her as far as the Group K church, where new papers are being prepared.

'I won't need new papers,' I tell him. 'Nicole de Wilde is still safe and unsuspected.'

'She's just been away, recovering in the countryside from a long illness,' Papa says with a smile.

When we arrive in Eupen, we have a meagre breakfast at a café not far from the station and I can't help noticing how much people stare at me.

'Why is everyone looking?' I whisper to Papa. 'It's not because of the wanted posters, is it?'

He shakes his head and almost laughs. 'Even your own papa didn't recognize you from those posters,' he tells me. 'No, I think, despite your efforts with the soap, water and comb, you still look a little' – he pats my hand – 'unusual.'

I'm wearing Papa's tweed cap to cover up my strange hairstyle. But my outfit is still unusual: the shapeless tunic and trousers over my tiny frame.

As he settles the bill, Papa tells the waiter I've lost my luggage and asks where we might be able to buy a few essentials. His story is simple and plausible. So close to home, I'm so desperate to get back that I might forget how careful we still have to be.

In the little clothes shop, Papa charms the saleswoman with the same tale. I've lost my luggage and I need a smart new outfit. He brings out clothing coupons and a food-rationing book and tells the woman: 'I'm sure we can come to a good arrangement.'

I choose a pale blue beret, a navy blue skirt, new woollen socks, a white blouse and a warm blue jacket with a high collar and a belt. It seems incredible to be able to buy so many new things at once, but Papa assures me it's OK.

I think fondly back to my lost grey jumper. I'm going

home, I remember with a jolt; maybe Grand–Mamie and Violetta will be able to find me another one. Grand–Mamie! I'm suddenly impatient with excitement to see her again.

'I'll wear my new things,' I tell the saleswoman, and lovingly fold up my grey trousers and tunic. I will always keep them, I will often think of how far I managed to travel because of them. Maybe one day I'll see Madame Rosen and Ettie again and be able to thank them.

'Have you been ill?' the woman asks me kindly, noting my cropped hair, bandaged hand and tutting at how loose the skirt is on my tiny waist.

'Yes, but I'm much better now,' I reply.

'This dreadful war!' the woman complains to my papa. 'We can't feed the children properly and they get ill much more than they used to. My sister has just lost her second child.'

Papa nods solemnly.

When we come out of the shop, I ask him, 'Do you like my disguise?'

'Yes.' He adds, 'I want you to look as well as you can for your mother. She has been lost in grief for you. She has mourned you, Nicole, as if you were already dead. She has given up hope and she will find this overwhelming.'

Eupen station is quiet and we board the train to Brussels without being checked by guards. In the carriage, I sit with my head on Papa's chest, his arm tight around me. I hear his steady heartbeat under my ear and I feel protected.

From the window, I can see that the very first green shoots of spring are starting to come, but nothing feels better for Belgium. The war still goes on, the Nazis are still here. When we stop at a station, a family gets on board wearing the Jewish yellow star sewn onto their clothes, even on the baby's cardigan. I sit up and stare in surprise. I've seen the stars in the camp before, of course, but not in ordinary life, marking people out like this. It's shocking.

'Everything is worse, Papa,' I whisper against his chest. 'Maybe we'll never get rid of the Nazis.'

He pats my arm, as if I'm a fretful child. Maybe I *am* a fretful child. 'Everything is worse,' he agrees. 'We're hungrier, we're poorer, we're more oppressed; they take more teenagers and Jewish people away every day. But because of this, thousands are flocking to the cause. There is sabotage three times a day. There is a spirit, Nicole, which refuses to die. Your badly drawn face on all the posters, it's inspired many others. When people are not afraid to die for a cause, then it can't fail.'

I think back to the moment when I shot at the grain silo. I wasn't afraid to die and I wasn't afraid to kill. I already know that when I've recovered my strength

I'll go back to Group K to serve with renewed determination.

When we arrive in Brussels, Papa checks me over once again. I'm still thinner and paler than even the oppressed Belgian citizens around me. But my shorn head is covered with the blue beret and I'm in my smart new outfit so I no longer stand out so vividly.

'Take my arm,' Papa says as we make our way along the platform towards the guards checking the tickets and papers of all the passengers. Nazi guards . . . my knees tremble at the thought of having to approach them. I wish I still had the pistol, which we left in the cellar for the baker, knowing it was safer to travel through checkpoints without it.

I hold tight to my papa. There should be no need to worry. I'm Nicole once again and her ID card is safe.

The guards look distracted and our papers receive barely a glance.

'Looks like something's just happened . . . or about to,' Papa says, giving me a little wink as we walk on. 'Every single disruption is good. It keeps them worried and gives the rest of us hope.'

Chapter Forty-Nine

We board a tram to take us to our part of town and I begin to feel as if I'm in a dream. For weeks and months I've dreamed of being free, and now here I am, out in the open, roaming the streets like a normal person. I've got a tram ticket, I'm sitting on board and I don't need to look over my shoulder and wonder who is behind me. It feels endlessly strange. I can't relax because I'm too excited to be going home.

When we get off the tram, Papa walks me close to our street, but then, as his pace begins to slow, I steel myself for what must happen next.

'You're not going to come with me, are you?' I ask him.

'No, Nicole. I'm an escaped prisoner, still in hiding, and I need to stay that way.' He holds out his arms and enfolds me for one last time. I kiss him on the cheek and his moustache tickles my face, something I remember complaining about when I was small. 'Take care,' he says, his voice a little strained now. 'Nicole, will you go back to the group?'

'Of course.' I know I'm going to be much more dangerous to the enemy now than I was before.

He hugs me all the tighter. 'Take care,' he says.

'You too, Papa. I want to see you again, very soon.'

'And I want to see you. I want to come home. One day the war will end, Nicole, and we will have overcome them.'

More than anything, I want to believe him.

'You have your papers,' he says. 'You've killed your biggest enemy, so you can go home.'

I walk down my street and it is a new kind of wonderful to be here. There are so many details I notice as if for the first time and yet it's so familiar. It's shabbier, the two cars look older and dirtier, the houses have peeling paint and no flowers have been planted in the window boxes for spring.

But to me, it's the most beautiful street in the world.

Then the person I'd forgotten all about is standing right in front of me, blocking my path. The guard: Stapenhorst.

'Mademoiselle de Wilde?' he asks without any hesitation. 'And just where have you been?'

I don't panic; I don't even flinch. I look Stapenhorst straight in the face. No one is going to stop me now. No one is going to take me in now, when I've crossed Germany, killed Richter, been reunited with my papa and made it all the way back to my very own street.

'Hello, Stapie, I've been away . . . for a long time. But now I'm coming home.'

A look passes between us. I want him to understand that it would be better for him to accept this now. No questions asked.

'I can't talk about it. You know how it is,' I tell him firmly.

He stares at me, uncertain whether to believe me or not. Finally he decides on: 'Welcome home, Mademoiselle. How are you?'

'I'm well. How are you?'

He shrugs. 'Not so good. My two brothers have been killed. I think my father might sell the farm and all the cows.'

'I'm sorry,' I tell him, although I'm itching, bursting to get home now.

'This war, eh?' He shakes his head. 'It's nothing like I thought it would be.'

'No . . . well . . . I suppose I'll see you around.'

'Yes.'

Finally he steps aside. Now I am just four doors away from home and no one, nothing, is in my way, I can't wait one second longer and take off at a sprint.

I bound to the door, throw it open and I'm brought to a standstill by the hall. I can't believe it's here – just the same, as if it's been waiting for me all this time. Coats on their pegs, shoes all lined up and a smell I immediately recognize as home.

I snatch a breath then rush into the sitting room. My darling Grand-Mamie is fast asleep in her armchair with Gaspar and her knitting in her lap. I fly up to her, kiss her on the forehead, sink a hand into the fur of my lovely cat and whisper: 'Never, never, never, *never* give in!'

Grand-Mamie opens her eyes and gives such a start of astonishment that Gaspar leaps from her knees and the knitting tumbles to the floor. But before she can say a word and ruin my surprise, I dash out, heading straight for the kitchen.

I open the door and there, with her back to me, her hands in the sink, is my beloved mama.

She's heard the door opening so she turns to look over her shoulder. Her hair, all threaded with silver, is caught up in a soft bun and her lovely face, deeply creased with sadness and care, freezes.

For a moment she looks as if she's seen a ghost. With a great clatter the plate she's been washing falls into the sink.

'I'm home,' I manage, my throat too tight with the sob that is about to burst from me. I can't move, I'm so overwhelmed to be here, back in the kitchen with Mama.

But then I run forward and throw my arms around her. Oh, we are two scrawny scraps whose bony chests, hips and shoulders dig against each other. My cheek is squeezed into her neck and her hands, all wet with dishwater, are clasped around my waist.

'Oh, Nicole, Nicole,' she whispers over and over. Her fingers touch my face, my lips, my ears, my neck as if she's checking to make sure it's really me. 'Nicole, I was wrong. Please forgive me,' she gasps. 'Oh, Nicole, girls can make every difference. Nicole . . . are you really here? Are you really home?'

Trembling, half crying, half laughing, we sink to our knees and can't imagine ever letting go.

11th November 1947

I always like to get there first, ahead of the crowds, so I walk briskly along with two big bouquets of flowers in my arms, and soon I'm where I want to be, looking down at a simple grey headstone. I crouch to lay the first bunch of flowers and I wipe the stone nicely clean with a handkerchief from my pocket.

My eyes trace the inscription:

Adele de Wilde
born 15th January 1859, died 27th December 1944
beloved daughter, sister, wife,
mother and grandmother

There is comfort in knowing that Grand-Mamie lived long enough to see the Allied troops marching through the streets of Brussels to liberate us. When she knew that her hero, Sir Winston, was going to win, she said she could die happily.

I stay at the grave for some time, talking to her. I give her all the latest news and tell her that Brussels is looking beautiful today: 'The sun is shining. Everyone is dressed in their Sunday best. I know today is all about poppies and Remembrance, but I've brought you pink peonies because I know they're your favourite.'

When I've finished updating Grand-Mamie with the news, it's time to move on to my other dear, dear friends. I approach this stone more slowly because it's much harder to come here. Grand-Mamie died peacefully with her ambitions fulfilled. But as I begin to read the words on this larger, white marble memorial, I feel deep grief and my eyes begin to blur with tears:

IN MEMORY OF OUR COMRADES,
THE BRAVEST OF THE BRAVE, MOST LOYAL
OF US ALL, THE FIGHTERS OF GROUP K
IN THE BELGIAN RESISTANCE

VIVIENNE FONTAINE, 'LA BELLE',
BORN 5TH DECEMBER 1920, DIED 26TH NOVEMBER 1940

NICHOLAS DURANCE, 'THE OWL',
BORN 21ST SEPTEMBER 1881, DIED 12TH DECEMBER 1940

DANIEL BOGAERT, 'RAVEN',
BORN 11TH APRIL 1915, DIED 16TH JANUARY 1942

PADRICE FOULARD, 'PLUM',
BORN 14TH FEBRUARY 1924, DIED 17TH AUGUST 1942

GEORGE DE WILDE, 'THE HAWK',
BORN 4TH SEPTEMBER 1894, DIED 2ND DECEMBER 1943

None of these fine people lived to see the end of the war. Not brave, teasing Padrice or kind and clever Raven. Not one of them watched as the Allied tanks drove straight down the Avenue de la Reine. Astonished crowds, hardly daring to believe it was possible, cheered them on their way, even as German snipers fired down from the buildings in desperate last attempts.

It seems very unfair that these good, brave people won't grow old in the country they fought so hard to free.

In the end, my beloved papa was not able to escape the dangers of his profession. Blowing up an important railway bridge, he left too little time to escape. He was hit by a flying stone and killed instantly.

The bravest of the brave.

I wonder, not for the first time, why I am not listed on the marble stone alongside them. I served the Resistance for another four years after I returned home, but it was not my fate to die for them. Like Hope, Jacques Janssens, Vivienne's brother the Torch, and a handful of others, I've somehow survived.

I'm now a fully qualified children's nurse. I work hard, long hours, but I bring my little patients all the care and comfort I would love to have brought Ettie and the bed full of waifs in Ravensbrück. Ettie and Madame Rosen did not survive.

'Rest in peace,' I murmur, patting the marble gently and laying my big bouquet of lilies, roses and more pink peonies in place. 'Belgium is still free.'

Finally, I allow my eyes to rest on the last name in the list:

ANTON MOREL
BORN 3RD JANUARY 1925,
DEPORTED TO NEUENGAMME CAMP, 24TH JANUARY 1941.
AGE 17. NO DATE OF DEATH ESTABLISHED.

Oh, Anton.

I still ache for you.

It's very hard to mourn someone who has no final date, no resting place. I waited and waited and hoped and yearned for Anton to come home. But this is the second year after the war, the camps are empty, the stragglers have all returned, enquiries have drawn a blank and I finally have to accept that he isn't going to come back.

All I have left of my brave and serious boy are these letters carved into stone, a heart-breaking poem full of love and longing which he must have posted to me on the way to the station, and my silver cross. Somehow, with the help of a former camp inmate and a scrap of an address, my silver necklace was miraculously returned to me, with the initials 'A+N' scratched into the back of the cross.

As my fingers trace the letters of his name, I try to smile through my tears. I've known Anton for as long as I can remember and he is still the best kind of boy. He won't grow up and he won't grow old. He will always have a tanned, square face and dark hair. He will always be honest and open, and through his brown eyes I know I would still be able to read his thoughts.

When we were young teenagers on the brink of our adventure, he told me if we survived we would have to make our lives wonderful, for the sake of everyone who died.

I know I have to do this for him. For Anton's sake, I have to move on now and let my wonderful life begin.

I often think of Monsieur Durance's words too: 'When one love comes to an end, the heart flies free and often settles very happily on another.'

Maybe it will happen for me.

I just have to be strong and keep looking forward to the future.

Afterword

My Grandparents' War

I was still quite small when I realized that I had grandparents who were on different sides during the Second World War.

I grew up in Britain where we cherish our role in that war. It was 'our finest hour'. We have endless books and films celebrating British heroism and the stiff upper lip which got us through quite impossible circumstances.

But I could never join in with the feeling, which still exists in Britain today, that all the Germans were evil – because my mother is German and my grandfather was a German soldier.

I used to spend my summer holidays in and around Frankfurt and Bonn with my German aunties, cousins, relatives and my Opa (grandfather). I spoke German like a native, and by the end of the summer I would even dream in German.

Compared to my small hometown on the east coast of Scotland, Germany seemed so brightly coloured and modern. I went to funfairs with toasted almonds and 'wurst' in a bun, visited the sunny wine-growing Mosel valley where my mother grew up. Germany is the home of many of my happiest childhood memories.

So when I learned about the Second World War and – even worse – the Holocaust, it wasn't just shocking, the way it might be for an ordinary British schoolchild; it felt like a horrifying betrayal. Why had no one I loved told me about this?

The next time I was in Germany I looked at all the men old enough to have been in the war and asked myself: 'What did he do? Was he a concentration camp guard? Did he round up Jewish people and condemn them to death?'

I really couldn't bear it.

My mother had little information about the war. She'd gone through fifteen years of schooling in Germany and it had never been taught. No one had any idea how to tell children about what had happened and what some of their parents might have done.

That's different now. Every German schoolchild visits a concentration camp museum and there is a real sense of shame and guilt about the past.

I still have endless curiosity about both world wars. I still want to know what it was really like to be involved.

The person who did talk to me about those days was my German Opa. He was a very fit seventyish when I knew him. He smoked a pipe, had lots of books and was always very well turned out. He'd moved from a village to a town to the city in his lifetime and was living in retirement in Frankfurt. We would go for long bike rides in the beautiful forests around the city, where I saw dragonflies for the first time, and sometimes he'd tell me about the wars, because he'd lived through both the First World War and the Second.

He was in kindergarten during the First World War. He could remember having to unpick woollens all day long so that the wool could be re-used to knit socks and scarves for soldiers. He talked about the terrible time after the war when everyone was penniless. People really did move money about in wheelbarrows because it was worth so little.

Both Opa and his second wife were always careful with money to a fault; they never wasted a scrap of food or bought anything that wasn't at hefty discount because of what they'd been through.

I wish as I grew older that I'd thought to ask for so many more stories before my Opa got Alzheimer's and couldn't talk about much any more. But what he told me about the Second World War was that he had wanted to be a journalist, but then the war came and he had to become a soldier.

Of his wartime experiences, the one he spoke of most was being on the hell that was the Eastern Front. He and his comrades had to fight the Russians in impossible, sub-zero conditions. It was so cold that men would lose fingers and toes to frostbite, their weapons would jam and – I always liked this detail – the snot would freeze in their noses. He certainly did kill people, and the photos of him in his German uniform still make me shudder.

My Opa was shot and severely injured but made it back to hospital in Germany. This was the thing that saved his life: not having to be on the Russian Front any more.

I didn't know my German grandmother, as she died when I was only a baby. But she came from a rural family with some land and a small vineyard. Her brother died of appendicitis in his teens. Her father died soon after, and she and her fierce workhorse of a mother ran the show. My own mother would tell me stories about this ferocious granny. How she got up before dawn on Saturday mornings to bake bread for the week ahead. How everyone's pinafores had to be washed, ironed and starched shiny white every single day. If you didn't finish your supper, she would serve it cold to you for breakfast!

Even in the 1950s, my mum led a life which hadn't

changed for centuries and was unendingly hard. Up at dawn to milk the cow, warm milk for breakfast, then Catholic mass at 6 a.m. She walked miles to school, then came home to help out in the fields. I have photos of her aged eight making haystacks with a pitchfork. She picked vegetables and dragged them home in a handcart, she helped harvest grapes in the autumn, but still did hours of homework, including Latin and piano practice, then up again at dawn the next day.

My mother still has a work ethic second to none. All the Germans I know work hard for what they have. They live modestly and there's no sense of a class system or being entitled to anything. The First World War, the Second World War, Nazism, and losing both wars swept all of that away.

My British grandparents were much luckier during the war. Grampa was a farmer, with two big farms and a team of workers to run. He didn't have to join up as increasing food production was a national duty.

On the east coast of Scotland, they were well away from bombing raids, and even rationing didn't affect them much as they grew grain, beef and vegetables and probably swapped their produce for fish, milk and butter, so had everything they needed for their young family.

They did their bit, of course. Grampa was a Home Guard – a volunteer army made up mostly of those past service age, but also including those in essential occupations – and he probably had to spend many long nights checking lights were blacked out and watching the North Sea for any sign of invaders. My granny, a five-foot-tall bundle of cheerfulness, drove ambulances in the district.

Although they lost many friends and relatives, my British grandparents were upbeat people who liked to talk about the war years as if it had all been good fun. The farms were manned by interesting prisoners of war and there were always RAF officers to entertain for dinner.

Because both sides of the war form part of my history, I've always been fascinated by the people who lived through that time, maybe especially on the European side.

Soon all the grandparents who fought in this momentous war will be dead. We need to preserve their stories and experiences. Teenagers need to remember there was a time when turning eighteen didn't mean being able to drink and go to uni; it meant you were old enough to fight, kill people and die for your country.

When I found out that fifteen-year-old girls were helping the Resistance, bombing bridges and killing Nazi soldiers, I felt I had to know more and I wanted to bring these stories to life.

I really hope you'll want to read more about these

extraordinary times too. *Cross My Heart* is inspired by real people, real events and real places; but the story and all the characters involved are fictional. I've compiled a blog which details all my research: the books I read, the websites I visited, the amazing stories I learned. Please come along to **www.carmenreid.com** and find out more about the extraordinary teenagers of the Second World War.

Acknowledgements

Many people have helped me turn *Cross My Heart* from an idea into a book I'm very proud of.

I'd especially like to mention my three editors at Random House: Kelly Hurst, Jess Clarke and Ben Horslen, for excellent feedback and many suggestions which really shaped the story and raised the bar every time. Also eagle-eyed copyeditor, Sue Cook. I'm so grateful to you all.

My husband Thomas was another critical eye who encouraged me from the very start. Huge thanks also to my teen reading circle: Sam Quinn, Murray Webster, Jonathan Honey and Zarah Ahmed, who took the time to read early drafts and gave me such helpful advice and encouragement. Claudie Quinn, I hope you're going to enjoy Nicole's tale too: she takes her fierce determination from you.

The Imperial War Museum library was an important research source and I'd like to highlight the auto-biographies of Yvonne Ridder Files, *The Quest for Freedom*, and Josie Villiers, *Granny Was a Spy*, plus Louis Paul Boon's novel, *My Little War*, for giving real insight into daily life in Belgium during the war. Jack Tickell's *Odette* was also hugely helpful. It was an obituary of Lucie Bruce which first inspired my story and my interest in the teenage Resisters.

Students of the Second World War will realize I've moved two important real events forward for the sake of the story: the sabotaging of *Le Soir* newspaper by the Resistance, and Sir Winston Churchill's famous Battle of Britain speech. I hope you'll forgive me.

For anyone who'd like to practise Group K code, here are the first twenty lines of Henry V:

O! for a Muse of fire, that would ascend
The brightest heaven of invention;
A kingdom for a stage, princes to act
And monarchs to behold the swelling scene.
Then should the war-like Harry, like himself,
Assume the port of Mars; and at his heels,
Leash'd in like hounds, should famine, sword, and fire
Crouch for employment. But pardon, gentles all,
The flat unraised spirits that hath dar'd
On this unworthy scaffold to bring forth
So great an object: can this cockpit hold
The vasty fields of France? or may we cram
Within this wooden O the very casques
That did affright the air at Agincourt?
O, pardon! Since a crooked figure may
Attest in little place a million;
And let us, ciphers to this great accompt,
On your imaginary forces work.
Suppose within the girdle of these walls
Are now confined two might monarchies